Scotch

S J Garland

MAPLE KAKAPO PUBLISHING
Napier, New Zealand

Title: Scotch Rising
Author: S. J. Garland
Publisher: Maple Kakapo
Address: 2069 Pakowhai Road,
                  Napier, New Zealand 4183
Format: Softcover
Publication Date: 5/2014
ISBN: ISBN 978-0-473-28490-9

For Andy, it can't be sunny every day.

Chapter 1

I have returned after ten long years to haunt these austere corridors. I was a boy seeking escape, pining for adventure and the wood-panelled walls, the smell of Lyme soap have long lived in my memory, though if asked yesterday to describe the War Office, I would not have thought of these details. My head crowded with the adventure to come, the happiness of escape, I would not have noticed my present self, sitting upon a simple polished wooden bench, waiting for an audience, a trial, the end of my military career. I was too young, too foolish, far too caught up in my own self-importance and cleverness at my escape from calamity to know how it might end; my boyish heart could not accept my gladness at having it come to an end, even in the face of an uncertain future, I would be free.

The knuckles on my fists stand out white, opening my hands, I trace the familiar calluses, scars, the marks of my trade with my eyes. Being a soldier is everything I have known in my adult life; it existed in a space of neither here nor there, never meant to be for a man from such a station. At least an hour has past, the corridor is cold and I must keep shifting in order to ease the aching in my limbs. The anticipation of the confrontation is always worse than the actual event. I learned this in battle.

"Captain Clyde-Dalton." Colonel Manners stood in the doorway to his office and I could glean nothing from his curt nod. He remained an efficient man, who spoke with conviction and authority, I do not know of any soldier who has disobeyed any of his commands.

I stood stiffly and briefly stretched my shoulders before following Manners into his sanctuary, prepared from my last meeting to greet the Spartan formality of his office. Looking around, I spied a fire burning in the grate, a luxury for the old soldier in the mid-November weather. His clerk's desk stood empty; this meeting would remain private, not a formal dishonorable discharge, perhaps I might be able to sell my commission and quietly step away from this life.

Colonel Manners' face, deeply marred by weathered lines, hold many secrets, the broad planes of his chin and

Manners' brows reached his slate iron wig, demanding my understanding. I only felt numb.

Grasping at my resolve, my voice grew insistent, "I should think, Colonel, my performance and spectacular fall from grace would only serve as evidence contrary to my commitment to the army, in fact I shall tell you now, I will not take up the post, I wish to be discharged of my duties, I no longer have the will to carry them through!"

"What you wish or what you think, has not been within your own power since you walked out of my door and joined the regiment." Manners stood and braced his hands on the desk, all attempts at civility gone, he became the avenging angel, the statesmen, the renowned military leader, "You will do as your damned well told, and I will have my way in this matter, Captain, or I will have you thrown back in the stocks and court-martialed. Your uncle may have turned a blind eye to your activities in the past, I do not believe he is likely to ignore a rather large black smudge over the family name brought about by an ungrateful nephew, far too cocksure for his own good."

Mouth pressed in a firm line, I nodded to indicate I understood the threat clearly. On this day there would be no freedom from the army. I wanted to drink myself into oblivion, live in the darkest places of London; I needed to punish myself for the death of Onatah, my wife, once the only future I could imagine, now I would be forced to carry on reliving my torment.

Regaining his seat, Manners once again took up his glass. "You acquired a certain skill set while with your regiment, unbeknownst even to your superiors, you successfully infiltrated the native population, even going so far as to marry one of them, yet you remained steadfastly loyal to your country. It will be important for your survival to draw upon these skills, where I am sending you." I leaned forward in my seat, curious despite myself. I do not want any part of this, my heart screamed. "The Act of Union put through Parliament this year effectively binds the Scots to us; we need to show those heathens we are watching their every move and there is no better way than through taxing their most precious commodity," Manners held up his glass.

"Whisky," surprise rang in my voice. It was not a tipple I enjoyed myself; beer remained the drink of choice amongst soldiers, with anything stronger reserved for great victories or defeats.

"I have been reminded it is imperative to be seen to tax alcohol equally on both sides of the border and, to aid in this endeavour, we are deploying soldiers, mostly clerks, to monitor alcohol production north of the border," Manners leaned forward, suddenly intent. "It might be said I am dealing lightly with you, especially as men have been hanged for less than your recent transgressions. Fortunately for you, I want seasoned soldiers up there and I want reports; the old pretender, James Francis, has a following who would like nothing better than to see a Stuart back on the throne of England and Scotland.

The mention of the Crown caught my interest. Manners knew how to goad soldiers into doing his bidding; here stood the successful commander, the same feeling of tension and excitement twisted in my guts, the way it had in Boston when the Colonel called in his special force. We would prepare for a raid against the French, the riskier the task, the more desirable the challenge. "How big a threat to the Crown? Surely, if there is a nest of vipers hiding in Scotland waiting for the old pretender, we can rouse them out with a small force?"

"The enthusiasm I once spied in your person has appeared once again," Manners smiled for the first time. "The treasury is severely low on funds; it has never recovered from Cromwell and his cronies, nor did it fare much better under the opulent spending of recent monarchs, the present Queen included. A full-scale operation is out of the question under the present tightening of purse strings, the placement of highly gifted and men loyal to us is the lightest option for Parliament. You are a soldier, Clyde-Dalton. I do not pretend to know of your hurts, but I think a stint in the Highlands of Scotland will give you a chance to rethink your present circumstances. Besides, there may yet be a reconciliation with your uncle, or you could easily take your place in society without him."

up and reached a hand out, I rebuffed him and walked back out into the darkened street; the shadows would hide my grief until morning.

Chapter 2

My eyes adjusted to the candlelight spilling from the compact windows of two rows of tightly packed stone houses facing the road with relief. The town of Markinch rose before me, my final destination and I turned my shaggy horse into the main street, following the main road whose path eventually led the traveller ever northward, into further wilds, towards Aberdeen. My bones ached after ten days in the saddle, it was not the hardest ride I had ever undertaken, but unfortunately after a month's incarceration followed by a fortnight's journey across the Atlantic with no exercise, my body needed to become accustomed to the gruelling pace. Coming to a halt under a sign for the Thistle and Rose, I made out the shape of a small figure, hidden in the shadows created by the light from the windows. The boy obviously believed he remained well hidden, because he did not shy away from his curious inspection of my person when I looked directly at him.

"Boy," the single word shot through the air, and made the lad jump, as I intended. Suppressing a smile I continued, "I am looking for directions to the Deoch-an-Dorus Distillery, or the Clunes estate?"

Large eyes shone through the darkness. I could not distinguish the colour, however they spoke of intelligence. The lad weighed his options as he finished examining me. He finally spoke with a heavy brogue. I strained my ears to understand his words filtering through the night air.

"Deoch is haud up for the night. Folk will head back again in the morn, the Clunes stead is back the away ye came, nae turn down tae Auld Reikie, an past the distillery up to the big castle." The lad finished his long speech on a breath of air, and looked up at me for a moment before continuing, "Most ay the men are here fur stoup of ale or a cap of Scotch mind, afair heading home tae their faimly."

Believing it might be better to give the lad encouragement rather than bothering with a repetition, I smiled. "Thank you, there must be someone inside with information," he nodded in agreement and I swung a leg over the saddle and dismounted slowly, letting my legs stretch as they hit the ground. I rustled through my saddlebags and moved to secure my mount to the hitching post, the boy cautiously eyed the creature, I could see his hair was overgrown and sticking up in places, his kilt in need of a good wash, maybe even a delousing, my horse returned his look of interest with one of unconcern.

"He's an unusual beastie," the boy put a hand out to pet his nose, "what's his name?"

The boy pulled his hand back as if it had been burned when the horse shied, I held him firmly by the reins and waited until he settled, "Put your hand under his nose, so he can give you a sniff," I watched the lad cautiously extend his hand once again. "Good, he wants to see if your friendly, I am fairly certain he does not bite, his name is Tasunke."

The boy rubbed the horse's forehead, while trying the foreign name out loud, "Tasunke," it slipped from his brogue and elongated into a double-o sound, he tried again with moderate success. "Where is that name from?"

"I purchased him from members of the Sioux tribe who passed near Boston while I remained stationed there, the name Tasunke means horse in their language," I stroked his thick fur, his coat was mostly white with large brown patches, no pure-bred fancy, a cross between a work horse and a wild animal, I loved him the moment I saw him. My wife, Onatah, and her brother, Hania, chided me for paying such a large sum for an unbroken horse, they said the Sioux tribe were full of back dealers, and the horse would probably die in the first winter. He proved them wrong, however, and with a bit of work and patience he became a good companion.

Wiping the memory from my mind before it led to unpleasant reminders, I turned to the boy, "I am trusting you with Tasunke while I step inside and speak with the innkeeper," the lad's face lit up and he stood a bit taller, "Make sure nothing happens to him out here." I smiled, Tasunke could be relied upon to watch the boy and himself.

Stepping through the portal into the crowded tap, I encountered the usual sights of a drinking house, a long bar, made of polished wood, tables set near the walls and longer benches across the room. A crowd of a couple dozen men lingered inside nursing drinks of different descriptions kept mainly silent except for a few whispers among neighbours, every eye trained upon one man at the far end of the room. Dressed in a red pleated kilt, one side draped over his heart, pinned with a silver brooch, the man held the audience's attention with ease, his intense eyes and flourishing hands punctuating his speech, drawing power to him and reflecting it back into the crowd in such a way as to make each man believe he spoke only to them. The old General in Boston remained the only other man I could recall ever having the power to match this one, who must have been the same age as myself, yet his demeanor rivaled the wisest of old men with the spirit of youth, such passion could be frightening in its power, its potential for misuse a destructive force.

The counter stayed relatively empty, I signaled the barman and ordered an ale, he gave me a curious look before turning to the barrels behind the bench. Strangers arriving in Markinch after dark were probably not a common occurrence; especially in the Highlands, the roads were dangerous at night, potholes, animals, even people making mischief given the right opportunity. I tried to listen to the thickly accented words of the mesmerizing man standing in front of the fire, however, my arrival had caught the attention of another man, who peered over his small glass of Scotch, thought for a moment and rose, lumbering more than walking over to my side.

The other man arched a brow, he stood a full head taller than myself, black raven hair fell to his broad shoulders, he wore the usual highland garment, a pleated kilt with one end draped over his shoulder, his bright blue eyes held mine, sizing up my courage. He spoke in a deep voice with a hint of soft brogue, his words much easier to make out than the boy's, "And who might ye be, sir? It's fairly late for a traveller tae stop looking tae sup an ale."

The large man did not appear unfriendly, his voice, however, held a note of strength used by men in positions of authority when giving orders; my army experience gave me invaluable lessons in sizing up men, this one could be a potential deadly enemy, not tonight though. "My name is

Esmond Clyde-Dalton and, as you surmised, I am a new arrival in Markinch."

"Captain Clyde-Dalton?" The other man spoke the question and tapped the sporran hanging from his belt, "I am in receipt of Colonel Manners' letter regarding your new post as Excise Collector, welcome to the Highlands, Captain," the other man nodded and gave me a wide grin.

I doffed my cap in response to the warm greeting, "thank you, I could not be sure if word of my arrival would reach the proper authorities, I was impatient to leave London, my business concluded." In truth I needed to escape the confines of the overcrowded city and avoid Mr Wick. I picked up the pint the barman placed at my elbow and took a deep pull, the flavour of the ale was dark and rich, sharp and not unpleasant. I contemplated the liquid as I set the cup down.

"A guid honest ale, made here in Markinch by the barman, though I canna say I indulge often being the manager up at Deoch-an-Dorus," I looked up at the other man in surprise. "I am afraid we were nae expecting someone tae replace the other lad so soon. We have a cottage the distillery rents tae the Crown fur yer keep, trying tae get some of our coin back, " the other man broke out into loud guffaws over his humour. "My name is Beathan Clunes."

Beathan's enjoyment over his own joke brought several glances sliding my way, some turned back to the speaker, others outwardly stared, marking each detail in my appearance, their scowls an indication of their feelings over my arrival in their village, I arranged my face into a study of boredom and stared straight back. I turned my head to look back at Beathan, my gaze fell upon the orator of the evening, staring back at me, mouth frowning in anger, I saw him look to Beathan and when he shrugged in response. The other man lifted his arm and pointed directly at me, "och, here is the gauger newly from London, and we hae Clunes making couthy with him, nae respect fur the fact it's our labour going intae those taxes."

Heads swiveled, eyes trained on my face, I was the focus of intense scrutiny by each man in the tap room, weighing the other man's words, searching my person for the truth of my crimes against them. I tried to remain a study in unconcern and brought the pint to my lips once again.

"Logan, you've had yer say, Markinch, nae Deoch, doesnae need any trouble from London, tae many jobs count on it, best ye and everyone else here this evening remember it," Beathan looked steadily back at the crowd, with an extra nod at Logan, the rabble rouser.

Unfortunately, the instigator was not to be put off, he stepped through the silent men, who watched, waiting for a spectacle, hoping for the new arrival to be shown his place. I had lived in the army for ten years, an institution perpetuated by bullying and submission, I stood my ground and hoped my look of mild curiosity stayed in place.

"It is the new gauger, how ready Her Majesty is when there is coin tae be collected, even all the way up here in the Highlands, taken from the pockets ay honest folk, I should give ye a creesh." Logan's final step placed him within arm's reach, anger rolling off of him in waves. I could pin him in one move, the other man was the same size as me, unfortunately he lacked the decade of fighting experience.

I stared directly into Logan's eyes, raising my voice so the whole room could easily understand, "I am Captain Esmond Clyde-Dalton, returned from fighting in the New World and newly stationed in Markinch as the Excise Collector," I emphasised the last two words, "as a representative of Her Majesty, I will fulfill my duty by any means necessary."

Logan frowned for several heartbeats, stunned by my aggressive approach. I thought this might be an end to it, until he produced a sly smile, raising his hand, he pointed a finger at my chest, stopping an inch short of touching my frock coat, "I think ye better bide yerself, Captain, there's many accidents can befall a man up here in the wilds."

"May I remind you, sir, an attack on Her Majesty's soldiers is considered an attack on her person? Treason is punishable by hanging, drawing and quartering, it would be a mighty shame to have your bits spread out in the four corners of England, though you might enjoy Cornwall as a final resting place." The threat met its mark, Logan gave me a look of contempt and his hand balled into a fist, a small feeling of achievement burst in my chest, perhaps I had goaded him into a fight, I needed to give someone a good, honest thrashing to lift my spirits, but as Logan leaned in to strike, Beathan intervened.

"Logan, you've caused enough tranchie fur one evening, the captain is right, he is a representative ay the Crown and should be treated as such, best be off, if ye still want yer job in the morn." A long look passed between the two men and Logan seethed under Beathan's words, before turning on his heel and stalking towards a group of men sitting in the corner of the room.

Conversations sprouted amongst the men, Beathan cleared his throat and attempted a weak smile, "Logan is the foreman up at Deoch," he watched Logan's back. "He's a guid worker and, as ye can see, motivates the rest ay the lads. If he stuck tae his job and left off the politicking, he would probably be more personable, such as it is, yer not the only one tae have a wee run in with him."

"A wee run in?" I repeated the words incredulously, "The man threatened a known soldier of the Crown, twice I recall. I have seen men hang for less, Mr Clunes, it is not my responsibility to keep such men from becoming problems, however, I warn you now, I will not hesitate to bring a speedy conclusion to this Logan's forays into disparaging the Crown." I finished the rest of the pint. Beathan stood silently beside me, an unreadable look on his face. "I think it's time for you to show me this cottage, Mr Clunes, and I will need somewhere to stable my horse."

"Please call me Beathan, Mr Clunes is my faither," the man gave a laugh, cut off abruptly when I did not join in. "Right, it'll be best if ye leave yer mount here at the inn's stables. Mr Turner, the previous tenant, did nae ride and I'm afraid the modest stable is in need ay some repair." Beathan shuffled his feet, and took a deep breath. "In truth, you might be more comfortable staying here at the inn fur a few nights, I received yer letter today and the cottage has nae been seen tae since Mr Turner, well, since he concluded his position."

I laughed for the first time in many weeks, my cheeks were stiff and the sound raw, it must have been the tiredness from travelling affecting my wits. "Beathan," I used the other man's first name in order to put him at ease, "I have lived in some of the lowest conditions a man might suffer, in all manner of hot weather in the middle of a bog, sharing a tent with my horse in freezing snow drifts, with only the thunderclouds and rain as my companions, I do not think a few cobwebs will diminish my constitution."

"Right," reluctantly, Beathan spoke with the barman, who sent his boy around the front to collect Tasunke. "I suppose we had best be on our way," his feet heavy, he opened the door and stepped out into the cool evening. These Scots appeared to be extremely fastidious, even the men.

After watching the boys for a few minutes, I left Tasunke to his and Kieran's ministrations before balancing my saddlebags on my shoulders and indicating to Beathan we should proceed, I fell into a purposeful stride next to him, trying to let my eyes adjust to the light from the lamp swinging in Beathan's hand.

"The cottage is nae far from the village, ten minutes' walk at the most, further up the road you'll find Deoch and further still is my family's keep," Beathan paused for a minute. "If the cottage is nae habitable, we can easily go back to the Thistle, there is a room available for the next few nights. Freya, the housemaid can tidy the place up in a trice."

I let my silence answer his nervous ramblings, the night air had grown even more chilled and a wind swept from the surrounding hills fiercely battering any exposed skin, it was mid-November, and it felt as if the deepest winter were only a few days away, I looked out and up at the dark clouds, tumbling across the sky.

Beathan noticed my interest, "Ground's frozen already, winter comes early here." He inspected my boots, hose and frock coat, "Ye might need some better hap-warms, a trip back down tae Edinburgh might set ye right, plenty ay guid tailors," Beathan rubbed his chin and looked back at the road.

"The rest of my belongings will be arriving by the next post, I have several winter garments from my time in Boston, I do not think it can be much colder here than there," I finished with an inspection of Beathan's bare legs, the kilt would keep the parts of him it covered warm, as for the rest, I could only guess. The houses of the village thinned and before the road veered sharply to the left, a stone building appeared out of the darkness, more a house than a cottage. Beathan stopped and went through an opening in the low stone fence, stopping before the front door to search through his sporran. With a grunt of satisfaction, he pulled out a long skeleton key and opened the door with a few jiggles. I followed him into the white-washed entranceway, complete with pegs for coats and a faded mirror, my companion halted a few feet away, next to another door.

He looked back at me with an apologetic frown before opening the portal and stepping through. I cautiously followed him and let my eyes adjust to the candles flickering to life on the tables and walls as Beathan walked around and lit several oil lamps. Blinking several times I peered around in wonder, the walls had been covered in slips of paper, a close inspection of the ones pinned nearest revealed mathematical formulations and a large board meant for chalk stood in one corner. Deciphering the numbers, lines and letters I was positive they must have something to do with one of Newton's theories. The room was a treasure trove of mathematics, the man who lived here before must have been a fanatic. Some of the equations would require further study, at a guess I would say the man was a genius. Moving further into the room to appease my curiosity, I abruptly stopped, a rope dangling from a beam in the centre of the space filling me with dread.

"Yer predecessor, Mr Turner, was a touch eccentric," Beathan appeared apologetic and began to stack a pile of papers on a desk near him. "Wee laddie from Devon, excessively clever, would sit in here fur hours, days if he could, working out all these maths questions, once he got a problem stuck in his head." Beathan's voice trailed off, and I walked further into the room and inspected the rope, I was fascinating in a macabre sense, and not dissimilar to the way the spectacle of public hangings enthralls a crowd.

"Once he got intae the tax ledgers, well there was nae stopping his need fur total accuracy, put a bug in auld Logan's ear." I looked over at Beathan in surprise, and he continued, "Harmless wee fellow though, could bowl him over with a breath of air, always the first in the village tae come down with an ailment. We naturally sent word tae Whitehall informing them of the tragic events, apparently his folk are all gone, Whitehall sent us money tae gie him a burial and told us tae dae what we liked with his belongings." Beathan's arms swept over the room, "As you can see, it would be better tae hae a professor from university organise this mess, than a housemaid."

"Perhaps a fortuitous circumstance has made this my new post, I am a member of the Royal Society and mathematics is not my main area of interest, however I am sure I can discover if any of these are worthy of publication." I watched Beathan who wore a dubious expression, "We might find a mathematical equation in here that explains how the whole world works."

Beathan nodded his head, "If yer sure ye want tae take on such a mess, I will leave ye tae it," he stepped around the rope. "Give me a moment and I will take down this rope at the least," he nudged a footstool into place.

I set my saddlebags onto the cushions of the settee, "There is no need to bother with it tonight, I will deal with it in the morning. Perhaps you might show me the rest of the cottage, it's been a hard ride up from the south and I would be partial to getting some rest," I wanted to be alone, and I did not want Beathan to fuss over anything.

Sensing my impatience, Beathan stepped down from the footstool, "We should get on with it, I suppose, I need tae get some work done before the still runs in the morning," he went back out the door and I followed him through to a room with a table set in the middle, seating at least eight. "This is the dining room, a bit large fur a single body, and the scullery is through those doors." Beathan waved in the direction of a door, "Freya comes with the cottage and she prepares the meals and cleans. There is a door tae the rear of the cottage, where ye will find the water pump, the privy and the stables."

I nodded to indicate my understanding and followed him back through the dining room door into the narrow hall. We took the steps to the second story and I was surprised to find four doors leading from a small landing. "This is a rather grand house for a person occupying such a lowly position as myself."

Beathan laughed, "Ye are right about that," he continued to smile. "This is the auld Clunes home, where my faither spent his childhood aiding his faither in making Scotch." There was a touch of pride in the other man's voice and something else, a sense of ownership over his own story, his own destiny. "Deoch soon became the Scotch of choice amongst the fashionable set down in Edinburgh and Glasgow, giving my faither the opportunity tae expand, and he bought the Markinch Castle and lands and built the distillery. I was born up there." He frowned, "My faither has never forgotten where he comes from and if I ever thought tae behave in a cruel manner, we would come down here and he would tell me our family's story."

Beathan appeared to be lost in thoughts from the past, I did not nudge him from his reverie; as a boy I wished for parents who might have taken some interest in me, I hoped with each year's visit my uncle would find something he might invest in and I would finally be the man he was proud to call a nephew.

Shaking his head, Beathan smiled, "This house is my history," he pointed to the rooms at the front of the house. "These are the largest bedrooms, both hae windows looking out tae the front, the two back rooms hae beds, though they are mostly used fur storage. I think you'll find sheets and other linen in there," with a nod he turned and walked back down the steps.

Beathan halted in front of the door to the drawing room, "Yer sure ye dinnae mind cleaning up this mess, it seems a trifle unfair fur ye tae be forced tae tidy up after the last excise officer," he frowned up at the rope.

"As I said before, it will be more of a pleasure than a duty. As a man of science, it is my prerogative to make sure no discovery goes without recognition." I studied the tapestry of papers and formulas, "Besides I have a feeling life in Markinch may make time for such personal pursuits."

"Yer correct if ye believe nae much happens up here," Beathan nodded his head and putting his hand on the front door, he hesitated a moment and turned back. "I won't go intae all of it tonight, I can see yer tired, I should warn ye, there are rumours in the village over Mr Turner's death, rumours I give nae credit, hae a guid night and I'll see ye up at Deoch tomorrow fur a tour."

I stared at the closed door, tired, drained, I let Beathan's comments concerning Mr Turner slide to the back of my mind, whatever the rumours regarding the other man's death, they could not have any bearing on the rest of my evening's activities, nor did I believe they would have any influence on my time in Markinch. One year would begin on the morrow.

After a closer inspection of the rooms above stairs, I decided not to bed down for the night in any of them, I shook out a couple of blankets from a linen closet and wrestled them back downstairs and into the parlour. A stack of kindling aided my attempts at getting a fire created in the grate and I searched the back of the cottage until I found a large wood pile, bringing in several arm loads, until the fire burned cheerily, the scraps of paper stuck to the walls shimmered in the light. A less than fruitful search through the kitchen yielded only a couple bottles of Scotch and a bag of flour. Freya the housemaid kept a tidy kitchen, which had much to recommend it.

Sitting in a large, comfortable chair near the fire, I uncorked the Scotch with my teeth and took a deep pull. Not accustomed to the strong liquor, I coughed several times as it burned down my throat, making my eyes water. After taking several deep breaths, I brought the bottle back to my lips. This was something in Scotland I was going to enjoy immensely. Setting the Scotch on a low table, I unwrapped the last of the cheese and bread I had purchased at an inn on the highway, the hard cheese still tasted sharp, unfortunately the bread had become hard, but I had lived on worse for more than one night in the past.

Chewing slowly, I looked around the room, trying to imagine the frenzied preoccupation of a man capable of producing this amount of work, his determined mind focused on solving the problem, I thought of where I should launch an attempt to find order from the chaos. Mr Turner's rope hung in the centre of the room, without preamble or malice, exposed and frail considering the life it snuffed out, the great mind it forced into submission and stasis. Even in my deepest despair I never thought of this as an option. I wanted revenge after Onatah's death and I sought out the man I knew was responsible, though he still lives and I failed in my task to kill him, he lives in disgrace and ruin, no longer the Captain of the Boston Militia, and I must live with the knowledge he yet breathes.

Perhaps if my will to live had been less, my mind not set on revenge, after anguish filled my soul and now set on seeking the shortest course to my own oblivion, the gentleman's way, through drinking and gambling, I might have used the rope, but I wanted to suffer as I know she suffered in her last moments. A hatred strong enough to propel me out of my comfortable seat stole over my senses, I loathed this contraption for the easy death, life is for suffering and duty, not made for quick exits. I stepped onto the cushioned stool and found the knot around the ceiling beam a foot out of my reach.

Stepping down from the footstool, I searched the room for a better ladder, I discarded ideas as frequently as I made them; until I spied a low table near the settee, dragging it over to the rope, I placed it underneath. Carefully, so as not to scratch the wood on the surface of the polished table, I placed the footstool on top, recognizing the elaborate needlework, I made an unsteady set of stairs; I first stepped onto the table and with a wobble carefully onto the stool. I could reach the rope where it was wrapped three times around the wooden beam, a knot on one side held the whole in place, I have never seen such intricate work and I studied it for several minutes before I tried to loosen it, unfortunately each time I tugged the rope one way, it would tighten in another spot and finally, frustrated by my lack of success, I heaved on the rope.

The extra downward force produced by my careless action resulted in a groan of protest from the cushion under my feet, I had time to think it might be a good idea to extricate my person from this precarious situation when a tearing noise ripped through the drawing room, sending my boots through the footstool. My arms splayed wide immediately and instinct propelled them in a similar fashion to a windmill, though how this action might halt my calamitous fall was beyond rational explanation. Unable to gain any purchase on the polished wooden surface of the low table with my ankles bound together in the sewing frame, I fell backward, slowly at first, then with a frightening rapidity. I was doomed, lost, there could be no escape from the writhing heap my body became as it hit floor with a solid thud.

Cursing loudly enough for a person on the road to hear, I rubbed the back of my head where it hit the edge of the settee. The rope slightly swayed, mocking my anger, "You may have won this battle, however a tactical retreat will see me fight again and the war is far from over, my friend." I reached down and untangled the footstool cushion frame from my feet and inspected the damage before throwing it with great satisfaction across the room. A good polish would see the table set to rights. Satisfied, I sat back in my previous chair and took a couple healthy swigs of Scotch, studying the knot in the rope. It was fancy work, and if Mr Turner were smaller than I, it meant there would be a ladder stored somewhere around the cottage, probably in the stables; the rope would have to wait until morning.

A volume on botany newly from the bookseller's in London sat unopened in my saddle bag, but I was too tired to concentrate on the plates and I set to finishing the Scotch before morning in the hopes it would chase any evil dreams away and let me sleep for at least a few hours.

Chapter 3

Head pounding, as I stood before the fire in the drawing room, shaving mirror balanced on the mantel in front of one of the large candlesticks, the remains of the Scotch bottle on the table making my stomach turn. It was still morning, not early however, as a steam whistle signaling the onset of the work day at Deoch went several hours beforehand, and I judiciously decided to wrap myself further in the pilfered blankets rather than face the day, my bones aching from sleeping on the floor. The squeak of the door opening at the rear of the cottage halted my shaving and I listened carefully to the slight footfalls in the scullery, opening and shutting cupboards, wood clattering on the stone floor.

Unconcerned with the intrusion, I continued my morning's ministrations, wiping my face with a linen cloth I robbed from the linen closet. After inspecting my work, I reached for my shirt, thinking I would be happy to have a couple of new ones as the buttonholes on this remained sorely frayed.

"Captain," a choked female voice croaked from the hallway, making her brogue even thicker. "I canna believe yer standing in the middle ay the drawing room completely unfleggit, nae mind tae mah purpie-smiles, and what hae ye done with my linen?"

Turning sharply, I caught a middle-aged woman standing in the doorway to the drawing room. Her head only reached my chest, however she was as wide as she was tall, a hand held to her heart and her face as red as the hair scraped back into a knot on the back of her head, she looked as if she might faint dead onto the floor.

"Purpie-smiles? I questioned and with as much haste as possible, I shoved my arms into the sleeves of my frayed shirt and frantically buttoned it down the front, in order to preserve her modesty as much as mine.

"My cheeks, my face, I must be rosy all over," the woman appeared to have regained some of her calm and she wrestled her eyes away from my covered body, she inspected the demolition of the drawing room, the blankets in a pile, the upturned table and finally the embroidered cushion that once graced the top of the low footstool.

Hoping to end the growing look of outrage on the woman's face, I decided to strike on the offensive, a handy tactical manoeuvre I had used in the past. "Freya, I believe Beathan informed me of your name last evening, it is nice to meet you this morning. As you can see, I was involved in a minor incident last night, I will of course replace anything broken.

Freya stared at the torn sewing, her small hands stretching the material and rubbing the loose threads between her fingers. "Mr Clune's mother sewed this cushion as a gift tae her husband, Beathan's grandmother, the damage is complete, I dinnae believe it can be fixed." Freya took a deep breath, I watched the anger grow in her stance, it made her taller. Chin up, she pointed the ruined cushion at me, "I dinnae know tae what purpose footstools are put in the New World, or in England, Captain, but here in the Highlands, they are used tae rest feet upon, and faimly heirlooms are treated with care, nae put to the Lord only knows what purpose."

"I am sorry over the cushion's damage," I thought of trying to explain my drunken logic over the rope and Mr Turner's death, however the look on the woman's face ordered appeasement and apologies, not explanations. I witnessed such a look many times from countless nannies and even my wife, "I am truly sorry, I am sure for a coin or two we can find someone who might fix it."

This was hardly an auspicious beginning to our relationship, which we would have to endure for an entire year. Freya glowered at me, shoulders hunched, "I've put porridge on the fire and there will be hot water fur coffee, if ye hae a mind," she turned and walked back out the door. "Beathan sent word this early this morning you hae arrived, but I hae two boys tae ready fur lessons."

I nodded at her explanation for being late and I ate two bowls of porridge in the hopes my enjoyment would soften Freya's contempt for me, but the silence during the entire meal extended to my exit of the cottage. Similar to other females of my acquaintance, I suspected she had formulated an intricate plan of punishment involving long silences and a pinched face. The walk up to the distillery aided in clearing my thoughts of the unpleasant interlude; my wife could be charmed with a few compliments and a token of my affection, perhaps Freya would not be adverse to something sweet brought up from London.

The air felt crisp, and by the formation of the clouds I doubted snow would be far off, the brown fields, spotted with heather, covered with a few patches of white, it gave the hills a feeling of desolation and I wrapped my frock coat tighter to my person. Logan's threats over the dangers of the Highlands, though misplaced, were correct; wandering into these hills could be treacherous, an unprepared man might find his death from cold and hunger before ever reaching help, not least the fact bandits and outlaws filled the hills, living out of reach of authorities. The rugged savagery of the place appealed to me, the lure of untamed nature only increased my enjoyment of the New World, once away from Boston, with Onatah and her brother, I was free to live as I pleased. These hills held men's secrets and the expansive sky protected the people who lived here from the weak; to make a life in the Highlands, one needed to be strong and have an aptitude for survival.

A crest in the road revealed several red buildings, along with a watermill. Men carried out the still's business, carrying sacks or chatting amongst themselves, a farmer and his son kept busy loading sacks onto a cart pulled by a donkey, the first building shouted to the world, Deoch-an-Dorus, Purveyors of Fine Scotch, Clunes and Sons. The sign spoke of success and permanence, giving the still and the business a foothold in the desolate landscape, the energy coming from the people working gave it a life and soul of its own; here a shelter rose for the people of Markinch, capable of weathering all storms.

I easily recognised Beathan's large frame further up the road speaking to a wiry man, knees protruding from a yellow kilt and a matching cap desperately trying to contain an erratic thatch of white hair, he turned to stare at me and said something to Beathan.

The other man turned and waved in greeting, I sped up to join them. "Captain, I hope ye enjoyed yer first evening in

Markinch, I sent Freya down tae the cottage this morn tae start her duties, I'm sure she made a good impression," Beathan finished on a broad grin and I wondered if word had reached him over the morning's events.

"Everything was satisfactory," I could wait until at least mid-afternoon before discussing my perfidy with Beathan; the village was small enough, I knew he would eventually come upon the truth of the cushion. I turned to the other man, "As Beathan said, I am Captain Esmond Clyde-Dalton."

The older man doffed his cap and nodded, "I'm Tavish, just Tavish and I will be showing ye around the place this morn, get ye up tae speed with the goings on here at Deoch. I am the former foreman, before I got tae slow."

"Come now. Tavish, ye speak as if we hae done ye a disservice," Beathan clapped the other man on the back hard enough to buckle one of his knees. "Yer only semi-retired, besides if we had ye going full time, folk would say I canna take care of my elders."

The old man took exception to Beathan's remarks and aimed a kick at his shins. "I've known ye all yer life, Beathan Clunes, and I am nae elderly."

Beathan stepped out of the way without much grace. "Captain, my faither sent ye an invitation tae dine with us this evening. I can see by the look of yer face ye would prefer tae decline, but I dinnae accept," he gave us both a salute and whistled as he walked away.

"The young hae a penchant fur wasting youth," Tavish said under his breath as he watched Beathan's back, turning to me. "Welcome tae Markinch and Deoch. We make the best Scotch in the world, if ye will follow me back down the road, we'll look over the malting barn," the old man wagged his overgrown white eyebrows indicating his excitement.

I mustered my enthusiasm for the morning's tour. Having enjoyed the product of these men's labours last evening, perhaps it was only fair I learned how they made their Scotch. Besides my only other business would be tidying Mr Turner's papers and it would force me to share more silent time with my brooding housemaid.

Tavish went forth with a bounce in his step that a few younger men of my acquaintance might watch with jealousy. I lengthened my strides in order to match his pace and watched while he greeted the other workers with a nod or smile. Reaching the first large barn on the left side of the road, Tavish opened a side door and indicated I should precede him. The warmth and the smell of the barn collided with my senses, leaving me momentarily dazed.

"Welcome, Captain, tae the malting barn." Tavish swept inside and walked over to one of the many long wooden boxes, which looked like troughs for water.

Stepping inside the warmth of the barn, I walked over to the row of troughs. Soggy barley filled each one. "This is where the germination process occurs, water is added tae the barley and we bide a few days fur the seeds tae germinate, fur the plants tae emerge from the seeds."

I decided not to inform him I was well aware of the process of germination, having witnessed many experiments in the process as a student at Cambridge and later as a member of the Royal Society. The older man needed to believe in my interest in the stills workings, so I nodded for him to continue.

"As Deoch prides itself on producing the best Scotch in the Highlands, we only use barley from local fairmers who we trust. Ye might nae be aware of this, Captain, but many diseases can befall guid barley and it is up tae the fairmers and us tae spot them." Tavish proceeded to describe in detail the various fungus and blight that ruined good barley.

Pointing to a set of stairs, Tavish indicated the second floor, the door firmly shut, "The barley is moved up to the drying floors." I followed him up the narrow staircase and slipped quickly behind him as he carefully entered the loft. My eyes burned and I blinked rapidly, the peat burning in the metal grate at the far end of the room heated the air to a pleasant temperature, however, there were no windows for the smoke to escape.

"We use the peat from the surrounding fens tae give our Scotch a light smoky taste, Markinch peat makes our Scotch special, there is nae other place in the Highlands hae as guid a peat as here," Tavish assured me with a smile.

I looked around the large space through watery, narrowed eyes. As best as my diminished sight would allow, the barley looked at least ankle deep. Pointing to two large rakes leaning beside the wall, "How are these devises put to use?"

Beaming with approval at my interest, Tavish plucked up one of the rakes and began to flick the barley over. "The boys come up here every so often and rustle the barley, its crucial the mixture isnae left fur too long otherwise ye get rot and the whole batch must be destroyed, cannae even feed it tae the livestock."

Tavish rewarded my interest by rushing me back down the stairs and out of the malting barn. Grateful for the clean air, I inhaled several deep breaths; even though the cold stung my face, at least my eyes halted their weeping.

After regaining control of my senses, I watched Tavish, who appeared to be lost in his own thoughts. The morning air began to seep into my clothes and the cold was uncomfortable after the intense heat of the drying floors. "Tavish, I presume there is another step in the process of Scotch we have yet to explore," I prompted lightly in order to get our bodies moving.

Tavish gave me a grim smile and dragged his feet towards the double doors of the watermill. I became exceptionally excited, here was an opportunity to watch the cogs and stone in motion, the curiosity of machinery never diminished as I left boyhood.

"The mill was built shortly after the Clunes purchased the Castle and surrounding lands," Tavish scratched his head. "I remember working on it along with the builder from Edinburgh; I was full amazed with how all the pieces fit together, took all the lads and oxen we had tae get the stone in place. Worth every shilling; we grind our own malt intae grist, saving time and coin by nae sending it off the mill down in the lowlands and we trade a grinding service tae fairmers if they sell us barley and they hae the rest ground," Tavish cleared his throat. "Mr Clunes, is an enterprising fellow."

Tavish opened a smaller door set into one of the larger portals with far less enthusiasm than when he explained how to look for small scabs of black on barley in order to find rot.

Ignoring the other man's apprehension, I boldly walked through to the first floor of the watermill. A man looked up from watching the grooved stones working together to grind the barley into grist, he shouted up to the second floor and another batch of grain fell from a chute to the middle of the stone circles where it would eventually work itself to the edges, ground and perfect. Without hesitating, I went up the steps covered in ground meal dust to the second floor, the gears would be located here and I was not disappointed. The waterwheel was driving the shaft, turning the pit wheel and meshing with the crown shaft in order to spin the main shaft down to the turning stones on the first floor.

My breath caught at the arresting sight, watching the fluidity of such a large machine in action, knowing man had been using such an incredible device for years in order to turn a crop, grown in the fields, inedible, into the basic staple of human survival, bread and of course in the case of the still, grist for making alcohol.

"Och, well, Captain, I wondered when I might be making yer acquaintance," a Scottish brogue echoed down from the loft above the gears, the face a replica of the man's standing behind me. I even turned to check Tavish stood at the top of the steps, perhaps this was a trick played on every new man in Markinch. "Uncanny, isn't it? Though I suspect I am the better looking brither, our mother told me as much, bless her soul, younger and handsomer than my older, dunce of a brither," the other man grinned with malice, his gaze focused past me on Tavish.

"Captain, may I make my younger brither, Angus, known tae ye," Tavish stepped beside me and frowned up at his kin. "He runs the watermill fur Deoch and any business with it goes through him," Tavish turned and tried to make a hasty departure to the first floor.

"Angus!" cried the other man from the top of the ladder, he threw himself down and chased after his older brother a moment. "Now ye arenae running the distillery, ye are nae longer entitled tae use our last name only, I am the Tavish and it is only fair ye call me as such!"

An argument between the two brothers erupted below stairs and I hurried to watch the outcome, the lad above stairs feeding the wheel nodded to the one watching the grinding stones and produced a worn silver coin. Meanwhile two floury faces appeared from below stairs with avid looks, the two brothers quarreling was an event.

"Ye know damn well, the oldest male in each family holds the family name. Faither has bin dead all our lives, making me the Tavish, it has naught tae do with the posts we hold, Angus," Tavish put emphasis on his brother's name in order to pin it there with force.

"If our mother lived, ye would know differently." Angus pointed his bony finger straight between the eyes of his brother, the mention of their mother appeared to galvanise both brothers.

Observing the two men, I tried to guess which one might win a physical fight. Tavish may have been older, but the two appeared so alike, one could not be stronger than his sibling. From the twinkle in each of their eyes, they did not look above fighting dirty and now the two stood toe to toe in the dusty millhouse. In an effort to inject some reason into the argument, I began, "I am sure your mother never intended you to fight over your last name at your advanced ages, did she not give you both acceptable first names to face the world?"

Two sets of piercing blue eyes bore into my face, all menace between the brothers dropped in favour of the destruction of a common enemy. "Sassenach," Angus's voice low, "ye better never, ever say anything about my mother ever again, nae tae me, nae tae anyone."

The anger radiating from the other man burned the air, more nods and coins exchanged hands and each brother flexed his fists, readying for a confrontation. I did my best to keep a straight face. As much as I would like to face each brother, they were at least twice my age, maybe even thrice, I bowed. "I beg your pardon," and turned to walk back outside, hoping neither would see the grin on my face.

The door to the mill closed. "Hae ye got a brither, Captain, or any siblings?" Tavish's sheepish voice came from beside me, as the old man scratched his head for a moment and reshaped his plaid hat before fixing it back over his flyaway white hair.

Crossing to the other side of the road, I spoke, "Ill luck left me as an only child, my parents died before I grew from my small clothes, my uncle did his best for me." The reply standard, any new acquaintance received the same distilled version of my childhood circumstances. For many, my situation did not appear unusual or hard.

Finally entering the last of the three red buildings, we stood next to two large polished metal tuns, an apparatus with stairs built around it for easy viewing. Tavish pointed, "These are the mashing tuns, the grist is steeped with hot water and eventually a mash is made, the end product is called wort. We brew the wort at least three times and this is where the excise comes in, the quality of this end product will determine how much spirit is finally produced."

I injected a comment here to show my knowledge, "At this time, I believe the yeast is added to the cool mixture and a rudimentary beer is produced." The operation at Deoch was large enough not to change any of its processes in order to cheat taxes and if they did make any hasty changes, it would be noticeable. Still, I did not want any trouble.

If I studied under Tavish's instruction, the look of joy on his face at my understanding of the wort process might have filled me with pleasure, for it gave me the opportunity to watch someone who truly enjoyed his work. He took pleasure from the simple chemical processes in making alcohol; here was not a soldier killing for wages, but a man who gained satisfaction from giving other people enjoyment.

"Captain, yer knowledge ay the process is correct indeed, the beer contains only a wee percentage ay alcohol, it's enough tae gie drunk from mind," Tavish pointed to two men, one busy sweeping the compact dirt floor and the other cleaning some instruments. "It's why we always hae two men in here watching the mash tuns and the pot stills, some workers hae been sorely tempted fur a taste in the past."

The thought of putting the wash back to my lips made my stomach protest over the amount of porridge I consumed earlier, the genuine look on Tavish's face confirmed the reality of such shenanigans. "It is well you have the matter in hand. Are those the pot stills?"

We walked to the opposite side of the barn where two large copper pot stills gleamed in the light of oil lamps, a man studiously polished the side of one while the run poured into another metal container, a glass box protected the newly distilled alcohol and I peered curiously at the iron padlock.

Wagging his eyebrows, "Ye can imagine if a fellow is tempted by the wort, how much temptation they might face watching this divine liquid spill forth; the padlock keeps us all honest." Tavish winked, pointing at the lyne arm where the evaporated alcohol cools and turns back to liquid, "Our arm is lengthier than any other in the Highlands, fur maximum cooling."

The device caught my interest and I walked up the narrow stairs and stood on the wooden platform surrounding the top of both pot stills, the lyne arm was indeed longer than the ones normally used for the distillation process, and it fell at more of a diagonal angle. "You Scots appear to have some ingenious ideas when it comes to making alcohol, now if only you could apply the same principles to your politics you might stay out of trouble."

"Och, Captain, never let it be said a Scotsman has nae nose fur making improvements tae Scotch, Deoch is one ay those rare places where new ideas arenae frowned upon. We like tradition in Markinch, and we like tae be the ones with best equipment," Tavish patted the still. "Ye might notice the shape."

"The gauger come tae inspect our stills, I am sure ye will find everything in order, Sassenach," the last word delivered on a hiss made every instinct in my body scream and come alive. Logan noted my presence at Deoch, as I looked over the railing at the kilted man standing below me.

I balled my fists and set my jaw with a snap, I buried the urge to shout back down at Logan remanding him for his rudeness. Instead I trained my gaze back on Tavish, "I believe you were going to mention something significant over the shape of the tuns, please continue."

Unsure at first, Tavish glanced down at Logan, gauging the other man's reaction and made a decision, "As ye can see, the tuns hae been reshaped, squashed intae more of an onion shape," Tavish's chest stood out proudly. "This slight change has made the distilling process much more effective; I convinced Clunes of its worth."

I clapped the other man on the shoulder, a reflex from my time as a soldier, camaraderie between friends meant in times of strife, when fighting might be fiercest, allies and friends became saviors and heroes. The action felt stilted with Tavish, however the other man's smile rewarded my presumption.

The man standing below did not take kindly to being ignored, "This is a cozy sight, Tavish making couthy with the Sassenach, hae ye any wonder over yer replacement by a younger man, I think ye should look back on this moment," Logan spat the words up at the older man.

Tavish's shoulders slumped, the light shining only moments ago in his blue eyes dimmed; he became a puppet of a man. Turning, I set my boots to the ladder sharply and quickly, not entirely sure of the logic spurring my hurried actions. My only thought to end the torment of an old man, stepping from the ladder, I strode with menace to where Logan stood, leaving only a hand's breadth between myself and him, I stopped abruptly, the other man swayed back to put space between us.

"In England, we have respect for our elders, it's a quaint custom, which appears to be on short supply here in the Highlands. No matter, I am happy to teach you the basics, even if I need to beat it into you." I kept my voice low. I knew it brought instant fear in other men. My focus tightened onto my prey, I knew Tavish stood at the bottom of the steps and the two men from the mashing tuns crept closer for a better view. The lad shining the still, stopped in mid stroke. Outnumbered, I relished the thought of a fight, I may not win against all of them at once but I was going to inflict some serious pain.

Logan blinked several times, his voice clear and reedy, "Last night ye were content tae hide behind Her Majesty fur protection, I find the change in yer attitude refreshing, though I wouldnae want tae be led intae a trap, it is treason tae attack a representative ay the Crown, I hear."

I let a smile creep across my lips, my eyes remained cold. "I am happy to remove my excise hat for long enough to beat some respect out of your hide. I think you have a big mouth, Logan, a big opinionated mouth I want to permanently shut, if you would step outside?"

A heartbeat passed and Logan commenced laughing and stepped away. "Yer nae milk and bread sop from the south, perhaps there's a bit ay Highlander in ye." I did not relax my stance, though Logan visibly forced himself into a casual position indicating the conclusion of the confrontation, "Ye might stand a better chance ay surviving up haur than yer predecessor."

"Another threat, Logan?" I asked mildly, letting my hands unclench. Logan looked nervous, surprised by my attitude. I did not back away from fights. "I suggest you keep your comments to yourself and out of earshot from me and you might stand a chance of not receiving a beating such as your father never dreamed of giving you."

Logan's lip curled into a snarl and I tensed waiting for impact. Surprisingly it never came, the other man appeared to be an instigator to his bones, however he could rein it in with a control few men possessed. Once again, I was impressed in spite of my annoyance with the man. Logan turned and yelled at his companions to get back to work.

Stepping in front of me, Tavish blocked my view of Logan's back as he stomped out the door, his bushy eyes contemplating me before he spoke. "I am nae right sure if I'm supposed tae thank ye. I'm the previous foreman, when Beathan took over, he replaced me with Logan, someone younger able to keep up with the demands ay Deoch, I'm still the master blender, along with Mr Clunes, of course."

"Tavish, I would like to make an apology to you," the need for honesty provoked me. "I think Logan and his rude treatment of you annoyed me, I let my anger rule my actions," the other man nodded and I tried to explain further. "The last few months have not been generous to me and I behave without thinking."

Nodding, Tavish walked back out of the barn and, once on the road, he looked around. A few men were gathered together smoking in front of the mill. He turned and walked up the hill out of the distillery buildings. "Markinch is a family name, nae long ago there was a Laird of Markinch and he owned all the lands and the Castle fur as far as ye can see," Tavish spread his arms wide to indicate the heather-covered hills.

Not understanding where this conversation might lead, I went over all the information Colonel Manners had provided regarding the post and Markinch. I had made a thorough study of each document on the ride north, "The information on Markinch and Deoch did not mention a Laird in the area, only the Clunes and several smaller landowners, unusual in the Highlands, yet not unique."

The other man waved a gnarled hand, "The Laird ay Markinch," Tavish paused for a moment before taking a deep breath, "I may hae been only a laddie but I remember him, stoatin brute ay a man with terrible wrath and even more enormous pride, made worse by his family's ill fortune. They were destitute, it's nae easy trying tae scratch a living frae these hills, envied the Clunes and their Scotch. Figured the troubles would be his turn tae make a great fortune and fur a while he and his son fought as mercenaries along with the rest ay the Scotch fur the Parliamentarians, raiding and fighting, taking anything ay value they could carry."

The terrible days of civil war only lived in the memories of boys reading texts now, as the men who fought had taken their places in the grave. Families pitted against one another, the shame of regicide still hangs over our Parliament like a plague, a generation of honourable men dead, only to return a king to his thrown, a terrible waste.

"When the royalists came up tae Scotland tae make a deal in Forty-Seven, promising reform and such, Markinch and his son quickly signed fur the King, hoping tae dae at least as well fur Markinch as done with the Parliamentarians." Tavish stopped and over a crest of the next hill, I could see the crenellated walls of a castle, "Guess their isnae a man amongst us who thinks they are gonnae die." Tavish looked long and hard at my profile before I turned to stare him in the eye, I only nodded for him to continue. "I suppose their maker had need of them as Markinch and his heir died the following year at the Battle of Preston, only his badge made it back tae the Highlands, presented tae his dochter along with a sealed letter frae the Sassenach declaring her faither and brither as traitors, all money and lands seized at once."

I gave Tavish a puzzled look, "Many families were torn apart during the civil war; I do not understand how the plight of the Markinch family has any real precedence over Deoch-an-Dorus now." I looked back to the castle, it could have grown from the ground in a great upheaval, its solid walls appeared hewn from the earth.

"I was a boy when Mr Clunes' faither made a deal with the Parliamentarians. He bought the castle and the surrounding lands, promising never tae rise up against them," Tavish chuckled. "He told the story tae the lads about how he travelled all the way to London. He waited fur days tae receive an audience with the magistrates and finally they gae it tae him without much pause as none of the fine Sassenach Lords wanted a castle in the middle of the Highlands. After he returned, Mr Clunes set tae expanding his business and kept Markinch away from the fighting in the south; none hereabouts had any taste for it, as it had naught tae dae with us."

Tavish scratched his bristly chin for a moment, "The point of this whole rambling tale is to tell you the story of Logan. He is the great, great grandson of the auld Markinch Laird, and he wears his jealousy of the Clunes' success on his sleeve."

Chapter 4

I spent the afternoon in Tavish's company, going through the old production logs. I insisted on making an inventory of all the grain arriving at the mill. Illegal stills could be using missing grain to make Scotch. Dusk fell as I walked back down to the cottage in order to prepare for my supper invitation; tiny flakes from clouds obscuring the sky began to fall, creating an atmosphere of hushed enchantment.

Walking through the front door of the cottage, I could smell peat burning in the grate, the pleasant smell of light smoke escaping through the chimney. Closing the door behind me, I shut my eyes and tried to conjure a picture of Onatah busily at work somewhere in the house.

"There ye are, Captain," Freya's voice rang from above and her stout figure filled my vision as she came down the stairs. "I hae tidied above stairs this afternoon, I aired one ay the front rooms and made the bed fur ye," she stopped on the bottom step and still craned her neck to look up at me. "Beathan has informed me ay yer supper invitation, sae there is naught in the larder," Freya paused a moment, looking uncertain. "You'll hae tae tell me if ye want meals made, otherwise I've got my own brood tae feed."

The morning's altercation forgotten, at least set to the side, I could only be relieved, not having much patience for women's moods and tantrums, "Thank you, Freya, I am sure the two of us will do our best to get along, please let me know of any expenses you incur and I will provide reimbursement."

"Of course, Captain," Freya turned her attention to the drawing room, and stepped closer in order to share in her confidence. "The Thistle and Rose acts as a market fur most goods and a tab will be run in yer name payable at the end of the month. They hae catalogues fur any items ye may want tae purchase from Auld Reikie, Edinburgh tae ye, or Glasgow," her look took in my sad frock coat. "We pride ourselves as having as guid a selection as anyone in town or Scotland. I thought tomorrow it would be appropriate fur me tae begin clearing away poor Mr Turner's work," sniffing dismissively. "I know it is wrong tae speak nae well ay the dead and I dinnae believe any ay the rumours circulating in the village. He never let me tidy up properly in here, I will hae tae fetch a ladder and a couple of my laddies to get the rope down."

What were these rumours? I wanted to ask for details concerning them, but a thought diverted me, "Take the rope down with a ladder, is there not one around? I thought Mr Turner's stature shorter than mine."

"Aye, he stood only just taller than I," Freya smiled at a memory, putting her hand to her forehead and grimacing up at me. "Sometimes I still cannae believe it. He might have been an odd body, however I never thought him capable, if I had," she took a couple of deep sobbing breaths.

Female hysterics were something I never acquired the ability to deal with; perhaps if my mother might have lived or a younger sister tormented me, I would have been more prepared to deal with them. I patted Freya on the back, "It's just as well, I want to leave the rope up; the knot is peculiar, there is something missing in the puzzle," I let my voice trail away.

Hiccoughing a couple of times, Freya frowned up at me and for the second time in one day, I could feel her approbation for a social misstep vibrating from her being. "Ye want me tae keep that horrible rope up in the drawing room, want me tae clean around it, knowing what happened in there, it's a terrible grizzle thing!"

I let my hand fall back to my side. Seeing her point, I grimaced, acknowledging the rope's macabre presence in an effort to placate her. "Until I finish my study of the knot, I think it's best for you to leave the drawing room off your list of duties. Besides I would enjoy going through Mr Turner's mathematical work; it looks incredibly interesting."

"Ye are an odd body, Captain," Freya stepped away, towards the door to the dining room. "I cannae condone such barbaric actions, maybe ye dinnae know how yer actions might affect my poor nerves," she sniffed. "The same as Mr Turner, strange behavioiur by folks from the south."

An urge to run my hands through my hair and pull as hard as I could came into my mind. Instead I fisted my hands and breathed deeply as the rear door to the cottage opened and closed forcefully. Taking today as a preview of the discord to come over the next year, I shuddered to think of the mess of nerves I might be left with in the end.

With heavy boots, I trod up the stairs to find what mischief Freya may have made while I spent the day up at Deoch. To my surprise, the results of her cleaning were not all bad, she'd organised one of the front rooms, lighting a fire in the grate, setting my shaving kit along with fresh water on the commode, even the heather in a small vase did not grate too much. Guilt washed over me, twice today I caused Freya to be unhappy and, in truth, I resolved to do my best to right our relationship once and for all in the morning.

After washing my face of the day's activities, I dressed in my best linen shirt and hose. Both made of good quality material, they stood the test of time. The hair on my head felt downy and I paused for a good minute, pondering whether to shave my head again or let it grow; in the New World, I had resolved never to wear a wig again, fashionable or no. A red ribbon caught my attention, and I picked up the delicate furbelow, careful not to disrupt any of the long strands of black hair it held in a curl, tears welled behind my eyes and I looked into the small mirror. I was a fraud, a disgrace to her memory; my wife lay dead and buried and I was to sup in style with the only society in the vicinity.

I smelled the hair, rubbing its silky texture on my cheek, I placed it carefully back onto lace set out by Freya; luckily she took precautions with my precious keepsake. I needed to cancel this invitation, not a month ago I stood rotting in the stocks in Boston, for attacking the man responsible for my wife's death.

Thinking of ways to bow out gracefully, my gaze fell upon my lapel pin, my only reminder of my place in society, of where I came from, the Clyde coat of arms set in gold with the family motto, Courage to the Last, written on the bottom. Never one for cowardice, I had attacked in the front lines in the New World, I would bear my burden.

Full darkness descended over Markinch, a lamp in one hand to light the way through the snowflakes my only companion on the road up and through the distillery. The workers either home or down at the Thistle for the evening, tucked warmly into their evening rituals, a night guard watched my progress from his post on the road in front of Deoch.

The lantern light reflected off the snow gathering in pockets on the ground, making it easy to pick my way over the rough surface. Just as I relaxed into the embrace of the wilds of the fens, lights from the castle were visible ahead, guiding me gently back to civilization, to the purpose of my evening's journey. The doors leading into the courtyard were open, in fact a quick inspection of the metal gate above my head revealed the fact it probably had not been down in some time. Large cauldrons lit with peat stood at intervals and I nodded to the workmen and servants before climbing the great steps.

I felt slightly embarrassed at the archaic formality of banging the large metal knocker on the door to alert the inside servants of my presence, surely they would have seen my approach. However, just as social niceties were different in the New World, so would they be different here in the Highlands. The door creaked open and a grim-faced gentlemen, wearing the same plaid as Beathan, peered out at me. Without speaking, I found myself ushered into a cavernous reception hall, resplendent with a blaze in the large fireplace and various bits of weaponry including muskets and rapiers adorning the wall. A large broadsword placed on the mantel caught my attention and I walked forward in order to make a closer inspection, the grim-faced clansman coughed in the back of his throat and indicated I should give him the oil lamp before proceeding with my curious journey.

Only a person twice the size of any man could wield this sword. Even with the added strength the warrior would need two hands to swing it. The hilt resplendently decorated with fine gold filigree and gems, with a large ruby set in the hilt, heavy scroll work wound down the blade and I squinted to read it properly.

"I thought ye may hae taken a wrong turn, Captain," Beathan's voice interrupted my deciphering and I turned with slight irritation to greet him. He held a glass out in his hand, "Welcome tae Castle Markinch, home ay the Clunes."

Accepting the glass with a smile, I nodded in return, "Thank you for the invitation to dine. It has been many months since I graced a seat at a proper dining table, I will concentrate on not making a bore of myself this evening." I lifted my glass to match Beathan's salute and we drank together. The Scotch tasted incredibly fine, much better quality than I ever sampled in the past and I turned the glass over to admire the colour.

"One of the perks of coming round fur supper," Beathan grimaced. "My faither is auld and tired and my sister is firmly on the shelf, hardly the best companions fur a meal. However, ye get to dip intae the guid stock." He winked, "We cannae hae folk around and drink the standard we send out tae the rest of the masses."

I gave Beathan another salute and took another pull, I could definitely become accustomed to the smooth, smoky flavour of this Scotch, the quality so different from the bottle I consumed the past evening, I never would have thought it came from the same family still.

"Beathan, I know ye would prefer tae keep the captain all tae yerself out there, however, Faither would enjoy meeting our guest," a firm, soft voice called from the open doorway, the brogue similar to Beathan's, light with only the touch of an accent to make it sound exotic.

My companion shrugged his shoulders in apology and led the way into a large, stately drawing room, oil lamps and a few candles lit the large space, a fire burned in a marble hearth set on the opposite side of the wall, two delicate couches faced one another in front, one occupied by an older gentlemen and a woman no longer in the blossom of youth, however far from old. Everything in the room spoke the success of Deoch, from the gilt picture frames and mirrors on the walls, to the rest of the furniture grouped together to form smaller parties of conversation in the room, even the thick rugs underfoot felt lavish.

"We dinnae stand on much formality here, Captain," the old man stood and swept his sharp eyes over my attire. I knew he missed nothing from my bald head to my slightly scuffed boots. His own jacket, worn over a linen shirt to compliment his kilt, spoke of an expensive cut made to look serviceable and he wore a small wig with the long white hair caught in a black ribbon.

I gave him a short bow, "A pleasure to make your acquaintance, Mr Clunes. Thank you for the invitation to dine, I informed Beathan on my arrival it is a rare occurrence for an old army captain." Pretty words and platitudes may not be my trade, however I was not above a bit of flattery.

"Nae, ye must call me Magnus, Mr Clunes is only fur folk who owe me coin or I owe them pose," he sat back down on the sofa with a huff, and took up his Scotch, an example of a man not born to wealth or privilege, who may have never even aspired to either, yet he sat in the drawing room of a disgraced Lord and reigned over all he surveyed; he earned respect.

Turning to the woman standing next to the sofa, I made another short bow. She politely returned the favour, and wore a curious rather than a friendly smile. "Captain, welcome tae our home, since my brither appears tae hae forgotten his duty tae me," she shot Beathan a mild look of annoyance, "I am Philomena Clunes, please spare me the Miss Clunes, it only grates on the fact I am nae miss at all."

"A pleasure to make your acquaintance, Philomena," the unusual name rolled from the tongue and threatened to trip the unwary speaker. Dressed in a simple gown, with no bows or ruffles, she wore her hair in a severe bun at the back of her head, no wig and no powder on her face, not even the hint of a black beauty patch marred her creamy complexion. If we met by chance in a ballroom, or even in the street, I do not think I would have given her a second glance, though something in her green eyes warranted a second look; intelligent, not striking as my wife's dark eyes and hair, any man meeting Onatah would fall immediately in love with her.

Philomena turned to acknowledge a discreet cough from another doorway, nodding she turned back, "I think Cook is ready fur us," she leaned down to help her father from the low couch and he held her arm as they led the way through to the heavily decorated dining room with a table set cozily for four, even though it could easily fit twenty diners. I tried to reconcile the fabulous display of wealth of both the drawing room and the dining room with the subdued appearance of my three supper companions; they gave no hint at the opulent tastes surrounding them; the room would be the envy of any society hostess in London.

Beathan leaned over from his seat next to mine and with a nod he indicated the room at large, "My late mother's tastes ran tae the fanciful, as an heiress from a great family she took pleasure in redecorating the castle tae current fashion." He smiled at Philomena, "If only my younger sister could delight in such pastimes, perhaps she would be seated at her own table this evening."

Sniffing in contempt, "I see nae reason fur me tae leave Faither's board," Philomena let the server shake out and place her napkin. "My absence would only result in a complete lack of female entertainment in this household, it isnae as if we were in danger ay yer wife making an imminent appearance."

Choking back a laugh into my soup – Philomena certainly knew how to expose a man – I felt myself relax in the presence of the two siblings, bickering looked commonplace between them and their father's smile showed a true affection for the two. It was rare to see a man take such concern over his children.

Philomena gently laid her spoon to rest on the table, frowning at Beathan before she spoke directly to me, "Captain, before my brither and I ruin this pleasant evening baiting each other with auld grievances, let us turn a new page. We hae heard ay yer recently being in Boston, please tell us ay yer adventures."

Three faces peered over the supper table eager to hear of the adventures of a soldier in the New World, to delight in learning of the hardships faced away from civilization, gasp over the brutality to be found and be warmed over the vast richness of the land I had left behind. My heart still beat across the ocean, "I am afraid I am not much of a storyteller and you will find me incredibly dull."

Magnus selected a portion of roast lamb from the attendant and waved his hand in my direction, "Nonsense, Captain, we are only the three ay us, except when Beathan or Philomena's friends come fur a stay in the country fur distraction. Though I secretly ponder what distractions

Markinch could possibly hold over the likes ay Auld Reikie or London, we are in want ay honest company."

"Indeed, Captain, ye will be doing me a favour by speaking on the subject," Philomena leaned forward in her seat. "Books on the New World are exceedingly hard tae come by all the way up here and I am currently waiting fur my copy of Dr Preston's newly published experiences ay his adventures in the Americas. My friends are reading it now."

"Dinnae encourage her, Captain, she is a bluestocking ay the worst order, Faither and I despair she will ever find a husband now she is well and truly on the shelf." Beathan gave his younger sister a condescending glance and turned his gaze to me, "I apologise fur my sister's lack ay decorum."

"Captain, let me make an apology tae ye fur my children's behaviour, ye might hae lived among the wild men of the America's however our own lack of genteel company has adversely affected the manners at my table," Magnus gave Beathan and Philomena a hard stare. "Perhaps ye could tell us why ye chose tae enter the military ranks."

There would be no escape this evening from topics I tended to avoid in all company, Markinch was no place to keep secrets and why should I be resolved to hold old wounds to my chest, my tenancy already at less than a year, "In fact I joined the regiment on a whim to escape my uncle's plans for a planned marriage." I felt strangely disappointed by the lack of response from any of my dinner companions, Beathan continued to dish roast capon into his mouth, Philomena's eyes glazed over and Magnus nodded sagely, as if he possessed a great understanding of the young and their foibles.

"As my uncle's only heir, he felt prompted to arrange a good marriage for me in order to continue our line infinitely into the future.," I pushed my plate away and tried to recall all the details of the late afternoon I was presented with the hand of the especially eligible and incomparable Lady Strathmore, the débutante of the season. She possessed every social grace that could be expected from a young woman of quality; she sang, played an instrument, spoke several languages well. She was rich and, not unlike other women of her station, she was cruel to those she believed undeserving of her attention. I had witnessed her pitiless behaviour firsthand.

"I knew from the first we could never suit, I pleaded with my uncle to end the engagement, he would not and I joined the regiment to escape." I thought of the look on Mr Wick's caring face as I pounded on the knocker at his townhouse, demanding entrance. "With some help from an old friend, I enrolled in my late father's platoon and was soon away to Boston."

"It is fashionable fur a man tae hae at least one broken engagement these days," Philomena remarked sourly, not meeting my eye, instead watching the serving staff clear away the plates. "Young men need a hint ay scandal in order tae get intae the best drawing rooms, where the incomparables are hidden away from the rest of society."

Magnus cleared his throat at the end of the table, "The papers speak of the immense riches of the New World, tobacco and cotton plantations spring intae life with nary a problem, huge shipbuilding yards produce vessels with the latest inventions, it is a land of opportunity where with a little capital, a man might make much fur himself."

"The papers have the right of it, most of the time, though it's a hard life for settlers away from the protection of towns or militia, especially as the French are wont to make skirmishes into our territory in order to expand their influence with their ungodly ways." I shrugged my shoulders, I was no longer an active soldier. I was a cog in a wheel of bureaucracy.

With the mention of the French, Beathan lifted his head from the next course and leaned towards me, "All the French be damned." Magnus raised his wineglass with a quiet "Hear, hear," while Philomena rolled her eyes. Beathan continued, "Did ye fight the dastardly fellows yerself, Captain? We only receive the barest ay news when it comes tae fighting in the Americas."

I studied Philomena's profile across the table. She had studiously ignored my gaze since I mentioned jilting Lady Strathmore; she clearly believed an alliance with her own sex much more important than civil conversation to aid in digestion, not unlike other high-strung females of my acquaintance. Finally, she turned her green eyes to meet mine, "I assure ye, Captain, any mention ay atrocities in which ye participated in the New World will nae make me think any less of ye."

The challenge hit the table, Magnus and Beathan watched the pair of us warily. "There are no real battles to be had with the French, nothing to give a complete victory to either side. Mostly because of the frugality of each country's government; the policy is to harvest the Americas with as little inconvenience as possible. The summer months mean the regiment and the Boston Militia are often away for long stretches, raiding enemy territory, harassing French towns and villages." I did not avert my eyes from Philomena's face, "The intent to terrorise the population into leaving with pain and murder."

Immediately I regretted being goaded into discussing the burn and pillage policy of the English Army. It was the same as the French side, but as a boy, I had imagined armies in a line, fighting with valour and honour, not the gut-clenching savagery of raiding a family farm, putting the inhabitants to death and stealing their food to feed ourselves before planning the next campaign of terror.

"The ladies of Boston must all be aflutter with tales ay yer extraordinary deeds done in the name of England." Philomena watched as a server placed a portion of blancmange on her dessert plate. "Tell us something nae connected with yerself, describe the savages who live in wilds, ye must hae surely met some while destroying the livelihood of innocent French folk."

"Magnus, you are harbouring a French sympathiser at your table," Philomena opened her mouth to argue however I continued swiftly. "The French are the natural enemy to England, you cannot be ignorant of this fact as it is splashed across the pages of history in both our nations in blood. In fact, it is the people ay the Americas who suffer the most during the conflict."

"Captain, I dinnae think anyone at this table would believe the French hae been anything but instigators ay conflict when it comes tae English happiness," Magnus once again cleared his throat loudly. "They hae even condescended tae ally themselves with us Scots on occasion, if only tae tweak the noses of the English."

This dinner would soon end in a farce if I did not regain control of my temper. I have never before allowed a woman to provoke me into behaving poorly, "The land as you mentioned before, Magnus, is full of promise, though it takes hard work and determination to beat back the wilderness and force it into proper production. Women and men must make huge sacrifices to gain returns. There is no one singular tribe amongst the Indians of the Americas; there are hundreds of different bands, speaking multiple different languages, all with their own customs and, depending on their territory, with different modes of survival. Some live from hunting buffalo over the Great Plains, others fish from the sea part of the year and hunt during others: it is all incredibly complicated."

"It sounds as if ye hae put some study intae such matters," Beathan smiled at Philomena. "Ere is yer first hand account ay the lives of folk in the Americas, if only ye could be patient with the Captain instead of haranguing him like an angry fish wife. Is it any wonder men cower in yer presence, even with yer large dowry?"

Philomena ignored her brother's jibe and focused her attention on me, "I hae read several articles depicting the Indians as total savages with nae remorse and nae regard fur human life, in fact I believe the English Army even removed one tribe, the Pequot, tae another location in order tae stop their barbarity against another group."

"It's true each tribe is fiercely protective of their hunting grounds and on occasion there are fights," I twirled the stem of my wineglass for a moment. "Not unlike the English going to war with France, or France with Spain, it is not always easy to rub along with one's neighbours. My own wife's tribe, for example, was the Mohawk, though they made alliances with four other nations for protection and are known collectively as the Iroquois, within the larger group, smaller nations are protected."

"Yer wife, Captain?" The look of shock on Philomena's face was worth every jibe I might receive from the more prudish residents of Markinch when they learned of my dead wife. "Never say ye are married tae a savage, it is unconscionable!"

"I was married to a member of the Mohawk tribe. She was not a savage." A memory of her sitting near the fire, chin resting on her knees, a smile playing on her lips as she listened to her brother, Hania, and I speak of our day's hunt rose before my eyes. I cleared my throat to erase it. "She was caring, generous and in every way the equal and better of most of the women who call themselves ladies in the ballrooms of London."

Philomena lowered her eyes to her plate in surrender; I only needed to expose myself to all manners of torment to cease her disapproval of my person. The hole in my chest where Onatah lived before her death ached in loneliness and I wished to be away from this table at once; I needed solace.

The silence lengthened and I feared that in my haste to see Philomena in her place, I had completely ruined the evening. Magnus spoke in a low voice, "Is it common practice fur officers tae marry Indian girls? We dinnae hear ay such things in the papers."

Laughing harshly, "You would not hear of a marriage between an English soldier and a native anywhere in the English realms, Magnus, though the practice is common enough even among the French. Women are a rare commodity, though I would have stayed with my wife for the rest of my days," I swallowed before continuing. "Most men leave women and return to England, creating dishonour for them."

"It appears ye arenae much better, Captain," Philomena stared across the table, with hard green eyes. "I have nae heard ay a native woman living with ye in the cottage, ye hae left her behind with a bevy of bastards in tow, I should think."

I stood towering over the table, I felt Beathan tense beside me, however he did not rise. I spoke the next words slowly, enunciating each one. "My wife is dead." The harshness of the words tore through the gilt dining room. "She was pregnant with our first child. They are both gone now. Please heap more agony onto my conscience if you think you could reach the top of the pile."

Philomena sat back in her chair, shock registering on her face, she was speechless, a state not often experienced by the young lady if judged by the look in her eye. Beathan whispered, "Perhaps ye should retire tae the drawing room with the tea cart, Phil, and leave us tae the Scotch."

The footman pulled her chair out from the table and Philomena rose a trifle unsteadily to her feet. She paused for a moment, an unreadable expression on her face. I was sure she might say something, instead she gave a short curtsey and swept from the room, shoulders square, chin up.

I closed my eyes, and turned to Beathan and Magnus who watched Philomena's progress from the dining room with surprise. "I apologise to you both, especially to you, Magnus," my expression hopefully conveyed my embarrassment. "You must think you invited a brute to come and dine with you this evening," I retook my seat and allowed the server to pour a Scotch.

"On the contrary, Captain, I think I hae invited a real man tae sit at the table," Magnus dismissed the serving staff with a wave. "My daughter is far too accustomed tae having her own way and she easily manipulates the dandies who come calling on her. I do believe she might be in shock," he raised his glass in salute and drank.

I raised my own and drank deeply, neither Beathan nor Magnus appeared exceptionally worried over my unsociable behaviour, all was forgotten of the ugly scene and the rest of the evening passed in amicable conversation, my thoughts drifting to the woman who challenged me so fiercely only once or twice.

Chapter 5

Magnus used the table to stand unsteadily, waving away Beathan's outstretched hand. "It has been an interesting evening, Captain. We only dined with Mr Turner on one occasion and I think the poor man wisnae want tae keep company." His voice trailed away for a moment, "However, ye must join us again soon, I want tae hear more ay the enterprises in Boston and how one might invest in them."

I stood out of respect for the older man, "Thank you, Magnus, for welcoming me to your table and to the whole village. It has been a privilege, I am sure our paths will cross soon."

Beathan and I watched Magnus disappear through the drawing room door, the clock on the mantelpiece indicated the lateness of the hour. "I should make my way home, I am sure you have early mornings down at Deoch, I heard the steam whistle this morning calling the workers."

"Ye are correct, Captain, however I dinnae think one last tipple will do either ay us any harm." Beathan filled my glass before I thought to protest. "Besides, much time has passed since this table witnessed such animated conversation, I need tae apologise fur my sister's rudeness earlier."

Cringing at the mention of the scene I orchestrated, "Please, Beathan, the discord was my own doing," the Scotch, wine and rich food worked together to calm my otherwise aggressive disposition of late. My mood much more mellow, allowing for confidences, "My wife is a sore topic and unfortunately it is one many do not understand. Perhaps I do not even comprehend it myself."

Swirling the Scotch in his glass to create reflections on the white linen tablecloth, Beathan grimaced and finally looked up. "My sister possesses a good heart, however she is stubborn, willful and far tae confident ay herself, all products ay my faither's indulgence and my late mother's failed attempts tae turn her intae a lady. Phil made it her life's occupation tae resist every plan my mother set fur her," Beathan laughed lightly before taking a drink. "As a bairn, I watched with amusement as Phil got booted out ay nae one but three finishing schools. After my mother's death, none dared mention she attend another or even spoke ay her having a season and finding a husband."

Never having known a true family, my parents long dead and my uncle only condescending to participate in the barest of contacts for most of my life. I felt unable to truly appreciate the frustration Beathan spoke of concerning his sister's non-conformity. In an effort to raise the other man's spirits, I raised my glass. "Family is something I have wished for my whole life, rather a disobedient sister than none at all."

The bleary-eyed expression I received from Beathan made me regret the attempt before he swallowed the rest of his Scotch. I did the same and stood, "I must be away, it would not do for me to fall asleep under the table and create a scandal as a representative of Her Majesty."

Blood rushed to my temples as I stood, closing my eyes for a moment. I could see slight points of light dancing around before I caught my breath. I looked over at Beathan, who appeared to be in the same predicament, "I think it is going to be an interesting walk back to the cottage this evening."

Leading the way out of the dining room, through the empty drawing room, Beathan chuckled, "Nae much ay interest ever happens in Markinch as I've told ye before, Captain, however if you're a wee bit intae yer cups I can hae a cart pulled around fur ye."

"I assure you, I am quite capable of making my own way home," inwardly rebelling at the thought of being too incapacitated to walk home. "I think the drink might have addled your wits, have I changed into an old lady in the past hour?"

"Now ye hae put the thought in my head," Beathan paused a moment for effect, scratching his chin and narrowing his eyes while giving me a thorough look over. "I think ye might hae an extremely bonnie figure in a frock, delicate ankles."

A moment's pause passed between the two of us as we eyed each other, before we burst into loud guffaws of laughter. I doubled up with my hands on my thighs, tears streaming down my face, and I could hear Beathan fighting for breath, the pair of us enjoying a joke like naughty schoolchildren. The noise alerted the silent butler who strode into the reception hall with forceful purpose, a disapproving look on his face and my oil lantern in one hand. Which he shoved in my direction once close enough, before disappearing back into the shadows.

Wiping tears from his eyes, Beathan opened the door into the night. "Safe journey home, Sassenach, mind dinnae leave the road fur any purpose, the fens are full of bogs, faeries and wee haggis, nae are fit tae play on a drunk man's mind."

"Not to worry, my big Scot, I shall keep my dainty ankles to the road." Beathan tried unsuccessfully to contain his renewed laughter. I held the oil lamp aloft and did my best to step daintily into the darkness.

It did not take long for the night's silence to close in around me and swallow the weak lamp light. The moon was still invisible behind dark clouds though the snow had stopped earlier, with only a fine layering covering the ground, merely enough to squeak underfoot, the only other noise the baying of animals. The evening might have begun poorly, however the general bonhomie between Magnus, Beathan and me was something I never thought to experience after the death of Onatah and my sacking from the regiment, all ties to humankind felt broken and irreplaceable.

A light from Deoch shone ahead signaling the halfway mark in my journey home, the cold began to penetrate my frock coat. I thought of my winter clothes making their slow progress on the post cart from London. I wished I'd possessed the foresight to bring everything up at once, instead of running away from London in haste. I shrugged deeper into the inadequate folds and thought of the peat fire still smouldering away in my bedroom. There were even a couple bricks, laid out by a thoughtful Freya, which I could use to warm my toes. I began to walk a bit faster, careful not to slip.

A crack rent the peaceful pastoral evening and I crouched and turned towards the noise, peering as hard as I could into the darkness to distinguish anything out of place. I blew out the oil lamp to cut out the light blindness and let my gaze adjust to the new dimness. I allowed several moments to pass, before deciding I could not investigate the noise in the dark. I fumbled in the front of my coat for the flint I always kept tucked into the inside pocket, a demand made by Hania, who always thought it important to practice good survival skills.

As the metal touched my fingertips, a loud explosion blew apart the night for a second time. Instead of burning out immediately as the first, the second blazed brightly in the distance, over the fens, shooting sparks into the night sky and illuminating a dark column of smoke. With quick fingers, I relit the oil lamp and walked to the edge of the road, the fens stretched out in murky darkness for miles around. I knew the dangers of venturing into them even in daylight, however in the notes Colonel Manners had provided for this post, he took great pains in warning me of illegal stills.

They only carried sixty gallons of liquid. The stills were easy to move to new locations. Thus easily avoiding the tax collector. A still combusting could have created an explosion and fire. This could be my only opportunity to catch a couple of criminals and perhaps have my sentence in Scotland reduced. I lowered the light and swept it along the ground, looking for human or animal tracks. I walked several yards in either direction before I found some hare prints. I carefully stepped over them, making sure not to veer too much from the bridle path, hoping the animals would provide a safe passage through the fens.

I paced steadily onward, towards the fire burning in the distance. Several times I needed to turn around and follow my tracks back to where other animal prints might be going in the direction of the fire. The night remained unusually silent despite the violent disruption; the residents of Markinch could not be ignorant of the blaze. Frustration with my lack of progress made me kick out at a clump of heather, it tore away from the earth and rolled several feet picking up snow as it went.

A glint from light reflecting off metal caught my eye as I looked for another bridle path; I squatted to inspect the foreign object further and discovered the bottom of a boot, the glint from a hobnail setting a new sole into place. I built a flat place from earth and snow for the oil lamp to rest while I uncovered the rest of the boot. Brushing snow and frozen mud away from the leather slowly, I followed the boot to where it should naturally come to an end and instead encountered a knee.

Falling onto my backside in the wet snow, I cursed several times, stood and carefully tried to walk around the body to where the head should be located. A fruitless enterprise, the body half-lay in a bog and I stood over it, hands on my hips, trying to decide on the best course of action. I was lost in the fens, the only light coming from the explosion in the distance and it looked to be burning out rapidly. I could follow all my clumsy steps back to the road with only a small chance of ever finding this location again, I needed to place a marker here to act as a beacon.

To remove the corpse from the bog would take care. I leaned down and tried to get a good handle on the boot. I pulled gently at first and again with more force until finally the body began to pull slowly from the murky half-frozen bog water. I could not risk leaving the corpse overnight; the weather might become milder in the morning allowing it to sink further into the earthy depths. I dropped the boot in order to catch my breath for a moment; I walked to the edge of the bog to investigate the position of the corpse in more detail. With the lamp raised in one hand, I could make out three arms. It did not matter which way I repositioned the lamp the third arm remained present, not a mere apparition.

A second body lay in the murky depths of the fens. Shocked to find one man here, I stepped away and took a couple of deep breaths. The sleepy village of Markinch held some grisly discoveries, and maybe even practices. Who were these men? What terrible fate met them here? All manner of gruesome deliberations swept through my head, did they murder outsiders in Markinch? Could this be a plot by a character from a fiendish gothic novel complete with witches and ghouls? I shook my head, trying to let reason guide me once again, though the Scotch warmed my more fanciful constructs.

I needed to get both bodies pulled from the bog before leaving to find help. I simply could not trust to let the matter wait until morning. The local magistrate must be called in and these men's identities made known. I replaced the lantern on the ground and once again gripped the boot tightly and pulled with all my strength.

With some difficulty I manoeuvred the first body onto more solid ground. Stamping down my disgust, I took hold of the material on the arm of the second corpse's frock coat and heaved with one great breath. It only budged a small bit; it took several minutes before the second man lay beside the first, and I panted heavily, trying to regain my breath before picking up the lantern and moving to inspect the gruesome faces of the dead men. In the army, I worked alongside a Dr Mathews a few times, who used various instruments to find the cause of a man's death. He remained the highest authority in such matters and I wished I were half as capable as him right now, from the decomposition. I could not even be sure when these men died.

Bracing my wits against the carnage I lifted the lamp light to reveal the twisted masks of the men's faces. Though not too badly decomposed, one bore the remnants of an agonizing death, before what appeared to be a bullet-hole fractured his skull in several places, in all probability killing him instantly.

The second corpse required further investigation, the head remained in fairly good condition despite the decomposition and insects and, after finding a single bullet-hole in the front of the man's frock coat, I surmised he must have died from it, though whether the wound caused instant death, I could not be sure. I did believe both men died at the same time.

My military days chipped away most of my religious sentiment. Watching friends die under the direst of circumstances. Killing the enemy for survival had hardened me to the prayers of salvation. My complete break from the teachings of the Church came with Onatah's senseless, merciless death; no God would ever have allowed her to die in such a way. A part of me felt moved looking down on these two men, who perished alone out here on the fens, who lay undiscovered for how many weeks, maybe even months. The savagery harked back to the terrible raids I participated in against French civilians. Hoping the men's souls might be saved, I repeated a small halting prayer from my childhood, even if mine remained damned.

Before going back to the nearest farmhouse or even back up to the castle in order to raise the alarm, I walked carefully around the bog. There might be clues to the reason for these men's deaths, perhaps a small scrap of evidence could point towards the killer. The light snow made the earth around the bog even more slippery and dangerous. I remained determined in my search. I slowly walked all the way around until I stood beside the top of each corpse. I thrust the lantern out over the bog, the light shining over the seemingly innocent water-filled hole, however nothing remarkable stood out in the light. I turned on my heel abruptly, aggravated with the whole situation, and one of my boots slipped. I tried to gain purchase on the solid ground with the other, but it caught on the lapel of one of the corpses, and as my arms went out from my sides to try and right my fall backwards into the bog, the lantern fell onto a clump of heather.

I hit the surface of the bog with a thud more than a splash, the cold temperature partially freezing the water and mud. This situation had not been covered by officer training and I lay facing the bruised sky, sinking by increments into the earthy grave of two unknown me, knowing that if I completely disappeared, I would never be found. The thought of my own death did not spur me into action. For the last few months, I had considered myself a person dead already, only going through the motions and social niceties required in order to carry on to the next day. I reaped no enjoyment, except for this evening, when the camaraderie lifted my spirits. Sinking a bit further into the bog, I needed to make a decision, lying here until the mud covered my face would be tantamount to tying a rope over a beam, making a noose and swinging, all by my own hand. I would have to try to save my life in order to keep my promise to Hania. I would die fighting as a warrior even though I would not see his sister on the other side.

Kicking my feet and moving my arms only made the mud pull at my body harder. Now I had made the decision to try and escape, a panic set in, escape would not be easy and I struggled all the harder, only making my predicament worse, until my body, legs and arms lay submerged. Only my mouth and nose remained barely above the surface, even my eyes became covered.

Conflicting thoughts hurried through my consciousness, I wanted to die, it would be similar to falling asleep and never waking. The suffocating mud snuffing out my life, yet the impulse to keep fighting, continue labouring for my broken and pitiful existence rode hard on the thoughts of giving up. Surrender did not exist in my nature. I could never be a coward and with one last gasp I tried to free an arm as my face sunk below the surface of the mud. I held my breath for as long as my burning lungs would allow, my hand finally freeing itself from the sticky earth I felt the burning cold of the night air sting my fingers. My trembling lips indicated I had no time left. I could no longer deny the natural need to try and breathe and I opened my mouth and sucked in a breath of water and mud, choking and gagging, my head becoming dizzy.

I imagined something touching my free hand. It must be a delusion, yet I felt it again, something solid wrapping my knuckles as incessantly as a bill collector on the knocker of the door. With all my focus I tried to grab the thin solid piece of wood, perhaps I could be saved. Hours seemed to pass before my mouth became free of the murky water. I heaved and coughed; throwing up the bog I had drunk along with the rest of the evening's meal. I did not care, icy air burned down my raw throat and into my depleted lungs. Sobbing and moaning, I continued to hang onto my lifeline with one hand as I continuously worked the other free.

Despite the sting of murky water, I opened my eyes to find my saviour, who still worked slowly, yet steadily, to free the rest of my body from the depths of the earth. My eyes found the head and shoulders of a small boy, the same lad who I first met outside the Thistle on the previous evening.

"Hauld on, Captain," Kieran repeated over and over, "I will hae ye free in a thrice, ye must nae struggle, try and relax." The lad pulled with all his strength, his face contorted with the effort. "Yer nearly there, Captain."

Throat burning with the effort to breath, I tried to nod my head in understanding, forcing my muscles to relax. I watched as Kieran struggled to free my heavy body. It could not be easy and with my second hand free, I gripped the stick more easily and my upper body glided haltingly along the surface of the mud, my boots and legs still weighted down with muck. My hands and arms finally reached the edge of the bog, it remained slippery, however with the boy's help I managed to pull the rest of my body free. Rolling away from the dangerous edge, coughing and choking, Kieran looked over me with a fierce glint in his eye.

"Thank you, lad, you saved my life." I tried to stand, and found my legs weak with cold and exhaustion. Kieran rushed to help support my weight, he might be small, however his wiry body was strong enough to help hold me upright. "Without your help, I would have met my maker, I owe you a blood debt." I used the term familiar amongst the Iroquois when acknowledging someone had saved their life.

Kieran's skinny chest puffed out, and he looked up into my face, with stern warning in his voice. "It's nae safe fur folk tae venture intae the fens at night, it's why all the cattle gets locked safe away in their beds. Even during the day, it's a terrible place, just look at these two poor men."

The wet and the cold made my teeth begin to chatter and my body shook. Between convulsions, I needed to ask, "Do you know who these men are, Kieran? Have you seen them in the village?" The boy appeared reluctant to look at the corpses. "One quick look, lad, before we go back to the village and get help." I felt determined to know the identities of these men.

Reluctantly, Kieran left my side and squatted near the heads of the two bodies. With no lamplight to aid his sight, he needed to lean quite close. After a minute he stood and came back to my side, put one of my shaking arms over his shoulders and tried to get me to walk. I shook my head, "Not until you tell me if you know those two men."

The lad hunched his shoulders together, and remained silent for a full minute, the only sound in the night air my own shivering, the boy finally relented. "Aye, I know the two men, it's the McKinney men," Kieran sniffed a few times and I could not see if he was crying with his head bent towards the ground. "It's a sorry place tae find them."

All the muscles in my body ached and I felt terribly tired. At this point I could not be sure I would make it back to the road, let alone the cottage. "Let us away, lad, you have done a man's work this evening. You should be proud," I clumsily put one frozen foot in front of the other, it was a painful process for both of us.

The lad required no light to guide him through the small trails around other bogs and pitfalls, instinct and previous traverse led him through safely and I could only be grateful. I needed every ounce of concentration to keep my fragile body in motion, conversation might help. "You know the way through the fens well for a lad."

"Nae sae much a lad," Kieran shifted under my weight belying his answer, his scrawny shoulders pressed into my side. "I'll be ten in two months, auld enough tae work at Deoch, Mr Clunes and Beathan dinnae take workers even a day younger, but I'll be ten and they cannae hae naught tae say on the matter."

"The village is surely large enough to support a school," I thought back on the number of houses in the village along with the workers cottages dotted around Deoch. "Surely there is someone around who teaches the children to read, write and complete sums?"

Kieran's voice indicated a frown settling over his lips, "Aye, the faither up at the kirk gives lessons in the morn for those willing tae pay the half shilling a week." The lad tried to shrug under my weight, "I can reid and write and dae some maths, I dinnae need any more learning tae work at Deoch with my faither."

The urge to sit and lay down on the cold earth became powerful. It required every bit of stubborn pride I possessed to urge my body forward; if I fell now, I would sleep and Kieran could not drag me the rest of the way. He was a brave lad, and I needed to reward his courage this evening with my own. I tried to resurrect the powerful desire to live I had felt in the bog, it fluttered and threatened to blow out.

We stumbled down and back up a small ditch, I felt the hard packed dirt of the ground through my now frozen toes and feet. I felt struck dumb by the increasing need for warmth, my vision impeded by a black fog on either side and I knew it would eventually spread to claim all my sight. Once this happened, I would be lost.

"Kieran, where the devil hae ye been, laddie, and what in the name ay the guid faither is this?" A stern voice erupted from behind us. "Ye better hae a damned guid excuse fur being out ay bed at this time ay night, let alone come out ay the fens. Ye better nae been poaching, laddie, otherwise I will take the fine out ay yer hide." Boots crunched on the frozen ground and I tried to turn and face the newcomer.

Instead of spinning around with my usual grace, my numb feet would not cooperate and, falling to my knees, I used the last of my energy to keep from falling all the way to the earth. Boot steps quickened and Logan's face loomed above mine. He squatted in front of me and looked at Kieran, "Get up tae the castle at once, tell them tae send a cart and warm blankets, and tell them tae send word to Freya."

"Faither," Kieran began reluctantly, holding his sodden cap in hand. "Faither, there is something terrible out in the fens," he looked to me for help. I opened and closed my mouth several times, the voice I normally commanded gone with the cold.

Logan slapped his son hard across the face, the boy staggered a few steps and lifted his chin defiantly. "Get up tae the castle and get help, we cannae waste any time on yer fanciful notions right now, if the captain disnae get warm, he will die." Logan stared at the boy hard and under the pressure of the light blue gaze, he folded and ran with jerky, exhausted steps up the road to the Clunes.

"I hae nae bloody notion what ye might be thinking of wandering in the fens at night without a guide." Logan put his hand through his long blond locks, and reached into his sporran pulling out a silver flask, decorated with a stag. "Sit, here let me help ye, take a good drink of this, mind tae get it down."

Shaking my head at first, I did not want to become any more befuddled and I felt more drunk now than when I left the castle. I needed to keep my wits, Logan however remained persistent and I let a couple of mouthfuls choke down my raw throat, at least the burning was from warmth rather than cold.

I focused my mind on one of my frozen hands, white with cold. I lifted it and grabbed the other man's wrist with the last of my strength, "Logan," my voice raw and harsh. "Explosion, I went to investigate." His face grew interested and he leaned closer to hear my whispered words, "Found two corpses, men, Kieran says it's the McKinneys." Shock registered on the other man's face and another emotion I could not understand as the darkness threated to take all my vision.

The shouts of men, rushing feet and a cart could be heard in the distance, I let go Logan's wrist, no longer possessing the strength to speak, think or even remain sitting. The darkness waited to take me into its embrace, a nothingness. I fought with the last of my energy; I did not want to go yet, I screamed in my head as the pain in my limbs and body intensified.

Hot hurried hands found my forehead, they took hold of my hand and burned me with their heat. "Captain," a small frightened voice spoke urgently, "it is Phil, can ye open yer eyes?" A violent fit shook my whole frame and she gasped, "He is still shivering which is a good sign, get those blankets around him, quickly, we must lift him intae the cart and get the warm bricks around him."

I could feel people rushing around, all business, and brisk movements; Phil's voice, earnest and instructive, took over the whole mêlée and brought industrious activity. Her small hands chaffed mine in a flurry of strokes, encouraging blood back into the digits. The pain of the cold could be as nothing to the pain I would experience once my body began to warm again. "Logan, ye must hae spoken with him, did he say why he walked intae the fens at night?"

"The last thing I said tae him as he left the castle this evening was tae nae venture intae the fens at night," Beathan's worried voice came from my feet. Suddenly I felt weightless, suspended in a blanket, carried by a few heaving men and deposited roughly onto the cart, as someone began putting hot bricks around my body. "He is a sensible enough, laddie, I cannae believe he wandered off the road."

Logan's voice lowered, perhaps he wanted to keep the information private or perhaps he felt it required a degree of delicacy I had yet to observe in the man. "Says he saw the explosion and fire, he must have decided tae try and investigate, bloody fool." He paused and ploughed on, words tumbling over themselves. "He found the McKinneys, Beathan, both dead, he says."

A lengthy silence followed, I listened to Phil give the driver instructions, I wanted to know Beathan's reaction and, from the delay, I guessed Phil wanted to hear it too. Finally he spoke, "Christ, I hoped, I thought they ran off. I knew Robert would never hae left Agnes behind, how did he identify them?"

"The captain could nae, having never met either of them," an aggravated sigh filled the night air. "Kieran found him and the bodies, out of bed, probably poaching again. I am sorry fur the lad's mischief, Beathan. Since his mother passed, I cannae seem tae dae anything right, it will be better once he commences up at Deoch and he will be far tae tired to indulge in any night time wanderings."

The rest of the conversation cut away and the cart lurched forward. I could not stay conscious any longer; the pain, the cold, the uncomfortable weight of living weighed down my mind and I let it finally drift away, uncaring as to where it might lead.

Chapter 6

I could hardly keep my eyes open yet dreadful visions and night terrors stalked across my feverish brain, the two corpses in the fens frightfully coming alive. Pushing me into the murky bog, blurring into the faces of men I killed, to Onatah's lifeless bloated body, swimming in blood and gore, her face contorted forever in pain, I could not leave her behind, I could not stay asleep. Jolting awake in a spasm, I shook and took several deep breaths to relax back into the soft bed. Under the covers, I should have been comfortable, however after hours, days, of rest the bedclothes felt itchy. My limbs too languid, I needed to stretch, to stand, to find out more of the McKinneys.

Testing each of my limbs, I tried to stretch them and gauge how much strength might have come back into them after the illness. Confused images of Phil and Freya swam around in my head, still foggy from the fever, the pain of feeling returning to my frozen limbs unbearable, I tried not to scream as my body felt struck by a million pins. At the time, all movement felt blurred, rushed conversations, quick diagnosis and swift footfalls as scalding bricks were eventually replaced by ice and snow to reduce the fever; those two women saved my life, not knowing it was hardly worth their tireless efforts.

With determination, I moved one leg to the edge of the bed. After taking a short break, I edged my way up the pillows into a sitting position, even these small movements required extraordinary concentration and I rested before moving my leg off the side of the bed. I breathed in a happy sigh of satisfaction, I could do this.

"And what dae ye think ye might be up tae, Captain?" The stern inquiry came from the door. I quickly looked up, caught like a naughty schoolboy in some such transgression. Freya held her hands on her ample hips, eyes narrowed, lips pursed as if she witnessed something so appalling it could only bring instant disfavour.

"Good morning, Freya," I stammered shrinking back under the covers. Unfortunately I did not possess the strength to lift my offending leg back under the covers, it hung there, a damning piece of evidence to my efforts at escaping from my convalescent bed. "I did not realise you might be around," thinking quickly, "I need to use the chamber pot."

"A guid sign," Freya announced as she bounced into the room. Fetching the brass pot from under the window, she moved to the side of the bed and rested her small hand on my forehead for a moment, "The heat appears tae hae left ye, yer fever broke late last night, the doctor did nae think ye could bide through another night without some damage." She began to lift the quilt from the bed.

"Madam," I growled, heat coming back into my face, I tried to slap her hands away from my person. "I beg your pardon, I am perfectly capable of managing on my own, thank you," I reached unsuccessfully for the piss pot, as she moved it out of my grasp, a frown settling on her face.

"Captain, it's nae time fur ye tae develop a bit ay modesty, I hae been helping ye with the pot fur two days." Freya sighed loudly as I remained as still as stone, a baleful look directed at her. "Well, I will leave the pot here, mind, and I will stay and watch if ye need help."

"Over my cold lifeless body, Madam, leave the pot and get out." I mustered every ounce of the army captain into my voice, I could not contemplate having my housekeeper stand over me, watching as I took a piss, the whole episode unseemly. "I can manage without your feminine assistance."

"It would hae been over yer dead body, Captain, without my assistance, nursing ye day and night, bringing down yer fever, and if ye think I've nae taken a good look, yer mistaken." Freya nodded giving an edge of spite to her words, flouncing towards the door, pride and hurt radiating from her body. "I hae got my own brood tae look after, ye know, I cannae always drop everything tae come to yer aid and not even get a thank ye for it."

I stared at the pot and listened to Freya noisily stomp back down the stairs, in a clear temper over my lack of cooperation. I sighed and tried to bang the pot on the bed for effect, however my weak arms made it look pitiful. I didn't even need the damned thing and my resolution from a couple of days ago to make peace with my housemaid shattered over the well-polished floor, even after she saved my life. Feeling comparable to the biggest ass in Scotland, I tried to sit up without the pillows at my back. I only needed to practice, my muscles felt weak from underuse and sickness. Once I pressed them into action, they would naturally return to their former vigour and I would be free to investigate the McKinney mystery further, perhaps Markinch would be interesting after all.

"Och, Captain, I think I now know why Freya is in one of her moods downstairs," Beathan's voice filled every corner of the room. Glancing at the door, the big man stood in the frame hunched over in order to get through, a tray of food in his arms and a tentative smile on his face. "Thought I might come around and look in on the patient, yer the talk ay the town, Captain, or should I say, half the talk of the town." For such a big man, I never heard him on the stairs.

The food on the tray reminded me I must not have eaten in days; this could also be the reason I remained weak. Beathan strode into the room and waited patiently for me to stack the pillows behind me. He set the tray down and walked back to the end of the bed, leaning on the poster frame with ease.

Excitement turned to mild disappointment with the fare, barley broth and a crust of bread, hardly the meal of substance I needed to get my strength back. I delicately took a sip and found the soup very good, immediately forgetting Beathan's presence at the end of the bed. I slurped my way through the bowl with satisfaction.

"At least yer appetite has nae been affected by your illness," Beathan chuckled as I wiped my mouth on the napkin and sat back. "However, I think I should enquire tae the reason ye left the road, after we discussed keeping yer delicate ankles from harm?"

A great feeling of shame and annoyance at my behaviour seized my mind and I thought of all the people who had been integral in saving me from my own foolishness. "I am sorry, Beathan, I truly am, I knew walking through the bloody fens held many different dangers at night. When I heard the explosion and saw the fire, I guess a bit of drunken courage prompted me from the road, I have to say I did not do half bad until I slipped into the bog."

"Unfortunately, everybody thinks they hae conquered the fens until one day or night their foot slips and they fall intae one ay those damned watery pits," Beathan grimaced. "Everyone heard the explosion last night, we're nae such damn fools tae go hunting through the darkness tae find the culprits, I would hae taken ye out there in daylight," he shook his head.

"I thought if I caught a couple of illegal still operators my sentence in Scotland might be reduced," I looked at Beathan sheepishly. "I have an agreement with Colonel Manners to occupy this post for one year, after which I can be discharged from the army and go, well, I am not sure where." My voice trailed away and I stared at the far wall.

"Ye better take a wee bit more caution if ye want tae live through yer year, I think, ye are hardly a week in and already faced certain death," Beathan raised his brows. "I hae tae say yer midnight ramblings did set some of Markinch's residences fears at ease." I frowned at him. "Ye found the bodies ay the McKinneys."

The image of the corpses rose up in my vision, "I could not imagine the terrible death they suffered out there in the bog," shuddering, as I nearly shared their fate. The relief when the lad saved me. I rubbed a hand across my face. "I was submerged in muck, Beathan, completely covered, I do not know how the lad found me or saved my hide, I can only be grateful."

Beathan looked nervous, he shuffled his great weight from one foot to another, and when he spoke, he could not meet my gaze. "There has been an inordinate amount of speculation in Markinch concerning the disappearance of the McKinneys," he sighed and finally turned to me, "and its probable link tae Mr Turner and his death."

"Mr Turner committed suicide, the evidence of his death hangs in my drawing room downstairs." I sat up straight and tried to rearrange the pillows into a more comfortable position. "It's possible the McKinneys could have something to do with it, the rope is tied to a beam too high for Turner to reach unless he possessed a ladder."

Appearing uncomfortable again, Beathan took a deep breath and set his chin, resolute to carry the tale forward. "Mr Turner possessed an obsessive nature, by the evidence left downstairs I think ye will agree," he paused and I nodded my understanding. "He became excessively curious concerning the McKinneys, who run a wee still on the opposite side at the fens from Deoch. Only a third ay our production, the Turret still manufactures a good tipple and they sell enough tae keep the accounts ticking over. Turner became obsessed with the notion the two men operated an illegal still or at the very least their buyers were nae as they seemed. He investigated everything tae do with Turret from the grain suppliers tae the distributers in Edinburgh and he never found a stitch of proof against them."

I listened quietly to the story, thinking of the man who would work for hours puzzling through a mathematical equation in his drawing room, mentally ticking off each avenue of solution until he finally found the correct answer. Only to recheck the result over and over until he could be sure of its validity, the McKinneys might have provided a problem he could never solve.

Lowering his voice to a whisper, "Folk in the village already thought Mr Turner a trifle odd with his mathematics and botanical walks, as he called them, searching fur specimens in the fens and woods. When the McKinneys disappeared, faither and son, leaving the mother, Agnes, tae run the still and with Turner's suicide at the same time, well, people are wont tae put the two together."

Mind racing for the obvious solution, I spoke quickly, "People believe Turner, fuelled by his suspicions, confronted the McKinneys and killed them when they would not admit to their crimes. After which he went home and, not able to live with his remorse, he killed himself," the last a statement rather than a question.

"You've got the right ay it," Beathan shook his head. "As I said on the first night we met, there are rumours going around regarding Turner I did nae believe. I could nae hae thought him capable ay murdering two men and hiding their bodies with such success, he was, as ye said, a small man, but now . . ." he let his voice trail away.

Finishing his thought, "The wounds inflicted on the McKinneys could only have been made with lead balls, one to the body and one in the head, a man of any size could easily have fired a gun. As you mentioned, his familiarity with the fens makes him a suspect. Perhaps he lured them out there." I sighed and let my head fall back on the pillows. "We will never know, all parties are dead, with no evidence pointing in either direction. I will need to go back out to where I found the bodies, search for any further evidence left by the killer." I rubbed a hand across my forehead. "I searched for anything out of place when I slipped into the damned bog myself, I did not see anything in lantern light." As an afterthought, "I need to have a look at the bodies before they are laid to rest."

Beathan frowned, "Robert and Everett's remains are in a grisly state." I did not change my expression. "They are laid out up at the kirk, all done with the proper ceremony, though I cannae say if Faither Tadgh will let ye make a close inspection ay them, he follows the kirk's rules strictly."

"I respect the rules of the Church, however my need for justice circumvents it in this case. I worked with a Dr Mathews in Boston a few times, an army consultant. He happened to be skilled in finding evidence of a man's death and the nature of his killer through close examination of the remains as well as the circumstances a body might be found in," I grimaced at Beathan. "It is the age of science and if it can solve the murders of these two men, I will use all my limited knowledge."

Freya's brisk voice cut through the silence, "I am happy tae see ye finished yer lunch, Captain." She bustled towards the bed and picked up the tray, "If ye manage tae keep the broth down, I will bring more up after ye rest," she stared pointedly at Beathan. "The doctor left instructions the captain would need rest tae recover fully."

Bowing slightly to Freya, and looking over at me, "I would nae disobey ye or the barber's orders." Beathan grinned at me, "Mind ye rest those delicate ankles ay yours, Captain, I'm nae sure how appropriate it is fur ye tae entertain men in yer nightshirt." He howled with laughter at his own wit and after receiving a scowl from me went out the door.

"Ye never mind what Beathan says, boys, I've got four ay my own, nae daughters tae soften them," she huffed as she walked through the door. "The taunts become worse if one ay them is sick or injured in some way, I sometimes think the male brain works in a completely different fashion than a woman's."

We are not irrational and taken to flights of fancy, I thought as I listened to her steps descend the stairs and the door close in the kitchen. I glanced around the room, not the least bit tired. I probably would improve more by getting out of bed. Unfortunately, I could not be sure of Freya's reaction if I decided to run for my freedom, nor regrettably if my body would betray my flight, only giving the woman more excuses to incarcerate me. I gazed up at the ceiling, I needed some occupation otherwise I might go completely mad.

Eyes falling on the nightstand, I leaned over and opened the drawer, hoping to at least find pen and paper. I should relate my current circumstances to Colonel Manners; he might relieve me of my duties for my completely foolish behaviour, maybe something good could happen from this debacle. Fishing through, I found a couple of graphite pencil stubs, shavings, a few loose leaf papers completely marked on both sides with mathematical equations and a leather bound notebook in the very back of the drawer, by the finish on the binding it must have been done in London at considerable cost.

Letting the pages open naturally to the middle. I found row upon row of numbers, without any break, flipping through the half-used book. I discovered all the pages contained the same neat scrawl of numbers. A comparison with the loose pages revealed the same hand must have written it, none other than Mr Turner. The information written in this book was important enough to Turner for him to take the trouble to write it in code. Whether it contained formulae for a mathematical discovery or his personal thoughts, he could only use so many ciphers.

I tore a page from the back of the book and wrote the alphabet along the top lengthwise, underneath I wrote the corresponding number from one to twenty-six, my time as a member of the Royal Society taught me the best explanations remained the simplest. I began to replace the numbers with the corresponding letter of the alphabet under the cipher. I wrote out a whole page, hoping to make some sense out of the stream of letters, however after trying different letter breaks, using one number as a space and even turning the pages upside down, I could not break the code.

On the opposite side of the torn sheet, I once again wrote out the alphabet, and underneath wrote in the corresponding numbers, this time from greatest to least, twenty-six to one. I worked my way through the same page, scribbling down letters until the page was full, after trying to connect letters to make words into sensible sentences, I gave it up as a fruitless endeavor, unless Turner double coded his thoughts, this did not appear to be the cipher either.

The morning wore on, though by the light of the windows, it would be hard to tell without my pocket watch on the bedside table. The sky only lightened briefly, the dark clouds too dense for the autumn light to penetrate, I lay back and tried to think of the next best cipher. Tucking the torn paper into the back of the book, and turning to a random page, I commenced looking for common groups of letters, four or five that might be the same word repeated over and over, this way I might find a small key to the whole puzzle.

I worked for hours making hardly any progress until I heard noise coming up the stairs. I quickly hid the pencil stubs and book under the covers, laying back into the pillows and trying my best to appear restful, though my mind raced, going over different ciphers and possible solutions.

Freya made enough noise coming into the room to give me an excuse to open my eyes. Her own gaze took in my state and if she guessed I did not spend the morning sleeping, she did not comment on it. Instead she fluffed the pillows at my back, "I've brought another tray fur ye, more broth, bread and a bit of cheese, and I know ye must be hungry."

"I'm starving, which is why I think you can dispense with the broth and substitute it for a nice roast leg of lamb or a pork pie," I waved at the contents of the tray. "This is all very well for an invalid, however I think my chances of recovery will be greatly improved with heartier fare."

"Ye will eat slowly and what is prescribed fur ye," Freya placed her hands on her hips. "I truly dinnae think ye realise how close tae meeting the good Lord ye came. Never mind the miracle ay Kieran finding ye out there. I thought the fever would finish ye, you've got something strong in ye, Captain," she patted the bed and turned to leave.

Sighing with irritation and resolution, "Freya, thank you for saving my life." Taking a deep breath, I continued, "Sometimes I take for granted what a stubborn bastard I can be, the only person I ever tried to accommodate in any way died, however, I will try to be more cooperative. " She did not turn around; instead she nodded her head and whistled as she went down the stairs.

A few minutes later I heard soft footsteps on the staircase, I put my spoon down, straining to hear any sound; it could not be Freya or Beathan, though the latter was lighter on his feet than his bulk suggested. These steps were as hesitant as a bird's, the intruder suffered a slight pause of indecision at the top of the steps. I thought to call out to them before a boy's apprehensive face appeared in the door frame, cap in hand.

"I heard Beathan tell my faither ye regained yer wits," Kieran bobbed a quick bow and I motioned him to come further into the room. He took up the place by the end of the bed Beathan had vacated in the morning, "I thought I might come down and see fur myself."

"Thanks to you, my boy, I am hale and becoming more hearty by the minute," gesturing to the tray of food. "Have you eaten? I can get Freya to bring something up for you." The boy's expression became worried and he shook his head furiously. I smiled, "Does Freya know you're up here?"

"Nae, I'm supposed tae be up at the castle with the cooper helping him bend the wood fur barrels, my faither says I'm tae stay put, punishment fur my night time wanderings." Kieran puffed his chest proud of his work, "It's heavy work fur the rest ay the afternoon and he doesnae need me, and as long as I fetch him a hare from my traps this week, he will keep quiet tae my faither."

"I will always be grateful to you for saving my life," I did not want Kieran to think me unappreciative. "However as my own experience must show you, roaming through the fens at night is a dangerous occupation, I would never want to hear of a similar accident befalling such a clever lad. How did you find me?"

Shrugging his shoulders, Kieran half sat on the bed, staring at the floor. "I needed tae check my lines; darkness provides cover, I saw yer light coming through the fens, following my hare tracks." An apprehensive look on his face, "I thought ye might be looking fur poachers," his face turned red, "so I hid. I never thought ye might try tae reach the fire at the other end."

"Kieran, if you saw the fire and heard both explosions, were you not tempted in the very least to check for the source?" I asked, exasperated. He did not turn his face towards mine; instead he steadily worked the toe of his boot into the wooden floor. "Is it because you already knew where the fire came from and who started it? You must tell me, it is dangerous for the village to have such goings on in the night; think of the danger if the fire spread through the fens to the village."

The lad remained silent, he worried his lip thinking over his options. I could well understand he felt the need to protect whomever caused the incident on the fens. I remained an outsider, a Sassenach, not even a Scots, if I wanted a test of loyalties, I found it in Kieran: he could not betray his own to me.

"I must ask this, as an officer," I waited until the boy's full attention finally rose from the floor to my face. "In your previous journeys through the fens, did you ever come across the McKinneys' bodies before, or have you ever come across anyone who might be trying to hide something?"

My questions remained vague, the sagging of the boy's shoulders and his attempts not to look me in the eye spoke of his unwillingness to part with any information if it meant he might get in trouble for it. I needed another route to the information. "Did you ever seen Mr Turner out in the fens?"

Kieran looked sharply at me and nodded slowly. "Mr Turner spent many hours walking through the fens and the woods, said it improved his constitution. Nae sure what he meant by it, but his cough scared away most of the game," the boy scratched his head. "He would pick different ferns and flowers and press them intae a great book he carried in his shoulder satchel."

The boy did not seem exceptionally afraid of Mr Turner. If he went mad with his suppositions of the McKinneys' guilt over an illegal still, it might be fair to say the boy knew of its existence and might be wary of the man. "Did you ever see Mr Turner speak with either of the McKinneys or anyone else out in the fens?"

A sigh and a look at the roof before shaking his head; the boy knew something, however he felt he could not reveal it until he knew me better. I decided to finish my soup and let him look around the room at my belongings for a few minutes. His eye caught the regimental sword I inherited from my father and he went to stand next to it for a better look.

Clearing his throat and speaking in a small voice, "I would be fond of going to the Americas one day, fight with Indians and the French, I would hae tae go as a foot soldier. I hae nae money tae buy a commission and cannae be an officer." The boy sighed and traced his finger down the fine filigreed silver and gold workmanship of the sword.

"The New World is a wondrous place. As you enjoy spending time in the fens and woods," I grimaced, "you would probably feel right at home in the deep, dense forests surrounding Boston, much more than I did at first." I hesitated for a second, "However, fighting is a terrible thing, war is a blight on all it touches, I hope it might never come here and taint you."

He turned to look at me, a curious and fierce expression on his face. "Men gain honour and spoils in war, they fight and it means something tae their folk and people drink tae them even after they are long dead." Kieran thought for a moment. "Men who fight in battles never die, their stories are told next tae the fire in the evening."

Kieran might be young, however I knew he did not get his ideas about fighting and honour from haggis out in the fens. It sounded as if Logan's stories might be influencing his son's impressionable mind. Some men who died in battles could be immortalised. Apparently his Markinch ancestors kept Logan and Kieran company on more than a few nights. Having already made Logan's acquaintance, I wondered to what kind of woman might have married him. I remember him telling Beathan she was dead. "Was your mother from Markinch?"

Shrugging his shoulders, Kieran walked back and leaned his hip into the bed once again. "I dinnae know, I never asked my faither, she died when I was young, my grandmother cared fur me until she died too; it's just me and him." He grinned, "It's fine because I dinnae hae tae wash like the other boys and I dinnae hae tae mind my manners."

"I can see how it might be appealing," I thought of my own lonely childhood. "I lost my mother as a small child and my father, who fought in many battles against the French and is part of the reason I joined the army." The contemplation of my own innocence made me cringe inside, yet if I never went to the New World, I never would have married Onatah and my sacrifices even now felt worth the trade.

"It's getting late," Kieran announced looking out the window. How he could tell the change in the sun's position in the flat daylight, I could not judge. "I must go and check my snares, Faither complains about the poaching, but he enjoys the coney stew all the same," with a wink the lad stuffed his cap on his head.

"Thank you again, lad, I would have died in a murky watery unmarked grave," I felt a tingle walk up my spine and settle behind my neck. "You saved my life and I owe you a blood debt, as I said on the night. You must come to me with anything, I will help you."

The heavy weight of the promise embarrassed the lad, he ducked his head and quietly stalked from the room. I did not even hear the door to the front of the cottage open and close. The lad definitely possessed a talent, and it would lead him into trouble if Logan could not keep a better eye on him. The father's help saving my life not withstanding, I do not think he would take advice on how to raise his son from me, a Sassenach.

Good fortune meant Kieran and I met with Logan as soon as we clumsily found the road. The boy and I were too exhausted and we needed a firm hand to take control of the situation. I wondered what he might have been up to out on the road so late at night, looking for his son or waiting near where the McKinneys laid half-hidden for another purpose. I did not know, I believed Kieran when he said he never saw the bodies before the night I found them. Considering his proclivity to roaming the fens it might be hard to believe, however closing my eyes I remembered the look of shock on his face after I forced him to identity the men, his surprise genuine.

My head hurt, I lay back on pillows and tried to get comfortable, closing my eyes, I thought of the events of the last few days, Markinch could turn out to be far from the sleepy village in the Highlands of Scotland portrayed by Colonel Manners in London. Perhaps Turner warned him, there was definitely a puzzle in need of some attention.

Chapter 7

Checking the road lay empty on either side of the cottage, I stepped into the world once again, with the knowledge Freya needed to run errands for most of the day and she hopefully would not find me gone until my return. Rupert and Everett's corpses were due to be interred in the evening. The bodies might hold evidence, which could solve their murder. Another slate grey day, the threat of snow oppressive, I walked slowly and evenly, stretching my limbs after the illness and forced rest, the porridge consumed sticking to the sides of my belly, providing a thick coating of warmth. The fens on either side of the road looked as they had on the night of my accident, beautiful and unthreatening in their rugged expanse, stretching and pulling towards the horizon.

I could hear the work day at Deoch bustling with activity before the red buildings became visible above the rise in the road. The white writing greeting me once again and reminding me where I existed, not in any village or town in the Highlands, in Markinch, at Deoch. As on my previous visit to Deoch, men studiously kept to their business, carrying grain sacks, walking with brooms, some speaking in groups. Today a farmer stood and waited for his grain to be milled, while another with the help of a young man shovelled wort into the back of their cart, presumably to feed their livestock.

Kieran waved furiously alerting the rest of the workers to my presence. So much for passing unnoticed. He shouted and every man turned to look from him to me, "Captain, I hope yer nae heading out intae the fens today," turning his face towards the sky. "Storm coming from the north."

The men quit their occupation to listen to our shouted conversation. Years had passed since I felt such embarrassment over my actions, I berated myself for my lack of foresight in walking through the fens and stared up at the sky. The air remained still, no wind from the north, I looked back at Kieran, "Taking a walk up to the church."

Several of the men nodded their heads; Kieran frowned and began to walk over, wooden rake in one hand. "Gonnae thank the Lord fur saving yer skin?"

Once he stepped closer and I was positive none near might hear my words, "I gave my thanks yesterday when you came to see me. You saved my life, not the Lord, I have seen and done too many things to know there is no higher benevolent force guiding our lives." Looking into the boy's face, "We must make our own paths, understand."

Wrinkling his nose and adjusting the rake over his skinny shoulders, "Ye speak like my faither." Sighing loudly he continued, disgruntled, "I'm still paying my penance fur being out of bed the other night," the boy's attention suddenly riveted on a spot in the distance, fear showing in his features. I immediately looked for danger.

Logan watched my conversation with his son intensely, propped on the large wooden doorframe to the still barn. One of us would have to break eye contact and I put a casual smile on my face as I resumed speaking with Kieran. "I will see you again soon, take care when you're out on your own," patting the top of his cap for affect I strode lazily away from Deoch. I did not find the boy's father intimidating, I did find him curious, he railed over the presence of Sassenachs in Scotland on my arrival, yet aided in saving my life the night of the accident, his presence out on the road while all others took to their beds or hearth raised questions over his motives.

I resolved to make a closer study of Logan, the displaced Laird of Markinch, my gut told me he could not be all he seemed. My fever and accident may have fueled my suspicions. Either way, as a soldier I learned to trust instincts. They had played a part in saving my life on more than one occasion and I would not ignore them now. A mêlée of boot prints, donkey hooves and cart wheels marked the spot in the road where Kieran and I had emerged from the fens. I closed my eyes for a moment and could hear the voices yelling to one another, Phil's murmured encouragement as well as Logan and Beathan's whispered conversation.

Beathan must have used several men to remove the McKinneys from their temporary gravesite; I could easily follow the path they took through the clumps of heather, boots stamping down the grass, any evidence left behind by the killer probably destroyed as a consequence and a rush of frustration pulsed through me. Part of the drive to solve the murders came from my natural instinct to believe there was an explanation for everything I could know and understand, the other part came from my position as an English officer taking over the post from another officer widely accused of these men's murders.

I needed to inform the English authorities if Mr Turner was indeed a murderer. The widow was entitled to compensation. If the trail led to another, they must pay the ultimate price for the McKinneys' deaths. I would see justice served either way. This conviction had woken me from my sleep that morning and stayed with me all through breakfast, not even Freya could break its hold over my mind with her idle talk. I needed to see justice done; I could not have any for my wife, however I would do my best for these men.

A firm grasp on my newly acquired principles, I turned north and headed for the stone church built next to the castle. Freya had mentioned she'd paid her respects to Rupert and Everett McKinney there the previous evening. Even in daylight, the path from the main road was not easy to spot, I did not notice it on my journey to or from supper at the castle. The small church stood isolated, a low stone fence protecting its walls and gravestones keeping watch over its parishioners.

Hesitating for a moment at the gate, I rubbed a hand over my face, what I had told Kieran of my beliefs surrounding God was true, I committed acts of barbarism fighting in the Americas I knew no fair being could forgive. I also thought He might have punished me with Onatah's death. Now I entered His sanctuary not seeking redemption, only justice. I closed the gate harder than I intended and walked past the grave markers, many hewn from stone of various sizes and shapes, a few of the larger markers carved with beautiful scrollwork, lovingly polished year after year, the purple heather grew in tufts, unmindful of the sanctity of the soil.

Two large plain wooden doors stood closed, I tried the handle on one and found it opened easily into a cavernous nave. I set the door closed quietly behind me and scanned the interior, row upon row of benches stood two by two down the length, an altar lit with candles at the end. A woman sat on the bench directly in front of the altar, her head bent in prayer. A priest by the look of his robes counselled her, while behind them a wooden carving of Jesus hung from the wall, looking down on them both with a baleful arms outstretched. My shoulders twitched at the sight and I looked for where the McKinneys might lie.

Spying a room off the side of the main chapel, I walked as quietly as I could in order not to disturb the confidence of the priest and his parishioner. Unfortunately my boots were of made of stern stuff, bold and unrepentant, they struck the cobbles underfoot with a confident clip, rather than a shy scuffle, the whispered conversation at the front of the church halted.

"My son," the priest stood, though he could not make out my identity from the front of the church. The windows set high in the wall let in only meagre light and not many candles burned at this time of day. "If ye would take a seat, I will be with ye in a moment," he called and I immediately picked up the pace.

I turned to wave, acknowledging his assistance, yet not pausing in my stride. The priest grew agitated as I went to open a side door. "My son, it is perhaps best I be with ye, when ye pay your last respects." I heard the other man's hurried steps rush down between the pews as I opened and entered the small room quickly, closing the door.

Walking slowly towards the table where the two men lay, peaceful and in a wretched state. I groped around in my frock coat pocket and I found a silk kerchief, which I pressed to my nose to ward off the sickly smell of decaying flesh. An unfortunate post-dinner conversation between soldiers after downing several cups of ale normally included a lively debate on which odour the more hideous, burned or rotting flesh. I remained firmly on the decaying flesh side of the argument.

The door opened as I reached the side of the corpse with the bullet wound in the head. It had entered the temple and, leaning down to examine it closely, I could see without touching the body it had passed through, blowing the back of the man's skull to pieces, instantly killing him. The shot must have been from close range, shot from arm level.

The rest of his body appeared to be unharmed. Any flesh exposed to the elements, such as the hands were badly decomposed. I needed to search for clues; I raised my hands and went to carefully open the man's pockets. A horrified gasp reminded me of my unwanted visitor and I looked up into the face of a middle-aged man, hands fisted at his sides, face barely concealing his gathering outrage.

"Those bodies have been shriven," the man squeaked. "This is the house of God, sir, and I pray ye respect the last remnants ay these two poor men before they are buried forever and can enter intae heaven." His stern gaze took in my coat and shaved head. "Ye must be the new gauger, the Sassenach, I suppose there must be some thanks tae yer presence, ye did find these two poor souls."

"Your right, Father," I tried to keep my tone neutral, the man appeared agitated and I needed access to these two bodies and information. "I wanted to pay my respects and perhaps have a look for any information leading to whom may have done this to them." Both reasonable requests, I used my most humble tone.

"Seeing as how ye recently almost met yer own death after finding them, I suppose I cannae deny ye the right tae make yer peace," the priest crossed himself. "Though as I said before, you cannae touch the bodies or risk angering God. Besides I watched Beathan go through each of the men's pockets, Agnes McKinney is in possession ay their belongings."

I nodded, and walked over to the second body, leaning in to inspect the bullet wound. "This is the younger of the two, so I assume it is the body of the son, Everett." Without lifting him, I could not tell if the round went straight through, but the information did not matter much. A careful search through the rest of his clothes indicated only one shot took the life of this man, his blood-crusted clothes implying a shot near the heart.

"Och, aye, ye are correct," the priest tripped over the word gauger and cleared his throat. "Captain, I dinnae see why ye need tae make an inspection. Yer nae the magistrate and folk know who killed these fine men and the good Lord punished him by ensuring he would never be buried in hallowed ground." I looked curiously at the priest, "Mr Turner of course, and his suicide, it goes against the laws of God and nature," the man chortled.

"Good morning, Father Tadgh," the priest and I glanced at the door and found Logan smiling at both of us. "I thought I heard yer voice in the chapel, giving one of yer sermons again?"

"I am reminding the Sassenach captain it is a sin tae take one's own life," Father Tadgh stood up straighter and adjusted his frock under the scrutiny of Logan. "It is comparable with the taking of a human life, so Mr Turner must be damned tae hell at least three times fur his terrible crimes, nae court on earth or in heaven can save his soul from burning."

Logan peered in my direction, a look of mild interest on his face. "I think the captain is well aware ay the consequences after death fur sinners," pausing he scrutinised the priest with a hint of malice. "He was, after all, a member of Her Majesty's army, committing unmentionable acts ay barbarity in the New World in the name of God and country."

A part of me, the soldier, ingrained and moulded into the English Army clamoured to protest Logan's unspecified yet malicious accusations. Duty, a part of my old life, demanded satisfaction, however I was too old and tired to rise to the bait. Instead, I endeavored to change the direction of conversation away from dangerous topics such as Mr Turner and my time in the army. "Have you come to pay your respects, Logan?"

"In fact, Beathan mentioned yesterday ye might hae some skill with inspecting corpses and discovering the method of death, even identifying the murderer through this evidence." Logan ignored the sceptical snorts from Father Tadgh, focusing his entire attention on my person. "As these two men were my friends, and technically members of my clan, I would like tae know if ye made any progress."

Or if I might have found evidence pointing to you as the gunman, "Beathan overestimated my knowledge. I told him I aided a doctor in Boston with such scientific queries, yet the progress in this science is slow and unreliable at best. It will be many years of research before it commences giving consistent answers."

"A terrible macabre thing tae dae tae a man after he is dead," Father Tadgh's face turned red once again with his outrage. "It is witchcraft, the thing of nightmares, only a truly horrible and depraved man wants tae fiddle with a corpse, it is disgusting and if this is the reason ye hae come, Sassenach, I suggest ye depart before I bring the heavens down on ye!"

"There is no need for the heavens to be out of countenance, Father Tadgh." I tried to placate the old man, Beathan had warned me of the priest's devotion to his God. "I have paid my respects to these men, any evidence from their bodies has been noted without disturbing their rest."

The mention of evidence made Logan inspect the bodies closer; I walked past him to the door. "A good day to you, gentlemen," I needed to make a quick escape, something in Logan's behaviour made me uncomfortable. I could be imagining it, yet I needed time to think, unfortunately Tavish's friendly face turned towards mine.

"Captain," the old man's voice rang through the stone church, a broad smile on his face. "I hae been meaning tae check on ye, thought ye still needed a few more days' rest." I shrugged uncomfortably, not willing to reveal my escape, he appeared to sense my reluctance and pressed on, "I need tae speak tae Father Tadgh, after that I'd thought perhaps I could get a couple of words in?"

Nodding, "I will wait for you outside, Tavish." One look at the priest's face speeded my surrender from his church. I walked with quick steps to the large front doors, made an exaggerated sign of the cross for my audience and stepped out into the flat light.

Logan escaped from the church and, as I found a spot to sit on the stone fence, I watched him wearily from my perch, waiting for another confrontation. Yet he did not break his stride to acknowledge my presence, only opened the gate and continued on his journey. Whatever his true purpose in coming, he never said, I did not think it to pay his respects. I tucked my hands into the pockets of my coat; I would walk down to the village today, my trunks should have made the long journey from London by now and I needed my wolf fur coat if my soft hide wanted to survive through the whole winter. I briefly wondered if the Highlanders wore a variety of stocking when the cold became unbearable.

Tavish waved from the church and I stood up. We went through the gate, "I am heading down tae the Thistle fur an early lunch, I've got the mashing tuns to deal with this afternoon and it will go well intae the night."

"I am heading in the same direction, I need to run some errands and try to get my affairs in order after my illness." Grimacing after the last word, I let my steps match the old man's. We walked in silence for a few minutes, he appeared to be gathering his thoughts, waiting until we cleared Deoch, waving away workers and enquiries. He began to relax as the red buildings disappeared behind us.

"You've only been in Markinch a short time," Tavish laughed grimly, "and an accident has befell ye, and fallen ill fur half the time, I think this doesnae bode well fur yer chances up here in the Highlands." He glanced at my profile and gave me a hearty punch in the kidneys. "You've got a strong constitution, only time will tell." Tavish removed the cap from his head and scratched around his ears before replacing it, tucking stray wisps under the rim, away from his eyes. "I think you're a decent enough fellow, fur a Sassenach. I've got a good judge of a man, I wanted tae tell ye, I dinnae think Mr Turner had naught tae do with Rupert and Everett's deaths. He might have been eccentric, but he was nae killer." Tavish huffed a few times before continuing, "And as fur the explosion, though I cannae confirm a still made it, I reckon and so do the villagers, the McGreevy boys caused it."

"I want to thank you for your trust, Tavish, I think it is something in short supply up here when it comes to Sassenachs." I tried to make light of the difficulties I encountered with the likes of Logan and Father Tadgh. "I have to say, however, even I cannot be sure of Turner's guilt or innocence in regards to the McKinneys' deaths, there is no real evidence either way."

"Here ye hae burst upon why I believe ye tae be trustworthy," Tavish beamed his approval. I could only stare in confusion. "Yer looking fur proof ay the murderer's identity; he could be a Sassenach, could be a Scot, but you'll decide when ye hae the proper confirmation."

Grimacing at the other man, "I can hardly do any more." I let frustration colour my tone, "Unfortunately, unless someone in the village knows more than they are currently divulging, the McKinneys' deaths will remain unsolved and Mr Turner will remain the lone suspect." Not wanting to dwell on the matter further, "Please tell me more of the McGreevys."

"Nae too much tae say, the McGreevys are relatives of the McKinneys from down south ways," Tavish furrowed his brow. "Several families came after the Laird Markinch died and his daughter was evicted from the castle. They wanted tae take advantage ay the fact there was nae law around the place without a formal laird, its nae uncommon and can be dangerous, however Magnus's faither saw the problem and bought up the castle, as I said before." Tavish looked at my cottage as we passed, a smile on his lips, "Still remember when the Clunes lived there," clearing his throat, "the McGreevys came and squatted on the edge of the fens, across from the McKinneys. There's a road leading up tae both families' dwellings beyond the village a ways, Magnus and his faither tried several times tae evict them. They always come back, I think as long as they bide the law in Markinch, Magnus leaves them alone."

I nodded at the old man, not sure where this tale might lead, he continued, "Some might think I'm a traitor fur saying this, there's only Beth and her two sons, Roth and Levy, up there these days. The boys are always up tae some mischief, mostly cattle rustling, though they keep from stealing folk in Markinch's sheep. They tend nae tae bring trouble tae the village, I've never heard of them working a still, it's possible they caused the mischief the other night."

Halting, I waited for Tavish to turn and wait for me before continuing, "Do you have any proof the McGreevys even own a still or are in the area? Has anyone from the village been up there?"

Tavish fidgeted for a minute under my hard stare, taking a deep breath. "Couple of folk reckon they saw them out in the woods before ye came tae Markinch; they tend tae stay away from the village. There are a few folk around who would like tae hae a less than couthy word tae them. If ye want tae find them best option is tae talk tae Beth, ye will need tae be mighty persuasive though."

Nodding at Tavish to continue walking, I thought for a few minutes. "Thank you for telling me of your suspicions. Tavish, I know it can be hard to trust strangers when you have lived in a small community your whole life." My wife's tribe remained insular for protection and, considering the devastation my presence allowed, I cannot blame them.

"Nae all folk in Markinch hates the Sassenachs, Captain," Tavish waved to a middle-aged woman standing in front of the first cottage as we walked into the village. "Some ay us, the Clunes included, benefited from the Sassenach civil war, I think we would rather excel in enterprise than dabble in politics, the latter brings nothing but misery and disappointment, look at Logan."

"Politics is power," I opened the door to the Thistle and Tavish walked smartly through. The tap room looked the same as the other night, with fewer patrons before noon. "The world is changing, even the lowly barber practices politics in Boston and everyone seems to have a say in the papers. Soon England and Scotland will be the same way."

"Ordinary men politicking, and making decisions fur the whole country," Tavish laughed and slapped me on the back. "Nae say it, we best leave our betters tae decide our fates and leave the rest ay us tae get on with what we know, like making the finest Scotch in all of the Highlands and consequently the world."

"You might not be able to hide up here forever." I waited in front of the wooden bar for the landlord to finish speaking with a couple of men seated at a table in the corner.

"Every day I pray for two things," Tavish threw the words over his shoulder as he nodded to two men. "One, the good Lord will give us an honest and true brew and the other is fur nae trouble tae come tae Markinch and change our lives, we are simple folk."

I watched Tavish greet the other two men and sit at the table. He was correct, I would not want to see trouble come to the town. Yet the possibility of an illegal still and Mr Turner's role in the deaths of two men made it impossible not to involve the English authorities. I would have to report my findings carefully.

After taking Tavish's order, the landlord stepped back behind the bar. "Captain, a pleasure tae see ye looking well after yer accident," he smiled and I tried not to look uncomfortable. "Yer trunks arrived from London this morning and I sent the boys up with them, they forgot tae take these with them." He rummaged through a stack of post.

"Thank you, I am much obliged, I am going to need my winter coat sooner than anticipated." I tried to make conversation, the other man only grunted and finally smiled handing over two envelopes, one with the tight, angular script of Colonel Manners, the other the wildly smudged hand of Mr Wick.

"Ye must be a popular man, two letters in one day," the landlord thumped the bar and I noticed a broadsheet with the Royal Society banner across the top. "Only the Clunes and Deoch receive two letters in one day."

"As these are the only two men in the country who might write to me, I doubt if it will be a regular occurrence." I did not think any of my army comrades would write after my hasty departure and Hania could not write. I pointed at the Royal Society sheet, "I believe that might be mine too."

The landlord inspected the paper and pulled it from another pile, looking up into my expectant face, he frowned. "I dinnae think so, Captain, this definitely has another destination, however if ye would enjoy having a quick look before the owner comes." He handed the sheet across the bar.

The door to the taproom opened and closed, I ignored the newcomer and set to reading the headlines from the latest Royal Society news. An extensive article on Antoine van Leeuwenhoek's single-cell organisms took up almost half the page along with some pretty drawings and a preview of the

Society's next experiment, a working replica of Otto von Guericke's vacuum pumps, took up the rest.

"It is good tae see ye looking so well, Captain." A female voice interrupted my thoughts, lilting in a familiar Scottish brogue, it haunted my feverish dreams. "Hae ye found something ay interest from my Royal Society paper?"

Bright green eyes inspected my face, taking in every line and smudge of fatigue before arching a brow, she must know of my escape. "Your Society paper, I was not aware you had an interest in such matters." I did not hand the paper over, instead I brought it closer to my chest for protection.

"I dinnae think our disastrous dinner conversation revealed much of my interests, Captain," she took a deep breath. "Only my ignorance, I can only apologise again fur insulting ye at my faither's table, it wisnnae well done of me."

Sheepishly offering her the broadsheet, "It is I who should be making amends. I was rude, I wanted to have an argument over my late wife and you handed me the perfect opening." I bowed slightly, "Please forgive my rudeness, anything you may have said after is forgiven as one of my saviours."

A light blush stained her cheeks where a row of freckles marched across in quiet unison. She blinked several times and I realised the woman who stood before me must receive few compliments. I smiled down at her and resisted the urge to touch the skin exposed between her glove and sleeve as she reached for the sheet. "It is nae great matter," she quietly remarked after clearing her throat and staring pointedly at my chest. "Freya is the most skilled at healing, with those four boys, it's nae wonder, I truly only helped her fur a brief time," looking up again, I saw a blush creep into her hairline. "She managed the tough bits."

Frowning at her reaction, I let her tug the broadsheet out of my grip. She looked at the innkeeper, who appeared to be just as shocked over her unusual response, and as he handed her the small pile of correspondence. She fumbled with the envelopes and they dropped to the floor. With a curse, she bent to pick them up, I was quicker, even after my illness, and I held them out to her. Her eyes darted and briefly held mine, before grabbing the offending envelopes from my hand, careful not to touch me, dipping a curtsey. "Captain, I bid ye a good day," she nodded at the landlord and tried to leave the taproom with as much haste as possible, skirts swirling.

The landlord and I watched the door close with some force. The windows rattled for a moment, he looked pointedly at me, a sliver of suspicion mounting in his brown eyes as he took in my surprised expression. "Never seen the lass behave in such a manner, wonder what it might have to do with?"

"Female vapours." I shrugged, who knew the contents of a woman's mind? Certainly not a man, the landlord eyed me sceptically, "Thank you once again for sending my baggage on to the cottage, please pass on my thanks to your boys." I turned and tied to catch Tavish's eye, however he appeared to be having an intense discussion with the other two men.

"Captain," he shouted across the room, before I stepped out of the inn. "Hae yerself a good day and mind what I said," the old man ignored the looks he received from his companions. "Stay out of the fens at night and get a damned guide if ye go venturing through during the day." The men beside him nodded sagely.

I tried to smile and be grateful for the advice, ducked my head and escaped the rest of the scrutiny. Outside flakes of snow began to fall rapidly from the slate grey sky, a wind picking up from the north burned its way through my coat and leggings. Kieran had correctly predicted the storm, how he could have possibly guessed was beyond my knowledge. Wrapping myself tighter into the folds of my thin coat, I turned and headed back to the warmth of the cottage, both letters tucked safely into an inside pocket, hopefully Freya would not have missed me and prepared a meal.

Chapter 8

I decided to take advantage of a break in the weather. After my investigations yesterday and Tavish's information on the McGreevys, my recovering body was forced into a rest period. No need for Freya to harangue me to sleep. I spent the rest of the afternoon dozing in front of the fire in the drawing room, alternatively reading over my correspondence and making an attempt to decipher some of the mathematical codes Mr Turner had left behind. I made only slight progress, whether the reason lies in its complexity or my ignorance, I can only guess. Feeling stronger today, with at least a foot of snow crunching under my boots, my warm wolfskin over my shoulders, I felt I could take on anything the Highlands could possibly throw at me, satisfied in possessing the right tools.

The courtyard behind the inn remained empty, people would try to stay inside for as long as possible today. A quick check of the sky determined more snow would be on its way before long. Guilt washed over me as I opened the door to the barn, the air a fraction warmer inside, it looked clean and smelled of sweet hay, a good sign. I had been a poor owner to Tasunke, not checking on his conditions since the accident. I walked down the row of stalls, the barn large enough to hold at least twenty horses comfortably, yet only a few of the stalls possessed beasts. I spied my loyal friend at the end of the filled stalls, he bobbed his head in steadfast greeting.

Removing my glove, I squeezed my hand through the bars, a lump of sugar in my palm, a small peace offering. Poor Tasunke whinnied and stamped through his passage from Boston, the ocean no place for a horse. He protested and shied away from London's crowds, now I neglected him in the wilds of Scotland. He eyed me with a bit of suspicion, before delicately taking the treat with his big lips, good old Tasunke. His nature did not allow him to hold a grudge for long. I gave him a good pat on the side of his neck before searching the stables for my riding gear.

I enjoyed the simple pleasure of brushing him down, removing the burrs from his mane, the smell from the oil used on the leather to keep it supple calmed my nerves. This is something I knew how to accomplish, it did not involve complicated relationships with people, between Tasunke and me, no secrets existed. Leading him out of the barn, a light snow commenced once again. I took a second to rethink my decision, however, I needed to carry on with the mission. I mounted, turning Tasunke from the yard and down the road, searching for the path leading to the McKinney and McGreevy dwellings.

The way turned out to be little more than a lane between two houses in the village, and I missed it the first time, and needed to turn back after realizing I was heading for Aberdeen. After a few passes, I determined this could be the only path north; it skirted the edge of the fens. Tasunke, sure-footed, long-haired beast, picked his way unhurriedly through the snow. No urgency propelled either of us forward, we enjoyed the lightly falling flakes, the silence, our own thoughts, much time passed since we enjoyed the luxury. After at least an hour the path ended, to the left and right lay further road. I knew from Freya, one led to the McKinneys and one led to the McGreevys. In my haste to be away from the house, I forgot to ask her which side each lived on. I would have to take a guess and be prepared to face either circumstance, the wife and mother of the slain men, or the mother of two outlaws.

In the end, I took my queue from Tasunke, who sidled to the left slightly while resting, as effective as flipping a coin. A mile or so up another road, found us standing in front of a small cottage and barn, smoke rising lazily into the snowing sky; at least there might be someone home. I dismounted a few feet from the cottage and led Tasunke towards a hitching post under the eaves of the cottage. When the door opened, a woman wrapped in a tartan came to stand on the front porch, a rifle in her hand pointed directly at my chest.

"State yer name and business," the woman shouted, her gaze and aim steady. Unfortunately, from the welcome, I could not guess which of the women this might be. "Dinnae get many visitors up here, nor less strangers, ye must be bringing trouble."

Holding up my gloved hands in a sign of surrender, careful not to let the reigns fall through my fingers, "Madam, I am the new excise collector from London, I have travelled up here to ask you a few questions." I could not add any further information until I could be sure which lady I spoke with.

The lady blew air out her nose and did not lower the rifle. "Nae many Sassenach around, I suppose, and even less who would admit tae being the gauger." She looked up at the sky and sniffed, "Ye better come in out ay the cold. Try anything I dinnae like and I will shoot ye, I've been told I've got great aim."

Quickly tying the reins and making sure Tasunke stood out of the weather, I slowly stepped into the cottage and closed the door behind me. I found myself in the kitchen and walked over to the stove to warm my cold hands. "Welcome tae the McKinneys.'" The woman's voice shook slightly, "I am Agnes McKinney, and I suppose I should thank ye fur finding my men."

I studied the top of the stove for a full minute, the heavy iron solid, this simple machine the heart of this cottage. It would have seen good times and witnessed hard scenes between family members, now reduced to one. Dread filled me as I turned and looked into the grief ravaged face of Agnes McKinney, to lose one's family was to lose one's soul. I studied her profile, Agnes had endured weeks of agonizing nights and days filled with torment. She would have questioned all the small and large things her husband might have said, sifted for clues in her son's actions, needing to know what might have befallen them. Hoping they might have run away instead of dying on the fens.

All I seemed to do in this village was make apologies, "Agnes, I hope I can call you by your given name. I have come to extend my condolences, not only as the man who found them, but also as a representative of the English authority in the village," I took a deep breath. "I did not know them, yet they have my sympathies as I became close in sharing their unmarked grave."

Agnes set the rifle on the table, and going to a cupboard, she pulled out a bottle of Scotch, two glasses and a plate of oat biscuits. I took her invitation to sit and she poured me a glass. "Beathan came round tae tell me the news, I was up at the kirk when ye came through." A sad smile turned one of the corners of her mouth up. "Ye sure know how tae cause a ruckus, Captain, Faither Tadgh remained up in arms fur the rest ay the morning."

"The father certainly has a way of making his beliefs known," I took a sip of the Scotch. Made only a mile or two from Deoch, yet I tasted a subtle difference. I studied the amber liquid, trying to gather my thoughts, never being good with delicate situations. "I have also come up here today to ask some questions concerning Rupert and Everett's last movements."

The woman nodded, drank off the rest of her portion and poured another one. Agnes did not appear to have any of the telling marks of one who drank heavily regularly, the alcohol ageing a person. Rather she looked to be clumsily comforting the wounds left by her men's absence. "I can tell ye what I told Beathan, I know it was Mr Turner, I can feel it in my soul," her dark eyes burned with fury.

No preamble, no complex questions to try and coax her suspicions from her, the accusation lay flat on the table. "I have been told by several sources you have some suspicions against Mr Turner, I need to know how you came by them. If he became involved with your husband and son in some way and is responsible for their deaths, the English authorities must be made aware."

Her face crumbled slightly and I looked away, uncomfortable in her projection of emotion. I looked back once she began to speak, "I dinnae see what can come of it now, my boys are dead, he is dead, all is fur naught." She drank down half the contents of her glass and tried to calm her breathing, taking long deep breaths. "Maybe something could hae been done, I dinnae know," she splayed her hands onto the worn wood of the table. "In the spring, we began getting our grain from another supplier. At first the farmer would bring it intae Deoch fur grinding and we would pick up the sacks there. It worked fine, until the farmer told us he could get the grinding done fur cheaper down south and bring up the finished product, ready for the malting. We are a small still, as ye can see, we need tae save money where we can and Rupert thought it would be best, so we stopped going tae Deoch. Mr Turner thought there might be something odd going on, he came up and inspected our barn several times. He never found anything, because there was nothing tae find, I would hae known if Rupert and Everett operated another still."

If the men kept another still, Agnes McKinney never knew of it, I could tell she spoke the truth, no lie marred her brow or coloured her eyes. "I understand Mr Turner also went through all your books and never found anything either," I prompted.

"Aye, went through and wrote down all the buyers in Edinburgh and Glasgow, in order tae make sure they existed," Lindsay shrugged her shoulders and leaned back in the chair. "Though I dinnae know why he'd bother, the tax is paid on the amount made, and we never tried tae cheat him, nae on the amount sold. It's up tae us tae sell what we make, who cares who is buying the end product as long as it sells?"

Her reasoning correct, where could Mr Turner's enquiries have led after taking down the addresses of buyers? As long as the McKinneys paid their tax on the amount made, how could it make a difference over the amount sold? "I do not want to intrude on your sympathy for much longer, yet I hope you might give me the addresses Mr Turner was interested in. Perhaps there is some clue we are missing."

Sighing, Agnes studied my profile for a full minute, before heavily standing from the chair. She walked into another room and stayed away for long enough I thought she might have forgotten my presence. When she returned, my Scotch glass stood empty. Holding a slip of paper out, she said. "Here are the addresses, dinnae know what help they can be."

I accepted the paper with as much graciousness as I could muster, after all, this woman buried her men last evening. "I do not want to be indelicate, only I need to know for tax purposes, will you carry on running the still without Everett and Rupert?"

"Need tae eat and put a roof over my head." Agnes watched me stand and adjust my coat, the fur overly warm in the kitchen. "I hae a widow cousin coming up from the south tae help me, I will send word once we hae the still going again."

Facing her in front of the door, I gave her a deep bow, far too extravagant for the social encounter and her place in it. However, I needed to convey my sorrow, her life already one full of hardships would only become a greater burden without her husband and son. "A good day to you and I look forward to seeing you again," the words swallowed by her grief.

The door to the cottage shut, I waited a moment or two before pulling the fur over my bald head, the better to keep it warm. I walked over to where Tasunke stood silently, under the eaves. I wiped cold slush from his rump and dried the saddle before easing my frame into it, now to the McGreevys.

Concentrating on the landscape, I tried to shake off the rawness of Agnes's grief. Her feelings were new, my own grief felt faded in comparison, the immediate pain had eased and I realised with shock, I accepted Onatah's death. A momentary panic filled my heart, soon I would move on, I could not let go, this grief defined me.

After passing the main road, I continued to follow the path on the opposite side, the way not as smooth as the McKinneys'. Tasunke's steps grew more cautious as he slipped in a couple of potholes stumbling, reviving me from my efforts to dive into the pain of my loss and wrap it around my person. I halted his progress and dismounted, taking the reins. I walked him forward, scuffing the ground with my boots, looking for danger and soon a rustic cottage and barn appeared in a small clearing littered with all manner of refuse.

I patted Tasunke's neck and led him forward, a curl of smoke rose from the chimney of the cottage, the roof looked in need of urgent repair, a quick scan of the barn revealed its own dereliction, there were several stones missing from the sides, I could detect movement and wondered if some poor beast tried to stay out of the weather. Or perhaps Beth McGreevy or one of her famous sons hid inside. Instead of walking towards the cottage, I changed direction. I thought only to speak to Beth, however if her sons were around all the better to discover their involvement in the explosion on the fens the other night. With the tomahawks Hania had taught me to use loosened on my belt along with the pair of ivory-handled flintlocks I inherited from my father, the trio of weapons had seen me through all manner of tight situations in the New World, I walked cautiously forward.

"What the devil dae ye think yer up tae, laddie?" A shrill female voice sounded from behind me. "Turn slowly, so I can see yer hands," obeying I turned and faced a woman, who wore a black scowl and pointed an old rifle at my chest. She looked skinny enough for one shot of the rifle to thump her into the snow-covered earth.

"Good morning, Beth McGreevy, I presume?" I kept my voice firm. "I am Captain Esmond Clyde-Dalton, the new excise man for Markinch, I need to have a couple of words with you regarding recent events. Thought I might settle my horse in the barn, out of the weather."

Squinting up at me, I watched any number of emotions dim her features, she was thinking hard. "Got some pigs in the barn, they will try and make an escape if ye open the door and I'll lose them out on the fens. Best ye settle yer horse under the eaves, better get out of the weather if ye know what's good for ye."

I took a quick look back at the barn. An uneasy feeling compelled me to investigate further, however Beth mumbled something under her breath I did not catch. I felt rushed to accommodate her in order to get the information I needed, both Beathan and Tavish had warned me of her temper.

"Thank you for inviting me in," I greeted Beth after settling Tasunke and taking another cursory glance around the yard. "I know it is dangerous to invite men into your home when you live alone up here." I sat in one of three wooden chairs around a table, one leg shorter than the others, making it tough to balance on the cobbles.

Beth smiled, enjoying my discomfort. She put two glasses on the table and filled each one with Scotch, pushing one in front of me. The glass greasy with fingermarks made my stomach protest at the thought of putting it to my lips. She did not notice my reluctance and downed her glass in one. I took a tentative sip.

"Dinnae get any visitors up here, except the law of course, falsely accusing my boys ay all sorts ay trouble." Beth took the chair opposite and settled her spindly frame, though without a cushion I could not imagine her being comfortable. "Dinnae run a still, never hae, I suppose ye are going tae accuse my boys ay murdering the McKinneys."

The accusation hung in the air, I never thought of it, mostly because of the rumours around Mr Turner's involvement. His connection planted itself in my imagination and now little else occupied my thoughts. "How well did your boys rub along with the McKinneys?"

"Och, well enough, I suppose," Beth poured another draught into her glass. "We are distant relatives, mind, from back when the auld Laird died. Though the McKinneys hae always been a bit tae big fur themselves, even though we come from the same place, think they are better than us." Beth thought for a minute, cleaning under her fingernail with a bit of splintered wood. "Rupert was the same age as my youngest, Levy."

Stomach turning at the sight of the small pile of debris building on the table from Beth's nails, I looked around the kitchen. Hard to say whether the boys were living here, the meagre contents could service one or three. "When was the last time you saw your boys, Mrs McGreevy?"

"Few months back," Beth wiped the pile of black dirt from the table with the sleeve of her gown. "They went down south tae find some work after the lambing season up here. Brought me more wool tae spin, should be home in a week or so tae take my work tae market. I dinnae leave the cottage unattended, there are brigands around."

None bigger than you, I thought to myself. Tavish would not have mentioned them to me if he did not believe they might be around, nor would Beathan be quick to accuse them. "I have to ask you if either of your boys has been operating a still, an explosion occurred on the fens the other night, not far from this cottage and there has been some speculation your boys might be involved."

"Lies," Beth slammed a surprisingly strong fist onto the table, it shook the glasses and the bottle of Scotch pitched perilously. I reached out to steady it, "bet ye heard it from those ingrates down in Markinch. Well, I will tell ye they hae it out fur my boys, they worked at Deoch and were accused of theft and fired, even though they had naught tae do with it. Now they go and find work where they can, I spin wool. If the two of them hae learned tae operate a still, we could be as rich as the bloody Clunes." A fire lit Beth's eyes and she appeared feverish, "They could stay home all the time, but I tell ye, Captain, I dinnae think they hae the brains, I love them, but stills are a complicated business."

She was lying, I could not prove it, however I felt it in my guts. Instincts warning me of her duplicitous nature, the only truth she spoke was her belief her boys could not run a still. This did not mean they were not trying. "Madam, thank you for taking the time to answer my questions, I should be off, back to the village. When your boys do turn up, I will be looking to question them myself."

"They are normally home fur Christmas," Beth stood and eyed my half-empty glass between narrowed eyes. I clenched my stomach, forced a smile and downed the rest in one swallow, breathing heavily to stop from heaving. She continued speaking, satisfied, "Nae much work around in winter for two lads."

Grimacing on a hiccough, "I shall perhaps see you in the village." I bowed smartly, pulled the fur around my shoulders tighter and headed out the door without a backward glance. Tasunke stood watching me with a baleful eye. He looked ready to slumber back in the warm barn, with a bucket of oats by his side.

I could feel Beth's eyes on me as well as someone in the barn. Out in the open and alone I could easily be taken down, the best way to take down an opponent was through surprise, it's the reason we used raids to harry the French. I climbed into the saddle, and saluted the occupants of the barn; I wanted them to know I sensed their presence. Tasunke's clever hooves managed the path and we met the road, a good foot of snow had fallen in the time I spent with both women, and I let him have his lead, he knew the way back to the barn and warmth.

I thought falling snow magical as a child. It drifted from the sky, swirling, as light as air, and it covered everything in cold drifts of ice. Such a simple instrument of chaos, roads shut under its weight, accidents befell the unwary traveller and all remained quiet, sleeping under its heavy silence. Relaxing into thoughts of spending the afternoon working through ciphers for Mr Turner's diary. I remained convinced the answers to his actions before his death would be revealed along with his involvement with the McKinneys. The lack of any other occupation in Markinch fuelled my need to solve the mystery.

The sound of a dry branch snapping echoed out onto the road. I immediately leapt from the saddle and loosened the weapons on my belt. Tomahawk in hand, I led Tasunke to the side of the road and waited for the cause of the noise to reveal itself. It may have only been a deer or it might be the McGreevy brothers following. Hania taught me the importance of stillness. We spent many autumns hunting together and he would teach me, sometimes with painful consequences, the true abilities of a hunter and a warrior. Those lessons saved my life in the New World; I never thought to have to use them here in Scotland.

Minutes passed, the cloud of white breath emerging from my chapped lips the only sign of my presence, I could wait for hours, crouched in this position, in the summer, in a comfortable temperature. Unfortunately the fast falling snow building up on my shoulders and head reminded me my clothes would begin to leak in time, exposing me to another chill. The thought of spending any more time in bed with a fever, relying on the feminine ministrations of Freya, spurred me into action. I decided to shout out and take a stand when a small voice emerged from the woods on the opposite side of the road, a few feet judging by the slight echo.

"Captain, it's only me," Kieran's voice shook with shivers and I immediately stood up. Tasunke lifted his head, studied my profile and fell still again. "I went around tae check my snares before the weather turned worse and I saw ye go tae the McGreevys'." Kieran stepped out onto the road, a brace of conies over his shoulder, shivering so hard I was surprised he could speak at all.

Quickly striding over to him, I took his frozen hands in mine, looking over his clothes. "For a lad who spends most of his time out of doors, I'm surprised to see you so ill prepared." I lifted him up and carried him over to Tasunke, placing him on the front of the saddle. Taking the hares, I slung their frozen bodies across my back.

"McGreevys are dangerous folk." Kieran chattered through his teeth as I tried to get comfortable in the saddle behind him, pressing his small frame into the warmth of the wolf furs. "I know Roth and Levy are up there, though they dinnae show themselves often and probably wouldn't tae a stranger. Thought ye might need my help again," I heard the grin on his face.

"You're a good lad with a good heart." I signalled for Tasunke to move forward again and we plodded at a slow pace; I could not risk Tasunke becoming lame with Kieran in such a state. "If you knew the weather would close in, you should not have stayed out. You must always have a plan to get home, lad," laughing under my breath. "I would hate to know what your father might do to me if he knew you fell ill while chasing after me."

"He doesnae hae a mind for such things, might nae notice if I took ill." For the first time Kieran sounded like a small boy. It was hard to think of him as vulnerable. "He wishes he lived in another time and place, maybe fur things tae go back tae the auld days; he wants his rightful life."

I let the silence grow; the warmth from the furs began to work their magic, Kieran's scrawny shoulders eased from shivering and he leaned back. Tasunke dutifully trudged along in the deepening snow, needing to break the silence. "And what do you want, Kieran?"

The boy shrugged his shoulders, he remained quiet for so long I thought he was either not going to answer or had fallen asleep. "I suppose I would keep everything as it is now. Faither working at Deoch, Tavish teaching me how tae make Scotch and always having time tae check my snares or look for fish. I would wish tae remain in Markinch. Except when I am fighting in the New World, as ye did, I shall be away from

Markinch and Scotch. I will be having stoatin adventures and be like my great-great-grandfather, the auld Laird."

Hoping to make light of his desire to become a soldier, I said "I for one would be terrified to come across such a fierce small thing in battle." Kieran sat up taller when I used the word small. "Size is not everything in a fight, there are many ways to take down a larger opponent, and not only with your fists, using your wits and playing to your own strengths."

The boy sniffed, "I dinnae believe it, Levy McGreevy is the biggest man around, and they say he is the meanest fighter. He never, ever loses." Kieran leaned forward and patted Tasunke's neck and ran his fingers through the horse's ice-crusted mane. "Besides, Jimmy's the largest lad in the village and he has never lost a fight, nae ever."

It sounded as if the lad might have some experience with the latter of the two village bruisers, I did not want Kieran to think I might be singling him out. "Tell me of Jimmy, does he pick on all the village children?"

"He's the landlord of the Thistle's son, so he can get intae the beer and Scotch," Kieran shrugged. "He only shares with his friends and if anyone threatens tae tell his mother, they get a guid bop on the head. I'm nae a snitch, I tried trading a couple covies fur a taste, dinnae tell my faither."

The houses of the village finally began to appear as dark shapes in the falling snow, we would soon be safe, out of the elements. "I assure you I am not a snitch, either, however I would warn you over the dangers of alcohol." Thinking quickly, "I have heard a few scientific studies on the effects of alcohol on size, and I believe it may cause men to stay small their whole lives."

"You never say," Kieran's voice sounded worried. "I've only ever taken sips, nae much, dae ye think it might affect my size? The auld Laird was as big as a bear, folk say, I need tae be at least the same size as him."

Legends tended to grow larger in people's minds with time. "I think the odd sip is fine, it might be best if you leave the drinking to old men such as myself, no more growing to be done, you see." The lights from the village windows shone weakly through the snow and we turned into the main road, not a soul moved on the street.

Kieran slid from the saddle before I turned Tasunke into the inn's back courtyard, I handed him the brace of rabbits and he snapped one off the braided sticks and handed it back. "It's still foul weather, I can take you all the way back up to your cottage at Deoch."

The boy slid a hand longingly over Tasunke's wet, icy neck. "Nae, I better make my own way home, never know what mood Faither might be in. Best tae keep him couthy after all, I'm still on my punishment fur my last adventure with ye." He doffed his cap and stepped lightly through the drifting snow. I watched until he disappeared.

Without prompting Tasunke turned into the narrow passage and did not stop until we stood in front of the barn doors. Dismounting, I spoke. "Well, old man, I think we have had an interesting morning, let's stay inside for the rest of the day, shall we?"

Chapter 9

I relaxed into my favourite chair in front of the fire in the drawing room, a plate of half-eaten oat biscuits and a pot of tea at my elbow, as I drowsily contemplated the falling snow through the front windows. Kieran would have made it home safely, yet I worried for the boy. He was far too adventurous for his own health. I resolved to report back to Colonel Manners, his letter prompting news from me aside. I needed to be sharp in order to present recent circumstances in a respectable light. The current mysteries in Markinch did not warrant a whole militia, the less military involvement the better for everyone.

Finishing the cup of tea, I took up my travelling writing case, the battered wood as familiar to my eyes as my own hands. I ran my thumb over the small brass plate with my father's initials, JD, carved into the metal in script, as I had hundreds of times before. Opening the lid on paper, ink and goose quills, using a small knife, I sharpened the end of one of the new quills. I closed the lid of the wooden box, set my paper in place and stared at the blank sheet.

My one of my last letters had been to Mr Wick, informing him of my purchase of a great swath of land to the north of Boston. I had told him of my plans to settle there, have a family and never return to London, finally at peace with the world. The minutes ticked past in mechanical succession, the clock on the mantelpiece reminding me of time lapsing. I put the quill to paper several times, only to discard my words and think anew of an opening. I questioned my motives for protecting the people of Markinch, they would hardly thank me for my efforts. Previous experience taught me; better to write something than nothing at all, and I wrote across the page in halting script, hoping to see my thoughts in order to organise them.

Colonel Manners, the year of our Lord, 1707, November.

I am in receipt of your letter having taken up the post in Markinch not over a week past. On the surface, all appears to be in order, the main distillery, Deoch-an-Dorus, keeps tidy records and is running at full capacity. The other smaller still at the Turret is no longer in production and has not been for several weeks. The reason behind this halt is a cause of concern for the English, as it may have to do with the previous post holder, one Mr Turner of Somerset.

I glanced up at the knot in the rope Mr Turner had used to end his life, it hung motionless, without pride or threat. I studied the intricate way it clung to the beam and how high the noose must have hung. Mr Turner could not have hung the rope without a ladder, someone else was involved in his death. Someone in this town, did the McKinneys have more to do with it than being victims? Questions frustrated my thoughts, I railed against Colonel Manners for not detailing Mr Turner's tenure here in Markinch. For not mentioning the worrying circumstances of his death, this information must have been important. I wanted to write my angry thoughts onto the paper, however, I knew Colonel Manners' character well enough to guess his less than cooperative mood should I try to scold anything out of him, I needed to remain aloof and use my wits.

It appears the man created a local scandal with his interest in the Turret distillery, believing they might be responsible for operating an illegal still or running Scotch, though he found no proof of these crimes. According to my sources the two men who ran the still, Mr Rupert McKinney and Mr Everett McKinney, disappeared on the same night as Mr Turner's demise, leading many in the area to believe he was involved in the men's disappearance. I could not discover any proof Mr Turner might be involved in the men's vanishing, although Mr Turner's obsessive nature gives credence to the accusations. The discovery of Rupert and Everett's corpses out on the fens in recent days has only led to further speculation over Mr Turner's involvement in their demise. I made a cursory search of the place where the men died and of their bodies, finding wounds consistent with shots fired at close range. I searched the cottage where Mr Turner lived and found no such weapons. The lack of the murder weapon does not make Mr Turner innocent or a knave, it only reinforces the mystery surrounding all three men's deaths. I will be continuing my inquiries into the matter and I will present any further information to you as soon as it becomes available.

After signing my name and closing the envelope with red wax and my personal seal, I thought back on every word and sentence. My complete omission of my own involvement in the discovery of the McKinneys' bodies might cause problems if he decided to send further soldiers to investigate the deaths. However, I remained confident Colonel Manners would see no reason to disturb the fragile peace of the village with further soldiers or a militia. Markinch did not appear to be a place of strategic importance to the Scots or the English. I would have time to solve the mystery on my own.

I should have informed Manner's of the McGreevys possible involvement with an illegal still. However I refused to convict two men on the basis of no evidence. Once I obtained conclusive proof of their guilt, I could move forward, but until this opportunity arose, they remained two boys, guilty only of disturbing their neighbours with unproven cattle rustling, which did not necessarily fall into my own jurisdiction.

I set the finished letter complete with direction next to the cold teapot. It would have to be sufficient to keep Colonel Manners apprised of the situation, without causing a panic resulting in an overreaction. After witnessing such instances in Boston, I wanted Markinch to stay clear of any trouble. Often the best policy lay in no policy. My actions based on the presumption I could find some solution to present mess without force. Still the question lingered, why was I bothering to protect Markinch? It must lay in my own apathy towards the military for not preventing Onatah's death. My trust lay battered on her deathbed, no longer the fool who would believe an army of men could protect anything, only destroy.

My tired eyes spied the letter from Mr Wick. I had read it several times the day before and once that afternoon. It contained all manner of protestations over his clumsy behaviour in London. He reminded me of his ineptitude at social situations, as a scientist, even as an old man, he often overlooked social niceties. I must please forgive him his trespasses. I had already forgiven him, many times over, as I left the pub, on my way north. I also was not worthy of our friendship, yet pride stayed my hand every time I reached for pen and quill. I loved Mr Wick as a father and it made his feelings over my wife all the more bitter. I wish I could explain to him how the feelings of grief over her death slipped away from me every day with a speed that broke my heart anew. Only in my dreams could I picture her face, smell her skin, feel her touch. Awake she remained out of sight away from conscious thought.

I closed my eyes and held my head in my hands, grief at her loss no longer as powerful as the grief of my own inconsistency. However much I loved her, all I possessed was my anger at the man who caused her death, not loneliness or sadness at losing her and my unborn child. What manner of man was I, to put such a beautiful creature aside so quickly; I had hoped to revel in my grief for years to come. I wanted to write to her brother, Hania, who would be living in the winter hunting grounds, preparing for his first winter without his sister, only his wife and sons to keep him. He could not read nor write in any language, and there would be none to deliver the letter. I could not use him as a source of fresh hurt, I needed to make a choice, to hang on to her or let her go.

The reply to Mr Wick might have been longer than the one to Colonel Manners, yet it only contained the briefest of apologies for my own behaviour. Instead I told the old man of some of the finds in Mr Turner's mathematical equations. I tried to copy some them from the slips of paper for Mr Wick's consideration. Mathematics might be an interest of mine, however, it was not my strongest subject. My intermediate skills could only follow Mr Turner's equations so far, I would become lost in a sea of variables and could only guess the conclusions were correct. A plea for Mr Wick to find an accomplished mathematician concluded my letter and I folded the paper, and sealed it with my crest. My chores finished for the day, the rest of the afternoon stretched ahead of me with nothing to entertain.

I stood, stretching out my limbs, needing occupation, pacing to the window; the snow fell thick and fast. It looked set to continue all afternoon, well into the night. Having been out already, I did not feel the need to face the elements again. Nor did I need to invite Freya's criticism over my actions. My outings over the last few days against the barber's orders and it appeared the Lord used the old barber as his messenger on earth. I felt I still needed to make amends for upsetting Freya on a daily basis. Turning from the window, I scanned the room, Mr Turner's opus remained spread on the walls, the chalkboard stood in the corner with a half written logarithm. I was not accustomed to having nothing to occupy my mind, even less accustomed to not having physical activity to enjoy. I took the tea and plate of uneaten biscuits back into the kitchen; perhaps if I put everything away nicely I would go up in my thorny housekeeper's estimation.

A few minutes later, everything put back into place, I walked out of the kitchen and hesitated before walking directly back into the drawing room. The copy of *The Merry Devil of Edmonton* Mr Wick had sent me as a birthday present this past summer lay in one of my trunks above stairs. Yet the thought of reading more of Peter Fabel's adventures as a magician did not summon much interest. I did however have Mr Turner's diary, the answer to all of the recent deaths in Markinch could be contained in those coded pages. I took the steps two at a time, as I had as a boy to irritate my nanny and quickly found the diary in the table drawer beside my bed. Tucking it under my arm, I raced down the stairs and grimaced as I stumbled to the bottom, thinking of Freya's downturned mouth at my antics.

Sitting back in my chair by the fire, my writing case on my knees once again, I opened the diary to a random page and thought of where to begin; the numbers did not reveal any pattern to the untrained eye. Sighing and scanning the room, I felt the equations mock my efforts, the cipher could be anything. Using the same methodical approach as the other night, I wrote out the alphabet on a scrap piece of parchment, remembering a cipher described in one of my history books, I shifted the number of the alphabet down three spaces. Caesar used such a cipher to encode his own correspondence, hiding his deepest thoughts; this did not save him in the end, his best friend and ally holding the weapon of his demise. Now under the first letters of the alphabet, A, B, C, D, and E I wrote the numbers 1, 2, 24, 25, 26. I proceeded to write out a half page of letters corresponding to the cipher numbers underneath.

I could not make any sense out of the numbers, I tried to form words from groups of letters, yet nothing meaningful appeared. I tried to further the Caesar cipher by shuffling the numbers down the alphabet by four, five, six places and still could not form any coherent sentences. The frequency of numbers used in each line led me to an interesting conclusion: perhaps some of the numbers corresponded to more than one letter of the alphabet. This could be the breakthrough I need to solve the puzzle; it meant the cipher could be anything from an important date to a randomly selected group of numbers. I studied all of the pieces of paper stuck to the surrounding walls. I truly hoped the cipher was in a date rather than one of these calculations, otherwise I would never find it.

While studying at Magdalene College, I was privy to a major scandal whose discovery rocked the foundations of academic spirit at Cambridge as a whole. An old professor who conducted various chemical experiments began to believe some of his students might be stealing ideas from his work and he tried to protect himself accordingly by encoding his workbooks. He used a code based on the date of his beloved wife's death, an event so far in his past he believed his students might never guess. Unfortunately for the old man, his son, an aspiring chemist himself and lacking any scruples, worked out the cipher as the day his mother died and stole his father's ideas, and when the old man accused his son of misconduct, he locked the old professor away. The son's actions came to light after he could not thoroughly explain how some of his experiments worked through rigorous testing, sadly the revelation came too late for his father, who had died of a broken heart.

Setting the writing desk aside, I began looking through all of Mr Turner's papers. He must have left something around the cottage with his birthdate, parents' wedding anniversary, the day of his acceptance letter to College. I opened the drawers in the desk to search through each one and I found papers on recent discoveries made by mathematicians, but little else of a personal nature. I stood and carefully turned on the spot, looking for places where Mr Turner might have kept his correspondence. Even if he did not have regular contact with his kin, he would have received and written letters to Colonel Manners.

Blowing air forcefully out my mouth in frustration, I walked back over to my seat by the fire. I heard whistling from the front hall and stopped before sitting and waited for Freya to come bustling into the room, a refreshed teapot in hand, the same biscuits displayed on a plate.

"Here ye are, Captain," Freya set the tea things onto the same table they had occupied before by my elbow and glanced around in the room. "I hope ye hae gotten some work done, Captain, although I dinnae see how with all this nonsense going on around the place."

"You could help me," I used my most charming smile. "I am looking for Mr Turner's private correspondence, anything from London or family members." Gesturing to the desk, "I looked through the obvious places and could not find anything."

A placid smile on her face, "Och, well, Beathan came down after the accident." Freya glanced at the rope and made a studied effort not to look back again. "He went through tae search fur family or relatives, wrote tae the official in London." Freya unconsciously wiped her hands on the apron around her ample waist. "Nae family, nothing."

My hopes of finding anything on Mr Turner sank and I wanted to kick out the leg of the low table in the middle of the room. "Right, thank you for your help, I hoped to find something with his birthdate or parents' anniversary, something with information concerning the man."

Freya's forehead wrinkled in thought, she smiled and I knew an idea struck her. "There is this wee book." She went over the mantelpiece, and lifted a silver candle stick, underneath a worn black book rested and she carefully picked it up in one hand. "I cleaned even though he forbade me from coming in here and I found this once."

She held out the book, the cover indicating the most popular form of reading material the world over, at least in the civilised parts. I took it carefully, the cover worn with age and gently opened it to reveal neat script from another time. "The illuminations are so tiny, yet beautiful, I have never seen such a beautiful bible."

Frowning, Freya avoided my face and looked down at the pages as I turned them carefully over. Someone, a monk probably, had taken great pains to carefully write out all the Bible's passages, even covering the edges in gold in some places, others with scenes of peasants and animals. "Maybe if he read it more often," Freya let the sentence fade. "I hae looked through many times, nae sure what tae dae with it, I couldnae bear to have it sent tae the wrong direction." Freya sighed, "I let it rest there, if you look on the back pages, ye will find many different dates." She patted my arm and left me to look over the bible alone.

Scarcely aware of my surroundings, I sat back in my chair and studied the dates on the back cover. James Turner's birth written in clear script the last entry, above him his parents' wedding day and above this his father's birth and death dates. His father predeceased him by several years. The death of is mother was written as a side note beside his father's in the same year and month. Mr Turner's parents must have passed while he attended classes at College. Searching for living relatives above his parents, I only found names and dates of deceased aunts, uncles and grandparents. He had been truly alone in the world.

I took up my travelling writing case, a fresh enthusiasm guided my hand as I wrote out the alphabet carefully once again. Underneath, I first used Mr Turner's birthdate. I knew the letters and corresponding numbers must have a short cipher. His birthdate, his parents' wedding anniversary, the dates of their deaths; after an afternoon of work, none appeared to be the cipher. I banged the small illuminated bible down with force and immediately regretted the action when the binding became loose.

"There is a nice coney stew on the fire," Freya's voice sounded from the hallway. She did not step into the drawing room, her face pinched. "I hae a pretty good idea where the wee beast came from, mind, and he should know better," she nodded her head. "Hae a pleasant evening, Captain."

I stood, not wanting to appear rude. I knew she watched me and made comparisons with my behaviour to Mr Turner's; perhaps she could see the same feverish light. I knew the answer to the mystery lay in these neatly scrawled numbers. "Please watch your step in the snow, Freya, and no need to hurry over tomorrow morning, I can manage."

She snorted as she turned, disappearing from view. I frowned, I could take care of myself perfectly well. I had done so for numerous years, even in the army; I might be on campaign for weeks, not seeing any servants until I returned to Boston. I looked around the room, the answer to the puzzle lay here. I needed to put my mind to it and return to my uneventful life in the Highlands for the rest of the year, after which lay the freedom to choose any path I desired.

I looked up at the ceiling and closed my eyes. I tried to imagine myself as Mr Turner, ensconced in the familiar room, musing over his day, writing his innermost thoughts in his diary. Information so private he could not bear to have anyone else read it. What could possibly act as the cipher? Barely registering the knock on the door, I thought of all the maths written around the place and the equations I transcribed for Mr Wick. The answer must lie in one of them; the amount of work involved in trying to find which one would be daunting. I ignored the noises coming from the hall; Freya must have forgotten some task or other. I needed to think, which of the equations held his interest for the longest? Was there another scholar's work he admired?

"Captain, I hope I am nae intruding, I met Freya on the way from the village and she assured me you wouldnae mind a quick visitor." Phil's quiet voice from the doorway of the drawing room focused all my attention. I opened my eyes and found her hesitating on the threshold.

A sudden embarrassment infused my thoughts, I stood staring at Phil, no words came to mind. The drawing room would look a mess to anyone who lived in the impeccably clean castle and along with all the papers stuck to the walls, could only cause alarm.

"Please allow me to beg your pardon," I scooped a number of stacked papers from the low couch and invited her to sit with a wave of my arm. "I did not expect visitors this afternoon." Sighing I mentally checked myself, as she sat and arranged the folds of her tartan primly, "Even if I had been expecting you, the drawing room would still be unprepared for visitors." I put a slightly maniacal smile on my face as she looked around frowning at the rope still attached to the beams in the ceiling. Her slender shoulders shuddered slightly and she closed her eyes. I could not explain clearly why I left it there and spying the teapot. "Shall I go out and boil some water for tea?"

Philomena caught my eye, her determination in not looking away steadied my nerves. "The weather being what it is, perhaps something stronger might be called upon tae warm my toes. It is past the evening hour and perfectly acceptable for a lady tae indulge." She gave a low, throaty laugh, appearing to have no notion of the effects the sound could have on a man.

Stamping down a blush, I was no green schoolboy, enchanted by the attentions of any female. Especially one with unusually large eyes and a permanent ink stain on her fingers from the quill. I replaced the teapot on the tray and went to the sideboard where the Scotch bottle and glasses kept company.

I handed her one of the glasses, half full, "Miss Philomena, please enjoy." I took my own seat, it did not feel as comfortable as it had before her arrival, sitting with my back straight. "I think you might recognise it as your own, not as good as the Scotch we shared over supper, however."

"Call me Phil," she took a long sip of the liquid, let it rest in her mouth for a moment before swallowing. I sat mesmerised by the play of emotions crossing her face as she enjoyed the Scotch, here a true connoisseur sat. "Philomena is the name my mother insisted upon and every time I hear it, her disappointment in me grows."

"Beathan told me she passed several years ago, I am sorry for your loss." I added while Phil gave me a strange look, "I know what it is like to lose one's family, my own parents died while I remained a lad."

A wry smile played around Phil's lips, she appeared amused, yet a hint of sadness creased her brow and she sighed. "I can only assume Beathan didnae mention the cause ay her passing and I am impressed with the inhabitants ay the village fur nae spreading gossip, they are more loyal than I can imagine. I am nae sure if Beathan mentioned my mother came from an auld and distinguished Scots family?" She placed her empty glass on the table and gathered her thoughts. "A poor yet noble family, her father lived the life ay a dissolute drunk and gambler, by the time she entered society everyone knew she possessed nae dowry."

The situation was not uncommon. I felt uncomfortable as Phil made to continue with her mother's story. She held up her hand to prevent me from speaking. "Please, Captain, let me continue. All will be revealed," she smiled. "She did possess an incomparable beauty and wit, these two things would save her father from debtors' prison. He made sure everyone in Edinburgh knew she could be bought fur the right price, tae gain entry intae his illustrious family as well as becoming the owner ay such a lovely jewel."

I tried to imagine Beathan and Phil's mother as an incomparable beauty. Studying Phil's face closely, details of her mother's face in the set of her eyes, her slim figure remained veiled by her father's heavy features. Phil could never be a great beauty, yet she was certainly far from ordinary.

"My faither, Magnus, went tae Edinburgh the same year, the fortunes at Deoch greatly increased with the purchase ay the Markinch holdings and after losing his parents. He realised the importance ay keeping the Clunes tradition of Scotch-making in the family. He naively went tae find a bride amongst the elite," Phil grimaced. "He possessed money and a few connections; he never thought tae aim so high as an Earl's daughter. Yet he fell in love with Lady Lindsay at first sight, though she would hae naught tae do with him, in the end, he bought her from her faither and she never forgave him fur it."

As a child I wished for a family, for my uncle to embrace me, as more than an heir to the title, yet he never did. "Your father seems to care for you and your brother very much. I wish my life contained such a man, my uncle only ever cared for improving the family's connections."

Smiling, Phil took up her Scotch glass again. "We are lucky tae hae such a man as Magnus in our lives. He says he never regretted marrying my mother, even though she spent most of her time in Edinburgh, carrying on with other men. The last one resulting in a pregnancy, both she and the child died and my faither picked up the pieces, he is a strong man."

Standing, I walked over to the sideboard and fetched the bottle of Scotch, refilling Phil's glass before she could refuse. I firmly believed a strong libation was required when discussed family. "My own childhood was marked by years of loneliness," I waved a hand in the air. "I was surrounded by tutors and nannies, yet I only experienced a real companionship when I met my parents' great friend, Mr Wick."

Phil smiled curiously and reached into a bag at her feet. She pulled out a folded broadsheet and handed it over the table. "Nae the same Mr Wick of the Royal Society? My true purpose in visiting this afternoon nae tae share auld family gossip, I came tae give ye the Royal Society papers, the vacuum pumps are an interesting invention, however I have been conducting my own small experiments with them and the information is nae new."

I took the papers from her and unfolded them. "One and the same." I did not have much interest in the vacuum pumps either "You have been conducting your own experiments, have you sent your findings to the Royal Society?"

A light pink infused her cheeks and she looked away, out the window into a world growing dark. "I dinnae think the Society would be interested in the results ay experiments conducted by a woman, an unmarried bluestocking, as my brother would hae everyone know."

"You might be correct," I scratched my chin. "There is much debate over women's involvement in scientific matters and whether they have the constitution to carry out the rigorous work involved in proving or disproving theories." Phil perked up in her seat, looking as if she might have an argument on the matter. "However, this is the age of science and if we can make a spark-producing machine, surely women can further science?"

"Hear, hear," Phil responded cheerfully and raised her glass. "Perhaps I could write up some ay my findings and send them in. I do find the Society repeats many ay their auld experiments with nae further innovations gained from it and some ay the time I think they try things only in order tae spectate the absurd."

Laughing at some of the experiments I witnessed in my time with the Royal Society before I left for Boston. "I must agree with you, I think the older, wealthier members use it as an escape from their wives and the boring social rounds they are obliged to do, especially when Parliament is in session." My eyes strayed to Mr Turner's diary, lying open on the travelling writing desk.

Phil spied the same volume, interest infused her features and she reached over to pick it up. A stray curl from the severe knot on the back of her head came loose. She used her free hand to gently wipe it out of her eyes as she studied the numbers. Flipping through the pages, her expression grew even more absorbed in the numbers. "This cannae be a mathematical question, hae ye written yer diary in code?" She looked up smiling. "Ye are mysterious, Captain, how clever."

A voice in my gut shouted for me to not disclose the true owner of the diary. I did not want to give up my rights to Mr Turner, I felt close to finding the cipher. Soon I would have the key to his innermost thoughts and they might lead me to a murderer. "Yes, a habit from childhood, one too many prying nurses, having my thoughts reported on to my uncle could be an unpleasant experience." I tried to artfully grab the book from her hands, she pulled it away and pointed to the failed cipher pages.

"And hae ye forgotten how tae decode yer own diary, Captain?" she leaned over to make a closer inspection of my efforts, knowing I might be lying, which did not sit well. With her attention distracted, I liberated the volume from her slackened hand. She watched me curiously, a taint of mistrust in her face.

"Sometimes I am too clever for my own good," I tried to laugh naturally, however it sounded hollow and perpetrated the idea I might be up to something. "You should probably be on your way, Phil, it is growing dark and I need to get back to work."

Phil rose reluctantly from the couch, eyeing me and the diary with outright suspicion, though she did well to hold her tongue. "I give my leave ay ye, Captain, I hope ye will enjoy the society papers and I will think on yer suggestion to make a submission."

"I am sure the Society would be very happy to hear from you," I ushered her quickly to the door. An urgency to have her prying eyes away from Turner's diary giving fuel to my actions. "There are several lady members. Good evening."

Giving Phil a quick push out the door, I clutched Mr Turner's last words to my chest and stared down the empty hall. Phil's perfume lingered and I enjoyed the smell of lavender for a moment before walking into the kitchen to fetch some stew.

Chapter 10

Splashing cold water on my face from the basin aided in dispelling the fog of sleep from the rest of my brain. I needed my wits in full operation today, if I had possessed them yesterday, I might not have handled Phil so poorly. The hurt look on her face after my sudden insistence on her leaving haunted the rest of my evening. I expelled her for finding interest in Turner's diary, an interest I could have prevented if only I had closed the book upon her arrival. My defence lay in the new knowledge that I am sensitive over who knows of the existence of the diary, something I did not foresee earlier. Otherwise I might have taken better care. I felt the knave for behaving roughly with her, especially after she revealed her late mother's behaviour and its obvious effects on her and Magnus. I could only imagine what it must have done to Beathan.

There would be some way I could make it up to her, all I need do was wait and the opportunity would hopefully present itself and all could be well between us, though it appeared Phil's and my friendship might always be tumultuous. I needed action, and repairing the damage I caused to Phil yesterday was not on the agenda. Instead I would investigate a certain pair of cattle rustlers who many believed to be Scotch runners, not only for my own pride but for Colonel Manners. If I could prove the pair posed no significant threat to English excise, I would have a solid excuse for excluding them from my first report. Better to take care of unwanted attention quickly and quietly than have a whole militia march through the village.

Besides, the unfortunate circumstances surrounding the accusations against Mr Turner would bring unwanted scrutiny on Markinch and its new excise officer; perhaps Colonel Manners intended this situation all along. Everyone knew the Colonel operated one of the largest spy rings in the whole of the English military. His informants slid through war zones and ballrooms as ghosts, melting into the fabric of society, none ever suspect. I rubbed the whiskers on my chin; the grain of stubble rough on hands already losing some of the calluses built by years of practising with firearms, swords and especially the tomahawks Hania gave me. Onatah's brother acted as a scout appointed by the government to lead the army into the wilderness. He knew the land and how to avoid detection, though he despaired at our ignorance.

We became fast friends on my first summer of campaigning. We raided villages and supply chains and, after saving my miserable hide several times, he took me under his wing. Told me I had wasted his time and now I owed him a debt. He taught me to remain unseen in the woods, to survive in the unrelenting harsh landscape of the New World. Where a simple mistake could mean instant death and a big mistake could mean a slow agonizing death. His constant reminders of the dangers the elements posed, the need to step lightly, to attack fiercely and retreat softly were foreign to me at first.

The opportunity to make my goodbyes with Hania never came to be, my imprisonment after my actions at finding Onatah dead meant I missed her funeral and Hania's departure for the winter hunting grounds. I might be a reasonably well respected captain in the English army, however I wondered if Magnus, Beathan or even Tavish were to learn the secret of the actions leading to my imprisonment and reassignment in the army, they would trust me again. There would be no further invitations for dinner up at the Castle. Shaking my head, none of this mattered. I only needed to serve out my year here and I would be off, living the rest of my life, in any manner I wished, preferably with less dissection of my past and present circumstances. The only matter I needed to attend today was the McGreevys: did they pose a threat to only themselves or the village as a whole? And from the explosion the other night, I thought the latter might be the case.

Staring at the only unopened trunk in the corner of the room, nostalgia for my previous life rose. It did not somehow feel tainted with Onatah's death, I walked over, unlocked the buckles, and heaved the lid open, the smell of stale air wafting in my face. The voyage had not been overly gentle to some of the items, a couple of tobacco pouches would have to be thrown outside immediately before they could taint any more air. Laying bare fingers on them wrinkled my nose, the winter deerskin pants and shirts lined with fur Onatah made me years before appeared serviceable enough. The fur-lined garments might mean extra warmth, the snow had halted sometime in the evening, however the temperature remained enough to freeze his bones. I dug out my fur-lined moccasins with the beads sewn on the toes for good measure.

I ate my porridge leisurely, hoping Freya might walk in and discover an American Indian in her perfectly clean kitchen. My hopes remained dashed however as she did not arrive before my departure out the back door. I did not want to attract too much notice with my outfit as I headed out into the wilderness alone, after much advice opposing such actions. If I kept my footing this time, I should be able to follow the rabbit and other animal prints through the bridle paths. The sky would be light for hours, no need to worry about darkness blinding my way. I stopped at the edge of what appeared to be the manicured garden and looked out over the vast fens. Taking a sharp deep breath, I stepped into the fens once again, the crunch of snow and ice underfoot the only sound in the vast emptiness. Staring straight ahead, I convinced myself I could be the only man alive for miles, no notion of a village or a Scotch distillery operating near.

Travelling through the fens towards the site of the explosion went quicker than I anticipated, I must have been in a much more inebriated state the other evening than I previously imagined. The soft deer-hide boots left hardly any imprint in the snow, however they did not give good grip on the icy path and I stepped carefully until finally reaching a small clearing. Although snow covered most of the debris, peat burning under the surface kept the ground free from cover. I stepped carefully around the perimeter of the burned area; some small fragments of glass lay in the midst of the mud and dirt, nothing else of a foreign nature.

The burnt and broken glass could be clues of a still, it could also be from any number of things, broken glass bottles from an earlier settlement or the sight of a previous rubbish pile. Kicking through the snow around the blackened space revealed nothing more than a frozen crust of bread, either forgotten or hastily discarded. Someone or a pair of someones had been clever in covering up their mess. They knew somebody such as myself would be along to investigate and must have cleared it before the big storm yesterday, otherwise their prints would be all over the site.

Releasing my frustration in a low growl, I once again made a circle around the burnt peat. Two bridle trails led away over the snow, one leading towards east and Deoch, the other led towards the west and the McGreevys' farmhouse. With the picture of Beth McGreevy and her shotgun in the back of my mind as well as a good imaginary picture of Levy McGreevy's size and weight I picked my way towards their farmhouse. Unfortunately, unlike the places I stalked through with the military in the New World, no trees and brush grew high enough here to hide my passage, the best way to stay unseen lay in crouching and moving quickly between small hillocks.

Even with this strategy, I remained hopelessly visible and easy prey to anyone looking out on the moors, especially from the east. I felt relatively safe from onlookers in the village as enough dilating ground lay between to restrict my movements; this same reason might have prompted the McGreevys to feel safe from prying eyes at the explosion site. Tracking came naturally to me, I picked up Hania's tips and movements quickly. Not the same as understanding the mechanical parts in a steam engine or rebuilding a winch in order for it to carry a heavier load, yet easy enough to feel the accomplishment in the task. My skill only increased my sense of belonging and eventually I became part of an advanced scouting party, going deep into French territory in order to find positions. Some of my fondest memories came from those missions, positioned on the edge of a knife with only my wits to save me.

I had been away with Hania and a few others when the attack on Onatah and the rest of the village occurred. Hania had warned me trouble could be close. I heard rumours the French remained near to Boston. Unfortunately, I trusted the remnants of the city's militia to do its duty and protect the village, while I saved the rest of their lives. I could not think of it now, I possessed a task to complete and I halted for a moment, resting my back on a small hill to catch my breath. My legs burned with the effort of crouching and running, my fighting fitness fading with every passing day. The edge of the fens appeared close, trees began to grow along the edge, providing cover. I needed to pick my way there carefully, someone could be using the trees as their own cover.

Checking the tomahawks and guns at my waist, I squatted facing the tree line and started out cautiously, taking my time to step through the heather and frozen earth, the only sound my heavy breathing. An echo from the trees instantly froze my body and I peered into the thick gloom, scanning for any sign of movement. Holding my breath, I listening for any noise giving away man or beast, all my focus on the scene in front of me straining, and nothing came. I knew an animal could not outwait me easily, smaller animals' instinct might be to wait a few seconds and rush to safety, while larger animals could wait for several minutes if they sensed danger might be near.

Either the animal making the noise was long away or the animal was human, waiting for me to move and give away my position, or hoping I would lose interest in their presence and again give away my position. In both situations I needed to assume a human, who did not want their presence known and knew my position. The potential for violence as yet unknown, they could have many reasons for not wanting to reveal themselves to a man dressed in a foreign costume; poachers remained rife in the area, the Clunes did not take much stock in handing out penalties for the crime.

I could not stay here all day, the fur-lined clothes made my adventure much more bearable, however they would only provide so much warmth; I needed to make the first move in order to control the situation's outcome. Steeling my nerves, the familiar rush of excitement and apprehension filled my guts and I felt alive again, in the throes of seeking out an unknown enemy. I ducked my head, squeezed my shoulders in tight, trying to create as small a target as possible and ran crouched towards the trees. A definite crashing sound came from ahead, my heart beating hard with every breath; I stood up straighter and tried to run with my full stride. The mistake cost me more than my pride.

The first shot rang out, and as I felt the lead race past my skull, the wind lightly ruffling my hair, I instinctively dropped the other shoulder. Hoping the loss of balance would throw off the shooter while I fell to the safety of the ground. Unfortunately, the second shot caught my left arm, above the elbow, and I grimaced in pain. The bullet was hot and warm blood began to seep down my arm. I grunted as I hit the ground hard, and quickly turned to face the sky. I closed my eyes and focused on my breathing, a trick Onatah had taught me to reduce blood loss. I forced myself to take long slow breaths.

Once the panic of the wound lifted, I took stock, stretching my ears and listening for any other movement, while using my right hand to investigate the damage. Gritting my teeth, I inched my hand up my wounded arm and finding the wound, I felt for an entrance and exit hole. The arm throbbed in protest at the invasion, however I quickly determined the bullet went straight through. Ripping a length of linen from my undershirt, I tied it clumsily around my arm. It would suffice until the barber could take a look. I forced the fingers on my left arm to open and close several times, I did not think there was any bone damage, but the waning strength in the limb might mean muscle damage. I could not throw a tomahawk with it and I might be able to hold a gun, but a shot would likely carry the pistol from my grasp.

I needed to make an escape. I was sure the shots had not come from the cover of the trees, they must have been shot from behind me. In my foolish arrogance, I thought none could possibly have an advantage over my superior skills and I'd assumed I was alone on the fens. Careful not to jar my injured arm, I made a brief scan of the immediate area, no signs of human occupation. I did not expect any, the shooter had had plenty of opportunity to seek me out after the bullet hit my arm to finish off his work. A mad picture of Beth McGreevy stalking me through the fens with her hunting rifle flitted through my brain. I shook my head; there was no way she could have pounced on a dairy cow let alone a man with my many talents, I hoped.

The safest way to get to cover would be to crawl on my elbows, I flipped quickly and tested the weight on my injured arm, the pain was not unbearable, and I started slowly at first, picking my way over the ground and proceeding with more urgency as I felt a new trickle of blood escape the bandage every time I put pressure on it. I thought of all the times I was injured fighting, of the time I thought I would die in the bog only a few days past, my heart beat steady and strong reminding me of a will to live I had no conscious control over. With the trees only a few yards ahead, I risked getting unsteadily to my feet and running the rest of the way, once inside the enclosed space, I fell onto a tree and slid down, unmindful of the bark pushing up the back of my deerskin, scratching my back.

Fighting the urge to close my eyes, I tried to keep them unnaturally open, using the muscles in my forehead to pry the lids up. The blood loss would make me more and more tired with each passing minute. I could not rest for more than a few seconds at a time. I needed to get to the village, I thought of the McGreevys' cottage not far away, however any one of the three could be responsible for my predicament. Agnes McKinney's cottage lay beyond, yet I would still have to travel unseen through the McGreevys land to reach her and I did not want to bring more danger to her lonely doorstep. She suffered enough, and perhaps at the hands of the excise officer.

The best place to find shelter and help would be the village, people would be conducting their daily business, others would stop at the Thistle. I clenched my jaw and stood, squeezing my eyes shut as a wave of dizziness rendered my faculties useless. I opened my eyes once again and focused on one point until the fuzzy edges in my sight refocused. I could not risk taking the main road, instead I would move through the forest, as a ghost from the New World, invisible and one with the wilderness around me. The edge of the fens where the trees grew at larger intervals would aid in my progress, and I tried to keep hidden and take advantage of the relatively clear path.

Concentrating on my steps I tried to jog through the brush with as much fleetness of foot as I could muster. After a mile, the energy to stay focused began to drain away quickly and my steps grew heavier. I tripped over an exposed tree root, unable to right myself or put my arms out to brace my impact. My face collided with the frozen ground and I coughed mud and dirt out of my nose and mouth with great heaving breaths. I wanted to give up, I wanted my will to be broken, yet my heart still beat with irritating regularity. I stood clumsily once again and dragged my broken body towards the village.

Tears threatened to completely impede my vision as the first of the village houses became visible over the horizon, smoke from peat fires burned lazily into the sky, unmindful of my cold, aching limbs and throbbing injury. Like the steam engines I adored, my legs pumped with regular fits, right and left. My hope of receiving help before the village grew slim, as the buildings grew larger and my blurred eyes spied none around in the flat light. Walking through a small cottage back garden, a dog barked through the back door furiously needing to investigate the intruder. I paused for a moment, however, none came to the door, no aid here and I continued with an increasingly shuffling gait.

I found the street after walking through a pathway at the side of the house. Still, not a soul roamed the street, all appeared to be industriously conducting their business by the warmth of a fire. A mad thought seized my consciousness, the sign of the Thistle lay a couple houses down, yet if I lay down in the road here. Eventually one of the villagers would find me, but I could not take the chance it might be the knave who injured me. I fought the growing tiredness, the loss of vision and stumbled the last steps to the Thistle. Leaned on the door and used my good shoulder to press down onto the opening mechanism.

The weight of my body thrust the door wide, the wooden portal banged off the wall with force and I fell to the floor with a shudder so hard it made my teeth chatter. I curled into a ball, knowing I had done everything in my power to save my life. A moment's suspended silence followed my arrival in the taproom, after which my ears filled with the sounds of men shouting, astonished noises escaping their lips, chairs scraping and boots stomping quickly towards me.

I released a sigh as an arm reached out and rolled me over. "It's the captain, in a native costume. He's been hurt," the person doing the speaking unceremoniously poked at the bandage over my injury. "Bad I think, better get the barber."

More shuffling of feet and the door opened, the cool breeze swept across my body, a familiar voice sounded in my ear. "Och, Captain, I am nae even going tae ask about the clothes until yer better, it's the sort ay friend I am." Beathan grunted as he lifted me from the ground, not an easy feat even for the big man. "I'll take him tae a room upstairs, if ye dinnae mind."

After being set on a soft mattress, I listened to the orders shouted above my head and decided I needed to try and regain some of my dignity. Opening my eyelids slowly, as they felt bruised. I looked around the room, Beathan spoke with the innkeeper, they whispered their conference. I cleared my throat several times before I could get any words out past my chapped lips, the room felt overly warm, yet my skin felt overstretched.

Beathan stepped to the end of the bed and started to pull my moccasin boots from my feet. "Dinnae try tae speak, Captain, the barber is on his way." He closely inspected the footwear, "I think I might need a pair ay these."

I smiled and my bottom lip cracked, I licked the blood away, annoyed. "You will have to get a nice Indian girl to make a pair for you." Beathan rounded the bed and helped me to sit up, I let my head fall to my chest, momentarily dizzy.

"Yer in a right state once again," Beathan helped me pull off the deerskin and fur jacket and what remained of the linen shirt underneath. My bare skin shivered for a minute, as he inspected the bandage, "This looks mighty serious, what the hell happened?"

Sheepishly I kept my voice low, "I went out into the fens to inspect the site of the explosion. Someone must have thought I was more trouble alive than dead and they shot me. The bullet went clean through, however as you can see the bleeding has not eased."

"Yer a damned bull-headed man, Captain Clyde-Dalton, after all the warnings we gave ye over nae venturing intae the fens," Beathan stared into my face and I tried to look defiantly back at him. "Well, who could ay imagined ye get yerself shot? Might only hae been one ay the lads on the hunt. However this has the stench ay the McGreevy boys on it, I am going to hae a word with them."

The sound of rushing steps echoed in the corridor and a small man with a leather case peered intae the doorway, a smile on his face. I thought he would probably smile even if it were the end of the world, "Ah, Captain, my favourite patient, let's see what ye hae done tae yerself now."

My eyelids lowered to half-mast at the implication and I felt my lips turn down, the last thing I wanted was for the barber to get too familiar. I nodded at him as he came into the room and set his tools down. I looked at Beathan, "Two shots fired, one right above my head and this one. If it were a hunter, they would have checked their kill."

Beathan studied me for a moment, eyes unreadable. He shifted to let the barber through and the other man began to unwind the bandage, clucking like a woman the whole time. Finally Beathan sighed, "Did ye see who it was?"

I winced as the barber pulled the linen from the poorly clotted wound. "No, the blighters came up from behind me. I did not see anything, only heard the shots. I found some cover in the woods when I finally made the tree line, however I do not know if the shooter was long gone or let me go."

"I am going tae hae tae wash the wound thoroughly, it might sting," the barber's cheery voice grated. "Yer lucky the bullet went straight through, merely a flesh wound."

Sniffing loudly at the obnoxious man, I focused on Beathan, "I am not saying the shots might not have been an accident, but whoever was out there did not reveal themselves to help and I am sure there was someone else in the woods, watching the whole scene."

"At least ye came through in one piece," Beathan glanced at the barber. "We cannae hae another excise man meet his demise up here in Markinch, the wrong people will start tae talk." His laugh rang out in the empty room and he sobered immediately. "And the next time ye decide tae go off on and investigate, take someone with ye."

I wanted to protest, yet my vulnerable position made me bite back the words. It appeared I was destined to look the fool in the Highlands, years of experience in the military drained away and I became a boy again. "I do not believe I need to go out and inspect the explosion site again, someone did a good job of cleaning up any evidence."

"A shame you did nae find anything after going tae all this trouble," Beathan eyed my fur-lined buckskin trousers. "I thought a couple ay the auld lads might hae fits when ye fell through the door, a real native in the Thistle."

I could not help but grin in response to Beathan's mirth, it must have been quite a sight, and I had not thought of it until now. "I only wore the clothes because they are warmer than my frock coat, hose and boots, plus the moccasins are supposed to help me stalk through any terrain unseen."

"Maybe in the New World, Captain. Perhaps they lost some ay their magic here in the Highlands." Beathan took a deep breath and appeared to be gathering his thoughts. After a moment, he pulled a chair out from the wall and settled his large frame. He watched the barber ready a needle and thread and looked at my face, "The Scotch trade attracts many different folks, we hae a new guard fur our Scotch delivery intae Glasgow, it's a rough city and we decided two would be better than one."

Wincing again as the barber slowly stitched my wound closed, I tried to follow Beathan's story. Perhaps it had something to do with the McGreevys and I needed the distraction from the low cheerful humming of the barber.

"I mentioned our new excise man was a Sassenach, newly returned from Boston. Through a short discussion, this new guard admitted he also was recently returned from the New World, one of his qualifications for our position being his recent time spent with the Boston Militia," Beathan watched for my reaction.

A hatred so powerful it turned my stomach rose to the surface from the place it must have been hiding for the past few weeks. The barber patted my arm and reminded me to relax or the stitches would end up being uneven. I needed to concentrate on not jumping from my seat. "Where is this fellow now?"

Beathan waved one of his hands, indicating I should relax. "The man is halfway tae Glasgow, I hope, with his precious cargo. He told me a story before he left of the scariest moment in his life, one he will never forget, the scene is etched across his brain." Lowering his voice, "The incident involves ye specifically."

I relaxed onto the bed, the barber grew quiet and reached for one of the jars in his case. Opening the lid, a foul smell permeated the room, I looked at him and the ointment disdainfully, and he smiled back. "Smells terrible tae be sure, but it will keep the infection out."

Probably scare away anything coming within a foot's radius, I thought to myself. So Beathan knew my secret, he knew why I had been locked in the stocks, I steeled myself for the same approbation I faced in Boston. "How much of the story did he tell you?"

Understanding lit Beathan's expression. "Only the parts he knew. The army must have done a good job in covering up yer marriage tae the native girl, the man didnae mention it. He only told ay how the Boston Militia was returning from an ill-advised failure ay a siege at Port Royal. The militia commander, John March, tried tae take the fort twice and failed. His troops starving and weak, the English army based in Boston were forced tae rescue the motley crew before disaster struck."

I closed my eyes. I had lived the rest of the story, hearing it from someone made my face wrench to keep the sorrow at bay. The stupid mistakes leading to the deaths of at least a hundred souls, it made me shake with anger, the barber patted my shoulder awkwardly.

Continuing in a low voice, "On the march back from Port Royal, the French attacked a small settlement near Boston, the inhabitants a group ay native women, their men fighting or working fur settlers in Boston, only a few escaped."

The vision of Onatah's body, lying lifeless among the rest of her village, her limbs and bloated stomach, so beautiful in life made grotesque in death, came before my eyes. Rubbing a hand over my eyes, a shuddered sob escaped before I could stop it; it was the first time I had cried with grief in a long time.

"The man didnae have any idea ay the carnage carried out while the militia was away." Beathan steadily recounted the story, as I forcefully rubbed the moisture from my eyes. "The militia were only happy tae be home, until a madman attacked them at their supper. Dressed as an Iroquois warrior, he went straight fur John Marsh, only tae be held back at the last minute by another Indian companion. However, the attacking man was not an Indian, he was a white man, with eyes as cold and dark as hell, intent on killing the militia commander and an inch from succeeding. It took five men tae hold him down, all suffering injuries in the process. The new guard, he swears the man is ye, and it took him weeks tae sleep through the night after the incident. Says you became the Devil himself, risen up from Hell tae extract vengeance fur John Marsh's mistakes."

"I wish I had been," I spoke quietly. Tears gone, I felt refreshed. "The bastard got away with his stupidity, while my wife and her folk lost their lives. He was reprimanded and went on with his life, I was sent to the stocks, imprisoned and quietly shipped back to London." I looked Beathan straight in the face, "Are you going to spread this tale?"

The barber inspected his handy work, with a grim smile. "I will be around the cottage tae check the bandage tomorrow, yer exhausted now and I suggest ye get some much needed rest. I'll send the innkeeper up with some food." He turned towards the door and stopped for a moment. "All consultations are confidential."

Beathan shook his head as we both watched the small man disappear out the door, before he looked back at me. "I dinnae see why ye are so afraid ay the truth getting out, ye were seeking vengeance fur yer own. This is something Highlanders understand well; we would never sanction ye for it, however I am yer friend and so I will keep yer secret."

I sighed with relief and gratitude, the events of the day and Beathan's story both worked to pull at the rest of my energy and I lay back on the covers of the bed. "Thank you,

Beathan, I want to move on, I think, and this story will always drag at my heels."

Chapter 11

I spent a restful night at the Thistle, regaining my strength and contemplating the identity of the gunman. Experience taught me anyone could shoot a gun under pressure, but to be a good marksman one needed practise and nerve. The attacker might have missed the first shot, aimed directly through my skull, however they met their mark in my arm with the second. From enough distance and in such a hiding place as I could not spy them among the snow-covered hillock, something of a mystery brewed here in Markinch, and now an attempt on my own life; I needed to resolve the matter quickly.

I borrowed some ill-fitting clothes from one of the innkeeper's son's and went out of the Thistle early, unable to sleep any longer, feeling somewhat refreshed. I kept my arm tucked close to my chest in order not to move it unduly and walked down the main street towards my cottage. I watched a few workers make their way towards Deoch before the work whistle, a few doffed their caps in my direction, most ignored my presence. I halted at the front gate of the cottage and watched them pass, for the most part they remained silent, others spoke in low tones, more to preserve the silence of the morning rather than any need for privacy. Each sported a plume of white cloud where their warm breath mingled with the cold air.

The chilly temperature finally prompted me to move, the light jacket provided by the innkeeper no match for the weather and my fur-lined buckskins, folded under one arm, needed a good working through. They had become stiff as boards from yesterday's soaking. I braced myself before opening the door. Freya had refrained from visiting me at the inn last evening, however she made her displeasure known by speaking loudly at the bottom of the stairs of my foolish adventures. Oil lamps lit in the drawing room indicated her presence.

The door latch clicked behind me, and a shrill woman's voice came from the kitchen. "Captain, I cannae say how relieved I am tae know ye made it through the fens once again," Freya's plump frame filled the doorway to the dining room.

"Och, well, I can see ye made it out in one piece, but ye smell as if ye fell straight back intae the bog. Get yerself upstairs and I will warm some water; I am surprised the innkeeper put up with the stench ay ye." Freya's nose wrinkled and she pulled a linen square from a pocket in her apron.

Frowning, I dropped the deerskin clothes on the floor and lifted my arm. I sniffed the inside of my armpit; heather and maybe a bit of old sweat, nothing to cause true alarm, yet I also could smell something. I looked down at the clothes on a heap on the floor.

She looked down at them too, stepped forward and leaned down, sniffing gently, "What in the name ay the good Lord do ye hae there, Captain? Its nae ye, it's this mouldy pile ay who knows what. I will throw it out fur ye." She made to pick up the items keeping them the furthest from her body as possible.

With the promise of a few days ago to be kinder to Freya in the back of my mind, I kept my voice as even as possible. "Freya, my wife made me those clothes, they are in a bit of state at the moment, however they have sentimental value, they need to be aired and oiled properly." I felt proud of not losing my temper.

My buckskin coat now occupied the space between us, Freya looked from the garment to me incredulously. "Clothing, this is nae fit fur a savage, Captain, and it smells tae high heaven. I cannae believe anyone could stand wearing such a thing."

"You cannot throw them out, they are my belongings and I do not care if you think they smell," I ground out as I made to take the shirt from her. "I will lock them in a trunk upstairs and deal with them later if they offend your proper sensibilities."

I suppose the thought of having the garments locked away where they might moulder and become even worse prompted Freya to make a compromise. "I shall hang them up in the barn, shall I? There is a fairly dry space in the back where they will be safe enough." She grimaced and picked up the trousers and walked back towards the kitchen. "I hae some porridge on the fire, I will bring a bowl out fur ye."

I rubbed a hand over my face, the woman would be the death of me. I walked further into the hall and turned into the drawing room, the one lamp shone at the back of the room, where the chalk board stood with the logarithm written out across the top. I walked slowly over to it; I felt positive I had seen this precise piece of work before, it could not be a Mr Turner original and I studied the numbers and read the small passage underneath.

Fear them not therefore: for there is nothing covered that shall not be revealed; and hid, that shall not be known.
What I tell you in darkness, speak ye in light: and what ye hear in the ear, preach ye upon the housetops.
And fear not them, which kill the body, but are not able to kill the soul: but rather fear Him, which is able to destroy both soul and body in hell.

I had found the Cipher, I felt sure to the marrow of my bones. It lay hidden here, written out on the chalkboard behind me the whole time, in plain sight. Excitement rose in my stomach and I turned quickly, searching for my travelling writing case. In my haste I jolted my arm.

Freya found me wincing and holding back a number of choice curses, shook her head and set a tray with porridge and a teapot onto the table next to my favourite chair. "Please try tae take it easy fur once ,Captain, nae shame in having a rest. I am sure the barber will be around this morning tae take wee look at yer bandages."

I wanted to shout at her in my excitement to start work on the cipher and decode Turner's diary. Instead I walked over to my seat and tried to become comfortable with her fussing over everything. I grabbed her hand when she tried to unfurl the napkin over my legs, "I am perfectly capable, as you can see, I still have use of one arm."

Sniffing, Freya left the room and I began to shovel hot porridge into my mouth, burning my tongue in the process. I needed to wait a few minutes for the pain to ease before tucking back into breakfast. I would reveal all of Mr Turner's secrets in due course. I finished a cup of tea to clear the tray and set it aside, looking forward to spending the rest of the afternoon unravelling some of Markinch's secrets. I had just leaned over to pick up my writing desk when the bell for the front door rang out.

Freya shouted something from the back of the cottage and I waited for her to answer the portal, exchange friendly greetings and usher the barber into the drawing room. The man beamed his approval at my leisurely state, I narrowed my eyes in response.

"Captain, I checked at the Thistle fur ye this morning and found ye hae up and gone." He bustled into the room and set his familiar leather case on the couch opposite my chair. "I am happy tae see ye are recovered enough to move from bed."

I bit back an impatient retort and let the man inspect the bandage. He hummed cheerfully under his breath, Freya watching every move he made, while I stared at the rope around the beam in the ceiling. After several minutes the barber gave his verdict. "I believe it is healing nicely, I will refrain from changing the bandage fur another few days, though I think ye should wear a sling."

Taking one look at my mutinous expression, Freya steered the barber from the room gently, picking up his case on the way. I only heard the beginning of the conversation. "I think the Captain can manage fine without one and I will be here all day tae make sure he doesnae engage in any strenuous activities."

The front door clicked shut and Freya bustled in once again to clear the tray. "Ye know, Captain, if ye insist on getting yerself intae these scrapes, ye will hae tae learn tae live with the consequences," she stood after imparting the sage advice and walked from the room.

Getting shot and falling into a bog were not my first intentions upon arrival in Markinch. I thought sourly. The woman thought I fell into scrapes on purpose in order to make my life more difficult, or perhaps she thought I tried to make her life more difficult. Either way, I could finally look forward to an afternoon spent in quiet revelations with the help of the logarithm. I turned in my seat to look at the numbers once again.

A small rapping on the front door hardly interrupted my thoughts, the damned barber must be back to hassle me. I used my good hand to retrieve a piece of blank paper and reached for a new quill; I did not want old thinking in the way of my new discovery. I read the numbers in sequence over a few times, sure I had come across the configuration before. It would come to me if I sat quietly for a moment and relaxed, the dull pain in my arm acting as a centre.

"Captain," the slightly nervous Scots lilt cut through my thoughts as cleanly as the bullet went through my flesh yesterday. "I heard ay yer unfortunate accident and I thought ye might enjoy reading another pamphlet." I turned in my seat to face Philomena who came through the door and watched me, as a bird might a cat.

Sighing, this morning I felt doomed to entertain every person who casually walked by the cottage. I damned the mysterious shooter for not only injuring me, but also making me an object of focus after potentially discovering the key to the whole mystery. I held out my hand to indicate the sofa, "Please sit, you are most welcome, Miss Phil," I stumbled not to say the rest of her name.

Phil beamed a smile and for a moment I felt its heat on my skin and sat back as she handed me a folded broadsheet. She explained while I clumsily opened it with one hand and inspected the illustrations, "It is an explanation of Jethro Tull's seed drill, an interesting device. I know yer interest in steam engines, Captain, and I thought this might interest ye. Tull is a bit of a maverick, I gather, he wanted tae improve the common seed drill used in his fields tae make them more efficient. He used the foot pedals from his local church's organ tae distribute the seeds in a much more even fashion. If you follow the first illustration . . ." finished with her short prelude, Phil sat back on the sofa, as Freya came to the doorway.

"I thought I heard someone in here, Miss Philomena, how neighbourly ay ye tae visit the captain while he is indisposed." Freya brought in a tea tray laden with scones and jam and I briefly wondered why I usually settled with oat biscuits.

"Naturally after I heard ay the captain's injury, I thought tae bring him some reading material tae alleviate the boredom ay remaining indoors." Phil smiled after hearing my loud sniff from behind the broadsheet. "I shall nae be staying tae long, these do look scrumptious."

Freya hummed under her breath as she left the drawing room, her happiness at Phil's comment making her steps light, and why should it not? It came from a genuine assessment of the tea and scones; I wondered why I never thought to say something as simple.

"Shall I pour the tea?" Phil made the statement as she delicately lifted the pot from the tray. I tried not to show my impatience as she handed me a cup and saucer. "Ye appear a bit on edge, Captain, I suppose it is tae be expected after yer accident yesterday."

"It was hardly a damned accident." Some of the tea splashed over the rim of my cup. "Some bounder shot me and I am positive he did it on purpose." I looked over my shoulder at the chalk board and down at the blank paper resting on the travelling writing case. "I must apologise, not only for my recent behaviour, the other day I behaved abruptly with you and for no reason other than my own nervous speculations."

Phil frowned more than smiled at me. "The blame lies with me, I now realise we nae hae a close enough acquaintance for me tae be snooping through yer papers, asking impertinent questions." Phil sighed and took a sip of the hot tea. "Every time I come intae this room, filled with maths, I suppose I find it magical," she finished with a blush.

"You have an inquisitive mind, there is no shame in it." I tried to console her, I knew how it felt to want to know how things worked, what made them tick, a thought made me sit up a bit straighter. "Phil, do you recognise the numbers written out on the board behind me? I am sure they belong to a logarithm of some variety, yet I cannot place where I might have seen them before."

Setting her cup and saucer down, Phil studied the numbers for a minute, her brow furrowed in concentration. Her shoulders sagged and I thought she might be giving up, when a light lit her features and she turned her bright eyes to me once again in triumph. "I believe it is John Napier's logarithm 'e', or what he refers to as the natural logarithm."

I stood up to make a closer inspection of the numbers running in a line, I nodded and turned my head to look at her in approval. "I think you have it, Phil. You are quite right, I could not place the numbers, even though I felt quite certain of seeing them before. This must be the code I have been searching for."

Phil stared back at me, I felt uncertainty roll in waves from her body, she wanted to show interest, yet she held back after her previous experience. I could let her in, her clever wits might prove useful, yet a knot in my stomach urged caution. I made a quick decision, "I have made some discoveries, Phil, and I must admit, I was not fully honest with you. Would you like to know of them?"

"I would be greatly honoured if ye shared yer knowledge with me." Phil took her cup up once again and drained it. "Nae since my days away at finishing school did I hae a person tae speak ay science with, I am afraid Markinch is nae bustling hub ay scientific research."

Sitting back down, I faced Phil and gathered my thoughts. "First I apologise for throwing you out the other day." I picked up Turner's diary from the floor next to the chair and, taking a deep breath, I handed it to her. "You were correct, this is a diary in code. It is not however mine, and I believe it belonged to Mr Turner."

Looking from my face to the book in her hands, Phil opened it carefully to reveal the now familiar rows of numbers inching across the page in perfect uniformity, running her finger from the top to the bottom of the page. "It is an amazing piece ay work," she flipped through a few pages. "And ye hae tried tae use all the popular methods ay ciphers, the Caesar, the date method . . ." her voice trailed away as I nodded.

"This script has frustrated me since my recovery from the incident in the bog. The persistent rumours I heard of Mr Turner's involvement with the deaths of the McKinneys drove me to find a key to his words, I hope to find answers to many questions in there," I nodded towards the book. "Only this morning I looked at the logarithm and thought it might act to decode the mystery."

Phil let my excitement infuse her face before she looked down, her expression hidden by the top of her head, a neat part in her hair running from her forehead beyond. In a small voice she continued, "Do ye believe he might hae written ay his motives fur ending his life?" Her eyes darted to the rope a few feet away. "I dinnae think I could believe he killed the McKinneys, he nae appeared tae be the sort ay man tae resort tae violence."

I leaned back in the chair and carefully studied Phil's expression as she looked back up, choosing my words with care. "Many times in the army, fighting, I witnessed a sudden transformation take over a man. If he believed he might be in mortal danger, he would commit acts he never dreamt of in his life." The stark truth: even I committed acts of savagery and barbarity, as Beathan said yesterday, I single-handedly took out a militia command while they supped. It was a minor miracle none of the men I attacked died, too focused on my main target to care of their lives.

Phil looked small on the couch. She appeared to be running my words through her highly tuned brain, looking for all the things I said and did not say. I did not think much escaped her notice. Her shoulders squared and she looked me directly in the eye, "Where do we start, Captain? I am ready tae face the worst."

Picking up the blank piece of paper once more, Phil helped to place the writing case on my knees between us and opened the ink pot. I turned to her, her face hovered close to mine in order to study the opened diary numbers. "With the same method I have used for dismissing the rest of the ciphers, as based on a process of scientific elimination."

I wrote the alphabet out over the top of the page as Phil watched. I could feel her excitement over sharing an interest with someone and I realised for a moment she must be bored living up here in Markinch, away from her friends. As I wrote out the numbers of the logarithm, I asked, "Why do you not spend more time in Edinburgh? I have heard it is a veritable hotbed of scientific learning, you might join a society?"

"There hae been many times I hae thought a move tae Edinburgh might be best." Phil sighed and looked across the room and out the window into the cloudless sky. "We hae a townhouse and it is hardly used; Faither hates town, I think because ay Mother. I feel as if I am abandoning him every time I contemplate leaving."

"Magnus appears to be the most indulgent of fathers," I looked up at her after finishing writing out the code. "He seems only to want you to be happy, surely he will not go without company with Beathan and Tavish around the place? You never know, you might find a man with the same interests."

Phil's eyes squinted for a moment and she studied me with an air intensity. "I hope my brother didnae put this bug in yer ear and if he did I would like tae remind ye ay yer lack ay subtle persuasive skills." She focused on the scrap of paper and used a slender ink-stained hand to slant it towards her.

We both stared at the paper, looking at the numbers and letters whose discovery might lead to the unravelling of secrets to recent events.

A B C D E F G H I J K L M N O P Q R S T U V
W X Y Z
2 7 1 8 2 8 1 8 2 8 4 5 9 0 4 5 2 3 5 3 6 0
2 8 7 4

Clearing my throat, I reminded myself to never mention eligible young men or marriage in Phil's presence again. "I surmised previously the cipher would have a sequence of the same numbers, rather than allocating two numbers for some of the letters, as you can see in the book," I lifted the journal. "The frequency of some of the numbers is too obvious."

"Well done, Captain," Phil shifted in her seat and looked up into my face, her over-large eyes pinning me and her encouragement seeping into my bones, she reached for the travelling case. "Shall I take over the writing duties fur the next portion and ye can call out the numbers? This way ye can make sure I am nae writing the incorrect letter down."

I reluctantly gave up the writing case, it was the only item I owned over which I felt possessive. I never let anyone use it, yet watching her place it on her dainty knees, it looked comfortable, as if the case waited for Phil to take it up and carry on my work. I shook my head and handed over the ink pot. "Let us begin?"

I used the last page of letters, speaking each number succinctly while Phil dutifully searched through and found the corresponding letter. The whole proceeded slowly because each number corresponded with at least two letters, yet we patiently worked through until I read out all the numbers on the last page.

"Now the real work begins," Phil grimaced at the mess of neat letters on the page in her own elegant script. She opened the lid of the travelling desk and carefully lifted another piece of blank paper from inside and set it next to the page full of letters. "I think we should work on it line by line," Phil patted the place next to her on the sofa.

Without thinking I stood and sat next to her, my larger frame towered over hers on the sofa. She was such a delicate woman, I worried I might crush her with my clumsiness. Yet she shuffled closer, so our thighs met under our protective clothing, the heat of her skin burned through and I shuffled an inch away for safety. She appeared completely unaffected by the contact. Already solving the first words of the sentence. She wrote down alternative spellings until a sentence formed, the effect of her closeness made it difficult to concentrate, even over something I had worked on for days.

"Nae tae give myself the credit, yet I think we might hae the first sentence of our cipher." Phil lifted her eyes to mine, excitement over the accomplishment shone in them. I looked down at her and the rest of the room melted away for a second. A pull I never experienced before urged my head lower until it remained only an inch from hers and I thought I would kiss her. Phil gulped down a nervous breath and the spell broke. I studied the first sentence to cover my clumsiness. I read it aloud, "Again today I watched Logan question the McKinney grain farmers." I stopped at the end of the sentence, the last words hung in the air, leaving me hungry for more information.

Looking over at Phil, the dimness in her eyes indicated deep thought as she stared out the window. I wished to intrude on her private musings, a strange desire to know her thoughts nudged forward my curiosity, "Do you know these farmers? Do you know of them?"

Phil glanced back at me, I could tell from her hooded eyes that she carefully constructed her answer. "I know a minor scandal broke in the community when the McKinneys commenced purchasing their grain from a farmer down south. Scotch in Markinch hae always been made with grain from Markinch." She smiled at me for a moment before retreating back into memories, "Markinch may be a backwater Highlands village tae ye, Captain, however we are a loyal bunch as it happens. Even when the auld Laird died in battle, we nae drove his kin away, we took care ay them until they could stand on their own, we hae principles."

I thought of the old clan system in Scotland; it appeared it still lived, though turbulent times might see it broken, even here in Markinch where no Laird ruled. "What happened with the McKinneys and the grain?"

Phil wrinkled her forehead in thought, "I dinnae pay much attention at the time; idle village gossip, yet now with everything ending in such a miserable fashion," she took a deep breath. "I think I remember Tavish mentioning the McKinneys even stopped having the grain milled down at Deoch, thought they could get it cheaper." She glanced back at my face. "Scotch is a craft, Captain, it takes patience and an understanding ay science, though my brother might tell ye it's all gut feeling. Everyone thought the McKinneys might be protecting their trade, though I dinnae know what would hae interested Logan."

Having experienced two sides of the man, "What do you know of Logan?"

Leaning back on the sofa, Phil rested her head on a cushion whose height only reached my shoulders. "I only know what everyone else knows, his bloodline meant he should have been the Laird, yet through a twist ay fate his position was stripped and he works at Deoch. I know Tavish resents him fur replacing him, yet Beathan comments on how hard a worker he is, stirs up loyalist trouble every now and again."

"It's a dangerous time to have loyalist tendencies other than to Her Majesty." I made the statement firm, I did not want Phil to have any illusions where my ultimate loyalty lay. "The Crown will not suffer any advances by the Stuarts; they have given up their right to the monarchy, nor those who support him."

The silence between us stretched. The only sound our breathing and the crackling from the fire. Not offended by my fierce loyalty, Phil studied my profile. I looked for words to offset the harshness of my first statement, yet I found I could not say them. The Crown always found traitors and after witnessing traitors' deaths, I would warn any over engaging in foolish activities.

"Captain, yer loyalty tae yer country must be applauded, none seeing ye would ever doubt it," Phil took a deep breath. "You fought fur yer country in the New World, however, I would hope ye would hae a wee understanding fur the loyalty us Scots feel towards our own people."

I could understand yet. "Our countries have long been united under one monarch, yet you struggle with what you believe is servitude under the English throne. When it was a Scot who came from Edinburgh to take up the post left by a childless English monarch. It is the Scots who must look to join with us."

The frown on Phil's face deepened and I braced for a blistering retort when Freya stepped into the room. I have never been so happy to see her, smiling at the cozy picture we made. "I hae a nice brace ay lamb fur luncheon, would ye care tae join the captain?"

Phil glanced at the clock on the mantelpiece, "I am afraid, Freya, I must hae lost track ay the time, we were so engrossed in our work." She looked at me and I knew the real reason behind her departure. "I must be back up at the castle for luncheon, otherwise Faither will worry over my absence," she stood and straightened the tartan over her shoulder.

"Thank you, Phil, for all your help today, I would never have remembered where I saw the logarithm before and your help with the cipher could provide some very important clues." I tried to make my speech as heartfelt as possible; I knew I offended her with not understanding her loyalty to her country.

"Of course, Captain, perhaps we could work together on another problem. Scotland and England working together as equals, a novel scheme indeed," she turned and nodded to Freya. "A good day tae ye, I can see myself out."

I listened with Freya in the drawing room as Phil fetched her cape, and shut the door behind her. Out the window I watched as she fitted her gloves onto her small hands. Tugging them tight before wrapping the fur-lined cape further around her slender frame and walking out of the small front yard and into the road.

Freya watched the other woman go, a curious expression on her face, before looking back at me. "It is a shame she cannae stay fur luncheon, such a nice piece ay roast. It would be nice tae hae a woman around the house, might encourage ye tae use the dining table rather than the drawing room."

Interpreting the look on Freya's face as one I saw many times before on those of the matchmaking mamas of London society, I could not suppress a shudder. I felt caged in the small drawing room, thankful of Phil's speedy departure. "Miss Philomena's company is enviable, however she has much to occupy her time up at the castle. She is a hard-working young lady."

"And very much alone most ay the time," Freya mused walking towards the drawing room door. "She is a bit long in the tooth, yet I cannae help but think she would make any man a splendid wife."

Gritting my teeth I sat back in my favourite chair and leaned over to fetch the writing case with my good arm. "I thought you had luncheon to prepare." I ground out and began to decipher the next sentence in the coded diary.

Chapter 12

I set Mr Turner's diaries aside with a small thump of frustration. After two weeks of searching through his private thoughts for answers to his involvement with the McKinneys' deaths, or even the madness tempting him to take his own life, nothing. My elation over finally discovering the cipher to Mr Turner' diary became tempered after reading the last journal entry, where he wrote of mundane happenings in the village. He wrote the lead for the McKinneys' buyers was a dead end, they all turned out to be legitimate purveyors. With this small piece of information, I set out to find more information regarding Logan in the diary and the findings only created more questions.

At Deoch today for the weekly run off check: all seems well. I found Logan out of sorts, even more so than his usual countenance, for he is a taciturn fellow if ever I met one. He spoke to several of the workers in disapproving tones of the McKinneys' decision to use another farmer for the grain; one from down south, apparently this is tantamount to high treason in the village. Logan noticed my presence and dismissed the workers back to their stations and I asked him why he should be so concerned with the McKinneys' grain, surely the matter could be none of his business, their still being so much smaller than Deoch's? He informed me all happenings in Markinch would always remain his business more so than any others, and none more so than my own, as the gauger. I sniffed at his comments, and walked away, not wanting to engage him in another argument over Scottish and English relations, besides I hated the term gauger and do find great offence in it. Yet after thinking upon Logan's words I made up my mind to investigate the McKinneys further; it is my job as the excise man to follow up on any potential illegal happenings.

Rubbing my hand over my face, I squeezed my eyes; this journal entry appeared a few weeks before the McKinneys' murder and Mr Turner's suicide. Whether Logan were directly involved or not, he knew more than he was divulging. After discovering his possible link to the mystery surrounding the men's deaths, I watched Logan carefully. I wanted to question him in private, yet he always appeared to be with one person or another and I needed to keep my enquiries quiet. I did not want to risk inflaming the village sentiment against me by singling out the man who spoke openly of his dislike for the English. I needed evidence and justification before accusing him of any wrongdoing, especially murder.

Sighing, I tried to turn my mind from these complex musings before they took control of my life. Christmas Eve arrived today with little fanfare from myself, I studied the green trim Freya assembled on the low table with mild disinterest. At least her decorations smelled nice, however I remained at a loss as to why a gentleman living alone would have any need of them. It remained unlikely I would receive any visitors except perhaps Beathan, his sister since giving up my company after our recent row over Scots-English tensions.

Stray thoughts of Phil penetrated into my preoccupied studies of Mr Turner's diary, even though I remained sufficiently busy to forget eating meals and neglect my own correspondence. Something in her manner could not be easily forgotten, perhaps her enthusiasm in helping with the diary cipher or the way she neatly fell into place on the sofa that afternoon sparked my attention, my writing case perched on her knee, brow furrowed waiting for the next numbers to be called. Whatever the case, our falling out over her not understanding where the Scots position in politics lay on our fair isle acted as a burr stuck under my coat, until it felt as though it would remain there forever unless I took steps for its removal.

Unfortunately, as with my Freya appeasement strategy, making amends with Phil had not been as easy as I anticipated. Growling with frustration I stood and swept away the dishes from morning tea and carried them through to the kitchen. I had insisted Freya take the holidays for her family, as she had her boys to look after. For my part, the gesture might not have been based purely on goodwill; after spending days listening to Freya murmur over Phil's virtues and why the lass might leave in such a rush. I needed some peace, otherwise I could not trust my thoughts to be my own. I tried several times in the village to engage Phil, however, whether strategic or by chance, she always walked with a companion, or her business was too urgent. All of this left me with the feeling I might be losing my way with women.

In honesty, I did not have much experience with the fairer sex, my mother's early death created a gap never quite filled with nannies and maids, all of whom were friendly in their own efficient way, yet not loving. My experience with women before my posting with the army in Boston came in the ballrooms and parties of the social set. For the most part, interactions between men and women in society followed prescribed rules, only to be broken if one wanted a certain reputation. Though several rakes roamed amongst my own peers, the desire to become one of their ranks never appealed to me. After joining the army, even though officers often received invitations to parties in the best Boston homes. None of the young ladies ever caught my eye. I preferred to spend my time with the less moral of the lot when needs arose and then I met Onatah.

I recognised her as a great beauty the first time we met. An instant attraction compelled me to seek her out, yet it took several years before I could build the courage to interact with her without making a fool of myself. She remained patient and wise, waiting for me to make the advance, knowing I would eventually. Through friendship and camaraderie our love was forged. We survived the hard conditions of the New World. I miss the everyday circumstances, which made up our lives.

I flexed my arm, the gunshot wound healed nicely. Despite my contempt for the barber, he appeared to be a good surgeon. I would suffer no lasting damage from the attempt on my life, or had it been a warning? I played the scene over in my mind, time and comfort made it difficult to be sure of guessing the gunman's intentions.

Leaving the dishes in the sink, I decided the best way to clear my head would be a walk down to the Thistle. I needed to have lunch and perhaps Beathan or Tavish might be in the tap with a ready ear. After snuffing the oil lamps in the drawing room and pulling on my new winter frock coat, complete with fur lining, recently arrived from Edinburgh. I stepped through the front door and out into the world. Each step away from the cottage took me further from my stale contemplations. I took several deep breaths and convinced myself the invigorating walk would refresh my thoughts and speculations. Upon entering the street of houses and shops, I greeted several people rushing through their business.

The inhabitants of the village rushed to complete last minute tasks before the evening's Christmas party held at Deoch. A tradition since the Clunes' expansion into the castle, everyone in the village and surrounding area looked forward to the social event. Including the excise man; despite some of the villager's stubbornness at accepting my presence as inevitable. There were enough friendly people around to create the illusion of tolerance. I entered the tap to find it empty of my two companions, Beathan and Tavish must be busy with preparations for the evening's entertainment. I stepped up to the wooden bar, where the innkeeper greeted me with a smile.

"Captain, Freya mentioned ye might be down fur a lunch as she has the next few days fur her family." He reached for a glass and began pouring an ale from a cask behind him. "I hae also received a couple letters fur ye on this morning's run from London."

Leaning on the bar I looked over the room, empty save for a couple of old men sitting near the fire smoking and chatting amiably. I watched as the innkeeper set the beer on the bar in front of me and went to fetch the post.

"Here ye are, Captain," he handed me two letters, a quick glance showed them to be correspondence from Colonel Manners and Mr Wick. "And it'll be roast capon this afternoon, with all the trimmings."

"Thank you," I nodded to the innkeeper and went to find a comfortable, suitably private seat away from the prying eyes of the old men. I settled at a table opposite them and took a long drink of the ale.

Not for the first time did I think it was a shame Deoch only made Scotch. The beer at the Thistle, brewed by the innkeeper for the village, could be one of he best I ever tasted. I placed both letters on the battered wooden table. Which would be first, work or family? My military instincts pulled my hand towards Colonel Manners' missive and I broke the seal with my thumb. I began to read the cursive script marching across the page with increasing alarm and I concentrated in order not to panic in front of the other patrons who might be watching my expression.

Having reviewed your alarming preliminary report on the situation in Markinch, I have grave concerns over whether you are able to handle the Queen's business on your own. Mr Turner was not my first choice for the post in Markinch, nor would he have been a choice I would make for any post. The administration arm of the military recommended him because of his gift with numbers. He had no field experience and little common sense. However, our lack of experienced fighting men prohibited us from finding an alternative candidate. As you know, I rely on men with gut instincts to inform me of any possible threats to the Crown. Aside from the omission of the fact you found the bodies of the McKinneys on a drunken misadventure, my source also informs me there may be an illegal still operated by local thieves. Your own astute nature can only lead me to believe you have purposely omitted both of these facts for your own reasons and may I remind you of the tenuous position you occupy after your misadventure in Boston. Treason is as easy as taking up a sword against Her Majesty or even knowingly providing fraudulent reports to your superiors. I suggest you bring the situation in Markinch under control. If you do not do this to my satisfaction I will be forced to send a militia to rouse the operators of the illegal still out from hiding as well as forcefully putting an end to the rumours regarding the two men's deaths and Mr Turner.

Manners' cursive signature completed the missive, the threat of violence seemed to echo through the taproom and I looked up half-expecting to see the old military man staring down at me with eyes as hard as death. To my relief, the old men continued their conversation in hushed tones, clearing their throats at intervals. The innkeeper disappeared further into the Inn and I sat back and tried to relax. The worst had not yet come to pass, Colonel Manners wrote he would send the militia if I could not solve the problems myself, which left me some time. Not much, yet hopefully enough to spare Markinch the threat of living under a militia. In my experience, the villagers' motives would be questioned forcefully, the militia men came from the lowest orders, mercenaries paid to keep the Queen's peace, who often used cruel tactics to find their answers.

I folded Manners' directive with purpose, placing it in the front pocket of my jacket, safe from prying eyes. The news of this potential threat might hit the villagers hard and I knew it would be imperative to avoid mass panic if I wanted to get the truth. Taking another long drink from the ale, I picked up the letter from Mr Wick and a small smile replaced the frown as he described his delight in researching Mr Turner's equations.

I have found an old mathematics dean willing to take the time to go over the equations; he should have some results early in the New Year. To think you may have found the work of a genius all the way up in the wilds of Scotland, it is simply unthinkable! Of course the gentleman in question was an Englishman.

Shaking my head, I read the rest of the letter. Mr Wick could never believe academic learning might come from anywhere but a college or a society; a picture of him meeting with Phil made me laugh out loud. The men at the other table looked over curiously and I nodded in their direction, I set the letter aside as the innkeeper came through the with roast capon.

As happy as I felt for Mr Turner to have his work potentially realised by his peers, it remained a small victory compared to the impending disaster of the militia descending on Markinch. I needed to put a halt to Colonel Manners' plans. My gut told me Logan was either involved in the McKinneys' deaths or he possessed imperative information. He might even be responsible for Turner's death, he was tall enough to fix the rope on the beam using a chair rather than a ladder. It was time to get more aggressive with him and where better than the Christmas party this evening at Deoch? He would be amongst friends and neighbours, the potential for him to overindulge through the course of the evening might have him primed to reveal more than he should. I only needed to approach him with the right angle.

His notorious hatred for the English because of their involvement in his family's downfall remained his biggest weakness. I needed to exploit it cleverly and I might have an early Christmas present for Markinch. Taking a large bite of the capon, I chewed slowly and thought through my plan. I could do this, the people of the village depended on me, whether they appreciated it or not.

I stood waiting outside of the malting barn. The inside had been swept clean and decorated by the wives of the workers, tables laden with food and drink lined the room and I could hear the musicians strumming a merry tune, excited chatter bubbling up. As a boy, Christmas was a time of longing. I spent it alone, amongst servants at the family seat in Pendomer, longing for the company of children my own age or even my uncle. As a painfully well-behaved young man, I attended the Christmas parties chosen by my uncle in London at the most fashionable houses, the entertainment refined, the food exquisite, the wigs ridiculously high and all downright boring.

In Boston, I attended the Christmas Eve parties held by the matchmaking mamas, hoping to snare a title and wealth for one of their offspring. Such events normally meant I dodged to the card rooms as quickly as possible. Even after Onatah and I married, she would go to the winter hunting grounds with her brother, as they had practised all their lives, and I would stay alone in Boston, with the rest of the army, looking for entertainment. Here I stood with the rare opportunity to enjoy Christmas with an entire village bent on making merry and I needed to savour it, in spite of my mission with Logan, as I would probably never have another chance.

Straightening my frock coat for the second time, I grabbed the handle to the door firmly, took a deep breath and opened it, letting the light, laughter and joy roll over me for a minute before stepping through. My eyes took a moment to adjust to the brightness, candles lit the room at intervals and peopled milled around in groups of two or more, eating and drinking. Children dodged through the crowd with Christmas treats, upsetting the older folk and amusing the rest.

"Captain, I began tae worry ye might try and cry off this evening." Phil came to stand before me, hands held out, her hair pulled back in its usual bun, yet her eyes held a merriment not seen before.

Perhaps it was the scene playing out behind her, or her warm greeting after our recent disagreement, yet when I looked down into her face, I thought she could possibly be the most beautiful woman I had ever encountered. I needed to clear my throat before answering. "How could I miss the opportunity to finally see you? Merry Christmas."

A light blush infused her cheeks. "Well everyone is welcome, Captain, and a Merry Christmas tae ye, let me help ye with yer coat." Phil fussed with the heavy garment and handed it to a girl standing next to her. "Mind, take care of the captain's coat."

"You have done a remarkable job with the place, the last time I walked in here, the grain bags were piled high." I wanted to make conversation in order to keep her by my side for longer, yet I could think of nothing more to say.

"Well, the ladies from the village do most ay the work, I am forced tae admit," she looked around the crowd and back at me. "It is the one time ay year everyone puts their differences aside tae come together." In a lower voice, "I hae been wanting tae ask ye, if ye found anything in Mr Turner's diaries."

The mention of the diary brought my focus back onto the task I had set myself for the evening. I scanned the room and found Logan scolding Kieran in a corner and dragged my eyes away from the scene. "Nothing of significance, I afraid it has raised more questions than it's answered."

A frown appeared on Phil's face, "I admit tae feeling some disappointment with the news. I thought he might have written ay his feelings, or . . ." she let her voice drift and dissolve in the crowd.

"I had the same notion," I needed to bring her attention back to me, if only for a minute longer. "Yet he speaks only of mundane happenings around the village and some personal mathematics projects, nothing to indicate there might be truth in the rumours."

"And what rumours might those be? The two ay ye are certainly having a couthy chat." Beathan's large frame blocking the rest of the crowd, he handed me a drink and looked sternly at his sister. "I hope ye are making couthy with the captain, Phil, it is Christmas, holiday spirit and all."

Phil glowered up at her younger brother, "I will hae ye know, I am always friendly. If the two ay ye will excuse me, I hae guests tae speak with, Merry Christmas, Captain." I watched her melt into the crowd with disappointment.

Saluting Beathan with my glass, "Merry Christmas." I took a sip of the Scotch and gave an appreciative smile. "The party appears to be a success."

Indicating a less obtrusive place to stand other than in front of the door, I followed Beathan further into the room. He stopped and watched the crowd. "It's been exactly the same since I was a lad, running through people's ankles," he chuckled. "The only difference, the faces get older and the young hae more energy."

People began to clear a space in the centre of the room, and the fiddle players honed their instruments before striking up a jig. The villagers swayed with the sound and after a couple of seconds, Tavish took to the floor. His wild hair sticking up at odd angles, he pulled his kilt up over his knobby knees in order to move his legs faster with the beat of the music. The whole effect made it appear the lower half of his body was trying its best to escape the upper half.

Angus took to the floor and commenced dancing even faster than his brother, which I could not believe possible, the duo eliciting shouts of drunken encouragement from the rest of the crowd. The frenzy of the jig made both men red in the face, and they took great gulping breaths by the last of the notes, each clutching their sides and giving the other wary looks. The band struck up a slower song, and couples invaded the dance floor, giving the brothers no room to continue their feud.

I watched as everyone enjoyed themselves, unaware of the threat hovering over them. I looked to Beathan who watched his father on the other side of the room speaking with some of the older men. I needed to warn him, he might not be the Laird over Markinch, but he took care of its people.

"Beathan," I said in a low tone, "I could be severely reprimanded for what I am going to divulge to you." He looked over at me curiously, his bland smile an indication to carry on. "I received some disturbing news from the south today. The Colonel who oversees the excise in the Highlands has become concerned with recent events." I decided not mention there must be a spy amongst the villagers or someone who passed through feeding Manners information. "He has charged me with finding the McKinneys' murderers and searching out the probable illegal still."

Nodding, "The presence of an illegal still is part ay yer job tae find, though I dinnae understand why he is so concerned with the McKinneys' deaths. It is a village matter and will be solved by its folk."

Sensing Beathan's increasing temper, "Colonel Manners is a cautious man; he needs to know all is well in Markinch." After watching the dancers for a minute, I turned back to Beathan. "It is no secret the old pretender intends to cause trouble in Scotland, if I cannot be seen to put the matter of the still and the McKinneys' deaths to rest, you can be sure Manners will send someone who can, perhaps using force."

As he narrowed his eyes, I felt controlled anger roll from Beathan. He did not keep the contempt from his voice, "I hope ye dinnae mean tae threaten me, Captain, or the people ay Markinch with a militia? Such a thing could only cause problems fur everyone, I hae a business tae run, a business whose employment keeps this village from sinking intae a poverty most ay the Highlands hae experienced!"

Holding my hands out in front of me, I tried to placate the other man, who finished the rest of his Scotch in one mouthful. "I am the last man, English or otherwise, who would want to see a militia from the south come and camp in

Markinch. For all their duty to keep the peace, they cause more trouble than not." I thought of the Boston Militia, I may have been part of some brutal acts as a soldier, yet I never took pleasure in it as some of the militia, men who lived outside society, unaffected by their rules. "Please know I will do everything in my power to keep the militia away. You have my word."

Beathan snorted. "The word of a damned Englishman, and a soldier to boot, I will believe in it the day I catch a damned haggis out in the fens." With the insult delivered, Beathan moved away into the crowd towards the drinks table, taut fury making his movements jerky.

Finishing the rest of my Scotch in one, I winced as it burned down my throat, almost making me choke. I tried to rearrange my face as I watched Logan make his way through the crowd, seemingly speaking with every person, yet watching my expression. When he finally stepped next to me and filled my empty glass. I felt wary, rather than excited to put my previous plan into action.

"The Laird of the Manor appears tae be a bit out ay sorts," Logan nodded a chin to Beathan, whose face appeared strained. "Funny, but he looked in perfectly good spirits until he spoke with ye. I hope there is nae bad news from the south, especially during this festive time."

I thought Mr Turner's assessment of Logan's character correct, certainly I knew not to trust the other man. I needed to take charge of the conversation before I missed another opportunity to confirm my suspicions over the deaths of the McKinneys. "I think Beathan is struggling with stress from Deoch." After making the excuse. "You appear to be in a festive mood yourself, where has Kieran run off to? I have not seen him since my short journey up to visit with poor Mrs McKinney. I felt it my duty to check on her well-being. After all, I did find her husband and son."

"I thought it might be yer duty since the dead man, whose boots ye hae filled, is the probable murderer." Logan stared at me full in the face, his mouth lifted at one corner and I forced myself not to act surprised over his bold statement.

"Rumours and will o' the wisps, only, Logan." It was my turn to try and put the other man on edge. "If one could be charged with the offences of every rumour. I have no doubt one of us would be swinging from a short rope, from a high branch right at this moment, yet the Crown still requires proof in the order of the law."

The mention of his activities and known feelings towards the English only made the man smile, showing perfectly straight white teeth. In a low tone, he glanced around once to make sure none might overhear. "Och, we both know, rumour is one thing, actual deed is another. I would be careful, ye wouldnae want the indiscretion ye committed tae land yerself up here in Markinch making the rounds of civilised drawing rooms."

He knew of my attack on the Boston Militia. The only way he might have heard the story was through Beathan or the hired cart driver. I smiled grimly. "You enjoy speaking with people, especially those from outside Markinch. I do wonder what the McKinneys' new grain suppliers might have said to you, all those weeks ago."

Finally the other man's smile faded and he peered at me curiously. "I would like tae know where yer information might hae come from, Captain. Tis nae secret I questioned the farmers, it's my job tae look after the interests of Deoch, one I take seriously."

Here an opportunity lay. "Seriously enough to kill for?" I watched closely as the accusation slammed into the other man's face. He stared at me incredulously, his meticulously built composure finally unraveling. I admit to feeling a bit of triumph at breaking the other man.

Squaring his shoulders, he stepped uncomfortably close, his index finger raised until it hovered under my nose, all vestiges of acted friendliness drained from his expression, replaced by cold anger. "Ye best hae a good reason for accusing me of any crime, Captain, especially the murder of two of my folk." Logan pointed across the room at Beathan without turning his face from mine. "He is nae the Laird ay this land, I am the Laird ay Markinch, whether these people recognise it or nae, and it is my duty tae see them safe through the coming troubles. I suggest ye take care in insulting me again," he turned on his heel and walked away through the crowd.

I took a deep breath and watched the dancers as they went through the steps of a country reel. Remembering the glass in my hand, I took a drink and found Beathan in the crowd; he appeared to have regained some of his earlier good humour and I felt thankful for not ruining his whole evening.

From Logan's violent reaction to my accusation, I could not guess if he might be guilty or not. Many men use anger to hide their guilt. It was possible his reaction was only over the insinuation he murdered the McKinneys. Either way, I did not trust him and neither did Mr Turner, two good reasons not to quit my watch. My suspicions he may have murdered Mr Turner only strengthened. Beathan's reaction to my news was not unreasonable, he felt protective of Markinch and its inhabitants. It appeared to be an easy state to fall into, the village also grew on me, prodding me to keep information from my superiors, and risk treason.

Even alone at the side of the room, casually observing people mingle and celebrate another Christmas. I felt part of them, a living family, much the same way as I felt when Hania brought me to the camp for the first time and I met Onatah; here people cared for one another.

Phil looked up from a conversation with a matronly-looking woman, she frowned and excused herself. She picked up her skirts and weaved through the increasingly drunken revellers, at one point, righting herself after a man ran past with a gaggle of children laughing and chasing him. Drinking the last of the Scotch, I set the cup on the nearest table and waited until Phil's long skirts brushed over my boots. She looked immensely charming with her bright eyes and slightly flushed cheeks.

Holding out her hands, "Captain, ye cannae stay all alone in the corner, ye must come and socialise, it is a time for making new friends." Phil lightly clasped my hands and tried to pull me from my place.

Her strength no match for my own, I easily pulled against her, making her take a clumsy step forward in order to keep her balance. "Phil, I have spoken to everyone in this room

I intended to this evening, the only task left on the list is sharing a dance with a beautiful woman."

Eyes questioning, she searched my face. "Ye are making sport with me, Captain, ye know I dinnae like it when people make fun ay me," she tried to pull her hands from mine.

Grinning broadly, I held my grip and lowered my face, so it hovered only a few breaths above hers. I listened to her breath hitch, as she peered up into my face, perhaps I had not lost all my luck with the fairer sex. "Would you please allow me to escort you in the next dance?"

"I never dance, Captain. As a confirmed blue stocking I will hae ye know, I am terrible and all my partners limp away with sore feet." Phil giggled, it was the first time I had heard her laugh and it forced me to do something impulsive.

"We shall make a pair, for I hardly dance a reel myself, we will be even," I straightened and pulled Phil onto the dance floor, and forgot my mission. The anger at my diminishing sorrow and the potential for calamity should the militia be sent north for the space of the next dance.

Chapter 13

I watched out the window as darkness fell over Markinch in the early evening, the birds hopped around, looking for scraps of seeds, the branches on the trees held still with the wind letting up for once. As Freya had informed me several times since Christmas, New Year or Hogmanay had only recently begun again. Old customs coming back into favour, she said, and I needed to observe them as much as anyone else in the village, or suffer the dire consequences of bad luck for the rest of the year. She firmly believed that, as part of my household, she would suffer a poor year if I did something to upset the careful balance of right and wrong in the Highlands. It was my duty to go around with the rest of the villagers and drink people's Scotch and ale. Since the prospect of ringing in the New Year in such a manner did not offend my sensibilities and I had the added incentive of once again seeing Phil up at the castle, I agreed to do my best.

Which is why I stood staring out of the windows, waiting for Freya to come and fetch me. We would visit the first couple of houses together until she decided I could be trusted to drink and wander through Markinch on my own. Ever since the near drowning and the gunshot wound, I felt as if I had a target placed on my back.

Beathan informed me Deoch closed for the holidays and would not reopen until the day after Hogmanay. As generous employers, the Clunes respected workers' families and tradition in a way I had never seen before in the south. Family meant a great deal to them and they wanted it to mean a great deal to the people who worked for them. The days away from work meant men with families spent the time at home, engaged in any number of activities. I watched as fathers taught their sons to hunt, while the smaller children sledged over the hills. The whole week brought memories of my own lonely childhood, coupled with the excitement I felt when Onatah told me I would be a father; the excitement, the worry I could never measure up to be the man I wanted a child to be proud of knowing.

Though I had been excited over the prospect of having a family of my own, at the time it was not something I yearned for. Now, however, I wanted to make this happen more than anything else. I wanted to carry a rosy-cheeked son or daughter on my shoulders, hear them laugh.

My eyes caught movement at the gate, Freya's wide frame came through and she huffed her way to the front door. I quickly quit the drawing room and ran to the front door in order to save her from opening it. "Good Evening, Madam, a Happy New Year to you."

"And a Happy Hogmanay tae ye, Captain," Freya stepped through the door and inspected my clothing. "Dinnae ye look fine bad the trig in yer new clothes, trying tae impress a certain young lady, eh?"

News of the dance I shared with Phil on Christmas Eve spread through the village like a pox in a whore house; a self-confessed spinster who never stands up to dance is seen enjoying a reel with the English excise officer made for a good recounting over the tea trays of Markinch. "Madam, as you said it is the New Year and as a representative of Her Majesty, it is my duty to be presentable."

"Ach, well, ye look presentable enough, on with yer coat, we'll visit auld Tavish before heading up to the castle." Freya adjusted the heavy scarf around her neck and stamped some of the snow from her boots.

After waiting all day, I felt keen to socialise and wasted no time in throwing my frock over my shoulders and pulling my gloves on. I stepped through the open door still buttoning up the front of my jacket as Freya closed the door firmly behind her.

The snow crunched beneath our boots and Freya remained unusually quiet. A family of four, mother, father and two children, trudged up the road ahead of us and I searched for a topic of conversation. "I thought your boys would be joining us, I have not met any of them yet."

Huffing a bit with the exercise, Freya shrugged under her layers. "Informed me this morn they were tae auld tae be seen on Hogmanay with their mother, they have gone off with Kieran." She blew air out of her mouth harshly, "I warned them both if they caused any trouble I would get the leash out and give them a good creesh. It's a disgrace the way Logan lets the boy run around Markinch, he is more wild than nae, it gives the other boys a poor example."

I could tell from the tone of her voice Kieran's freedom was a sticking point between mother and sons, probably used on numerous occasions to justify their actions. Loath as I was to defend Logan, I wanted to placate Freya more. "I am sure Logan does the best he can with the child, it is not easy without the presence of a mother with a guiding hand."

The smile lighting Freya's face and her nod meant I might have said the right thing for once. Maybe this signaled a change for the better in the New Year? The buildings at Deoch loomed ahead of us, sconces lit on either side of the road welcoming the villagers to pass through.

Waving a hand to the left, where a small road veered before the first main building, "Tavish's workman's cottage is this way." Several villagers stepped off the main road and followed the path ahead of us. "He hosts one ay the more popular at homes before midnight, his brother hosts the other."

I nodded as the first notes of a song played on bagpipes shattered the night and we found Tavish's cottage. A queue greeted us outside and we joined the end. I looked around trying to get my bearings, "Who lives in the other cottage?"

"Logan and Kieran," Freya studied the other dwelling with a critical, matronly eye. "It is up tae each ay the cottage dwellers tae maintain their premises," she sniffed at the peeling paint on the door.

Not wanting to defend Logan twice in one evening and hoping to keep the good bonhomie with Freya. "It looks and sounds as though they made the right decision to be away for the evening." I winced as the bagpiper played a high note, even Freya shivered under her coats.

Stamping our feet for warmth, we finally rose to the front of the line. The door shut, Freya looked at my curious face before she knocked and said in a whisper. "It is tradition fur each person tae knock at the door, whether the homeowner knows they are there or nae, this way everyone is greeted in the same manner."

Narrowing my eyes, I was going to ask why it mattered when the temperature felt as though it dropped every minute we stood outside, when the door opened to reveal Tavish, a spring in his step, cap askew and merry glint in his eye.

"Welcome, welcome," Tavish shouted as if we stood several yards away. He grabbed my arm and shoved me inside with a half hug and did the same to Freya before planting a wet kiss on her cheeks, making her blush to the roots of her red hair. I thought it looked disgusting.

Inside the small cottage all was chaos; the people who had waited ahead of us in the queue drank from small earthenware cups. Several others sat or stood in groups with their coats and caps in a pile in the corner, while the piper tried to maintain his bearings in a drunken stupor and play a correct note.

Tavish thrust two small cups into our hands. "Here ye are, and Happy Hogmanay tae ye both," he downed the contents of his cup in one and poured another libation from the bottle in his other hand.

"Good health tae ye, Tavish," Freya took a dainty sip of the Scotch and with some encouragement finished the rest of the cup, only to be refilled by our generous host.

"Happy New Year, the best to you and yours," I downed mine in one and, through watering eyes, watched as Tavish refilled the cup.

A knock on the door diverted Tavish's attention for a minute, turning to us. "Looks like this is going tae be my busiest Hogmanay so far. With these numbers I shouldnae wonder if any soul turned up at my brither's place," he cackled evilly and went to answer the second knock.

At Freya's insistence, we stepped further into the room, in order to give the new arrivals some space, in as low a voice as she could manage. "Most folk go tae both at homes. The brothers never talk so it's easy tae nae offend either one."

Taking a sip of the Scotch, I let it roll down my throat without breathing, the concoction much stronger than anything I had yet tasted in Markinch, even the vile stuff at the

McGreevys' tasted better. Curiosity drove me to ask, "Why do the Tavish brothers quarrel?"

Coughing on her own drink, Freya peered up at me with watery eyes and a smile. "Och, Captain, it's like asking why the gowans bloom in spring, or why the mavis song is so sweet in the morn. They hae always been at odds, since boyhood, I heard tell, over their mother's affections and later over a woman's."

"Yet I thought them both confirmed bachelors," I looked around the cottage at the sparse belongings organised into their proper places without one furbelow or frill in sight, the place definitely lacked a woman's touch.

"It's a sad story," Freya glanced around her and surreptitiously moved to one side, out of earshot the rest of the group. "I was only a lass when it happened. Both Tavishes fell madly in love with the same girl, they competed fur her at every chance, made a right spectacle ay themselves. Finally the young lass announced she would make a decision and chose one or the other brither. At the time, mind, I thought she acted a bit ay a strumpet." Freya crossed herself. "The night before she made her choice, she caught a fever, fell asleep and died shortly after." She made he sign of the cross again.

"If they were both young lads at the time, neither could be tempted from the grief to bestow their affections on another young lady?" I furrowed by brow, I did not want to be indelicate over the tragic death of the young lady. "Many years have passed since the young lady's tragic death, and neither of them ever courted another?"

Freya drank the rest of her Scotch and set the cup down on a table laden with shortcake. She chose a fat piece and chewed it appreciatively. "It is only natural for people to move on, memories fade and the survivors must get on with the business ay life." She sighed deeply, "The problem lay in the brithers competitive spirit, each vowed they could out-grieve the other. As a result if either ay them ever tried tae court another lass, all thought ay moving on pushed aside in order tae beat the other brither."

I took Freya's lead and finished off the rest of my Scotch, the Tavishes story might possibly be one of the saddest

I had ever heard. Not to mention the fact I contemplated doing the same thing, mourn a woman for the rest of my days. Glancing around the cottage, I felt convinced men were not meant to live this way.

Bowling over to the host, Freya planted a kiss on his cheek. "We are off, Tavish, hae a couple ay rounds tae make before the New Year's bell, hope tae see ye up at the keep." Freya waved me along and I followed her after giving the old man a pat on his shoulder.

Back out in the cold, Freya huddled into her wraps further and I quickly pulled my gloves on. She looked up at the star-filled sky. "It is a cold one, Captain, I suggest we finish with the tour and walk straight up tae the keep, most folk will wander up before the midnight chime, it is tradition."

"Lead the way, Madam." I tucked Freya's hand over my arm and the two of us walked back onto the main road where we found more people walking to their Hogmanay destinations. Freya waved to several people and shouted greetings, yet kept us moving at a brisk pace.

"Nae need to brave the winter chill more than necessary," Freya picked up the pace as much as her short legs would allow.

I agreed whole-heartedly, the night might be clear and beautiful with the sky twinkling above, the moon lighting the fens on either side, making the whole landscape appear ethereal in blue and silver, but it remained cold and biting. The last rise revealed the familiar shape of the castle standing with quiet dignity over the surrounding harshness. Large cauldrons of peat glowed at intervals along the path, giving light, and a wreath of evergreen decorated the main gate. Inside the main courtyard, more fires warmed the evening air and a couple of ladies in servant's livery roasted chestnuts over the open flames.

With a smile of anticipation, Freya pulled more than lead me over to one of the ladies and asked for a couple of the warmed nuts, and I smiled as she handed one over to me. "There ye are, Captain, a real treat," she quickly peeled the brown skin away and popped the mushy flesh into her mouth.

I tried to smile. However in truth I hated the damned things, on one of my trips into London for the holidays the Thames froze enough for my uncle to host an impromptu small Frost Fair at his home on the Thames, where I was force-fed roasted chestnuts. I could still remember the earthy potato taste. I peeled mine and popped it into my mouth, smiling, as Freya looked on with excitement. "Delicious," I managed, trying not to gag. In a few moments we would enter the keep and I would be free to follow my own company.

Beaming, Freya marched to the door and banged the knocker several times. "Much better chestnuts here in the Highlands, than ye could ever get in London, Captain, I hae always believed we hae the better produce, it's the weather."

Saved by the taciturn butler, I followed Freya inside where more servants divested us of our outer coats; the butler indicated we should enter the drawing room where Beathan, Phil and Magnus all resided, speaking with other guests. The butler did not announce us; instead he gave Freya a warm smile and myself a look indicating he would be counting the silverware. Slightly affronted by the rude man, I turned back to watch Freya join a group of ladies in one corner, as I found Phil speaking with her father and felt pulled forward, wanting to join her.

After a few steps, Beathan stood in front of me, we had not spoken to one another since our argument on Christmas Eve and I did not want to engage in a scene here in his own home. I thought he might ask me to leave and I braced for it.

Instead the other man extended a large hand and grimaced. "I dinnae say this often, Captain, so ye better take heed, I may hae been hasty in accusing ye ay threats and I am sorry fur it. I know it isnae ye meddling intae Markinch, yer only the messenger and ye took a chance at telling me secret information."

I took the other man's hand and smiled with relief, "I also should apologise, the Christmas Eve gathering at Deoch may not have been the best time to reveal the English military were breathing down my neck. I often speak on impulse, it is a trait I have never learned from, it appears." Grinning with relief, "I thought you might be coming over to remove my English presence from your house."

Beathan waved a hand. "I realised the next day what I fool I made ay myself, the Scots temper gets the better of me on occasion." I stared at him incredulously, in all the time I had spent in Markinch I never once saw him angry. "Ye might be surprised, Captain, I can throw an impressive fit ay temper. I know ye hae nae love for the militia, past experiences make fur the harshest ay lessons." Beathan caught the attention of a server and handed a glass of Scotch to me, "Hae ye made any progress since we last met?"

"Progress on what?" Phil joined us, something looked softer in her appearance, her hair arranged in a much more fashionable style, the cut of her dress more current. Under the watchful gaze of Beathan, I sketched a bow and took her hand for a quick kiss, "Happy New Year to you, Philomena."

She blushed and gave me a quick curtsey. "And tae ye a Happy Hogmanay, Captain, I hope the next year brings ye only joy."

"The next year inevitably will if ye keep up with yer new beauty regime, sister," Beathan received an ugly frown from his sibling. "Och, come on, I am happy tae see ye take such an interest in these things, a lass ay yer great age must take care ay her looks."

Punching him in the side as children might, Phil shook her hand; Beathan looked as hard as a tree trunk. In an effort to steer conversation away from her appearance, she asked. "What is this talk of progress, Captain? Hae ye got any further with Turner's diary?"

I tried to fill the awkward silence. Beathan stared at me, Phil looked between the two of us with a sheepish expression and I felt stupid for keeping the diary a secret in the first place. Shrugging casually, "I found Mr Turner's diary while I recuperated from my accident in the fens, the contents a mystery, written in code." I watched Beathan's eyes widen and his expression show interest. I sighed heavily, "Phil helped me finally crack the cipher." I smiled at her, "And I read through most of it, but I know what you are thinking, and you will be as disappointed as I, Turner makes no mention of any motives behind his death, only a bit of suspicion against the McKinneys."

Beathan's shoulder's sagged, he cleared his throat, "Well, I cannae say as I'm nae frustrated Turner kept a diary and it holds nae answers tae any ay the mysteries, especially with the English breathing down our necks and threatening us with violence."

A sharp intake of breath brought my attention to Phil, one of her hands pressed to her lower neck and the blood draining from her face. "What is this talk of the English threatening violence? Surely they cannae believe we caused Mr Turner's demise?" The words tugged from her throat.

Unmindful of Beathan's presence, I took Phil's other hand to comfort her. The fingers felt small, vulnerable, not part of the capable hands who I watched write with confidence. "There is no need to worry. Once I find who is responsible for the McKinneys' deaths, all will be well and I have a good lead on someone who might have some valuable information."

Phil shook my hand from hers, I felt stung at the rejection and tried to hide the reaction. It was foolish, she looked up at me with an unreadable expression. "The deaths ay the McKinney's are nae concern fur the English, and nae concern ay yours, yer only the damned gauger."

I never minded the term used by others towards me, yet when it spilled from Phil's mouth, it took on a meaning of its own, for her to see me as someone who relentlessly ripped money from the mouths of her people. It felt as if a bullet entered my chest. My only refuge lay in civility, "Mistress Philomena, as I am sure you are aware, Mr Turner has been linked to their deaths and this rumour makes it my business."

Whether my tone or the use of her proper name disturbed her the most, Phil physically stepped back, looked to her brother who wore an expression of non-commitment. I knew he would not fight her battles for her, as so many siblings did, as I had wanted someone do for me as a child. The urge to apologise immediately welled inside however, the clock chimed saving me from making a fool of myself. The three of us looked over and watched woodenly as the rest of the room counted down to the New Year. Smiles and good wishes exchanged, the chimes ended and everyone gave a great cheer.

A brief silence ensued, everyone turned to stare at the three of us, still near the entranceway, a firm knock on the door relieved us of any further awkwardness. Phil sprang into action and walked briskly to the door where a second round of knocking commenced. Pushed along by Beathan and the rest of the small crowd, we made a semi-circle around the door, with a breath of anticipation; Phil opened the portal for the first visitor of the New Year, the one who would bring good fortune to the occupants of the house.

With a mild grimace, I recognised Logan standing in the threshold of the door, to what might have been his own castle had his family's fortunes been different. Offering a black bun on a silver plate to Phil, the mistress of the house. She accepted gracefully and invited Logan inside. Kieran followed closely behind him, he looked through the crowd and winked at me, his cheeks indicating he may not have taken my advice over the consumption of alcohol.

Beathan held the plate while Phil used a knife to cut into the cake, took a small piece and ate it, smiling. I watched her thank Logan, he replied with a gracious nod and everyone crowded around for a piece of the cake. Instead of returning to the small drawing room, the butler ushered us through the opposite door, into a grand ballroom, decked out with festive decorations, tables of food and drink and the same musicians from the village as were at the Christmas Eve party.

Relieving one of the waiters of a Scotch, I walked into the room, it must have been the castle's old hall. The windows set high in the walls for defence, the ceiling held up with enormous beams of wood, a platform still stood at one end of the room, where those who dined above the salt would have enjoyed their meals. Not having a coat of arms, the Clunes decorated the walls with antlers and swords; the effect might have been slightly over-dramatic if the great fires did not burn merrily, bringing warmth to the whole room.

Phil and Beathan eased their way through the growing crowd. Tavish took up a place next to Magnus who sat near one of the roaring fires, looking as if he might not be able to stand for much longer. With a thought to walk over and thank my host, I commenced walking across the room and halted when I noticed Logan standing near the other end of the hall. He stood for a moment searching through the crowd and disappeared through a doorway.

I immediately changed tack through the crowd, I nodded to a couple of people I recognised, one man I was sure I had never met gave me a hard pat on the back and a drunken smile. The other guests would not miss me. Gaining the end of the hall, I faced a set of old flintlocks, organised in the shape of a starburst on the wall, muzzles pointed to the centre. I spied a small service door, probably used by the servants to bring food and drink into the great room without disrupting the main hallways. I slipped through the door and waited a full minute in the darkness on the other side, I needed to be sure none of the guests had watched me pass through and would come to investigate; I could not explain I was following Logan whom I believed to be a murderer or at least held potentially damning information.

Eyes adjusting to the dimness, I found a staircase immediately in front of me, it led both up and down the stairs. A quick search of the wall revealed no handrail and I descended a few steps keeping my ears strained for any noises. After only a couple flights I could here banging and shouted orders, the kitchen lay below stairs. Deciding Logan would not have bothered to make his quiet exit if he meant only to visit the kitchen. I cautiously headed back up the steps, the stones felt old and dangerous underfoot, and I tried to make as little sound as possible.

A door abruptly swam before me and I took care to ease it open, revealing a long hallway. It looked empty save for a luxurious carpet running the length and several high tables along the sides, standing between several doors, all of which could be hiding Logan. Making my mind up to keep following the trail, I stepped from my hiding place, closed the hidden door with a click and walked down the middle of the hall, using the carpet to mask my footsteps. Six doors faced the middle of the corridor, two by two, I stopped in front of the first one on the right, and listened carefully, ear pressed to the wood, and no sounds emerged.

I went across the hall and used the same technique, still nothing, the two middle doors also hid their occupants. Finally without much hope I listened to the second to last door and before pressing my ear to the wood, heard a chair scraping the floor. Peering back down the hall I realised nothing could hide my large frame, and I quickly and quietly rushed the opposite door, thankfully finding it unlocked, I stepped through into darkness.

Holding my breath I listened for noises in the hall, after what seemed an eternity, I heard a click from the door closing opposite. Counting to ten, I gently turned the knob and opened the door a fraction and with one eye I strained to identify the figure hurriedly making his escape. Broad shoulders and blond hair tied with a leather strap at the back of his head; I did not doubt it was Logan. I could not see the end of the hall and I counted to thirty before opening the door wider and glancing back down the hall.

It appeared empty again, Logan must have used the passage to join the rest of the revellers in the ballroom. I closed the door behind me and crossed the carpet, I tried the door and it did not open, the bolt remained shut.

Swearing in frustration, I tried to use a bit of force, hoping it might be stuck, however in the end I conceded defeat. Logan must either have a key or he was proficient at picking locks, something of which I only possessed the vaguest knowledge, and that, at this moment, seemed odd, as they were only tiny mechanical machines.

"Captain, I dinnae know what ye are up tae here in the family quarters." a young girl's voice sounded from the end of the hall and I winced in response, I had been caught out for all of my carefulness.

Thinking quickly, I staggered a couple of times and turned to face the young girl, whose eyes widened at my exaggerated drunken state. "Ah, girl, it is well you found me. I have been looking for the privy for ages, must have taken a wrong turn some whereabouts, might you point me in the right direction?"

Turning red at the word privy, the girl came forward a few steps and coaxed me forward. "Och, ye surely hae taken the wrong way, ye cannae use Master Beathan's office as a privy tae be sure, bring the whole castle down around our heads, ye will. Ye follow me and we'll both stay out ay trouble."

At least I now knew what lay behind the locked door, unfortunately it only raised more questions: why would Logan be visiting Beathan's office during the New Year's eve party? The rational part of my brain insisted it could be nothing. He could have a perfectly legitimate reason for being there alone, he could be conducting Deoch business, for example. I followed the small maid back down the main staircase. She pointed to another door leading from the front of the hall, curtsied and I gave her my thanks. At least none from the party saw my descent from the upstairs rooms.

I walked back into the ballroom and searched the crowd. I watched as Phil spoke with an extremely animated Freya, whose glass tipped precariously with every sudden embellishment, and on to Beathan who stood with several of the workers from Deoch. I finally found Logan whispering in low tones to one of the workers I had seen around Markinch, who kept to himself. Logan looked up and caught my eye. For a minute we stared at one another across the hall, he must know of my suspicions, know I followed him. My mind might be trying to convince me of one thing, yet as Logan looked back to his companion, my gut told me he broke into Beathan's office for some reason of his own. The man I watched had a plan.

Chapter 14

I wriggled my shoulders a couple of times, and walked through the boisterous New Year's crowd. Musicians set up on the dais at the other end of the hall encouraged dancers onto the floor and the whole appeared as a jumble of tartan and men's legs. Every so often a buttock might make an appearance to the hilarity of most. After my failed attempt to stalk Logan above stairs and discern his mission in Beathan's office, I decided to keep a close eye on him. The crowd made it easy to blend in, the alcohol compelling people to be friendly and accepting, I spoke with several of the villagers as I walked over to Tavish and Magnus.

I found the two arguing over the best consistency for wort. With one eye on Logan's position in the room, I interrupted their conversation. "Magnus, a happy New Year and thank you for opening your home to me this evening and, Tavish, I thoroughly enjoyed your at home, thank you." I gave the older men a short bow.

Magnus nodded his grizzled head. "Thank you, my dear boy, please forgive me if I dinnae stand, these bones became tae auld years ago," I could see tiredness creeping into his eyes. "I am well canty ye decided tae join us fur the celebrations, I dinnae think Mr Turner thought much ay parties."

Tavish turned bright eyes to look up at me; he appeared to have garnered a second wind since he first arrived at the celebration. "I think he might hae been misunderstood," he paused for a moment. I searched his expression, an emotion passed over his features, regret, sadness, guilt, it flew away in the next instant and I could not be sure of what I saw. He continued. "Seventeen hundred and eight is our year, going tae be the best year fur Markinch and fur Deoch we ever had."

"Hear, hear," Magnus raised his glass in salute. Tavish and I followed suit with cheers of our own, I only hoped Tavish's prophecy would be correct, too much death had visited Markinch already. Yet with Francis Stuart causing trouble, there could be more hardships to come for the village.

"Ye out tae find my daughter, Captain," Magnus winked up at me. "I never saw her dance half as well as I did when she stood in yer arms." I caught myself before I could let my expression turn to schoolboy embarrassment over his cheek.

All three of us turned towards the group of people dancing and laughing. My gaze wandered to a couple making use of a dark corner to indulge in a quick New Year's kiss. I quickly looked away and directly into Magnus's over-perceptive eyes. I coughed a few times to hide my thoughts, however, I felt sure he knew I imagined his daughter in my arms in the same dark corner, doing precisely as the couple.

"I believe I will find Beathan, I have not spoken to him since the beginning of the evening and it is growing late." I bowed to each of the men and they nodded in return. "I do not want to stay abed all tomorrow."

Glancing around the hall, I realised I had lost sight of Logan during my short conversation with Magnus and Tavish. Turning quickly on my heel, I scanned all the faces in the crowd until I finally found him standing under the arch of the doorway to the entrance hall. He did not face into the ballroom, rather into the entranceway. Something prompted him into quick action and he strode the rest of the way through with a determined gait.

Whatever might interest the deposed Laird of Markinch, would also interest me a great deal and I tried to tack as quickly as possible through the drunken villagers. All of who decided tonight they would put their English prejudices aside and claim the excise man as one of their own. It would have been endearing if I had not been in such a rush. I did not want to lose Logan again, he could escape to any part of the house or even outdoors and I would not find him.

Extracting myself from the hard hug of one of the mill workers, I walked briskly into the entrance hall; it remained empty except for the sour butler. Not wanting to miss the opportunity to follow Logan, I put aside my objections to the man and asked, "Did you see Logan come through here? Which way did he go? I have business with him."

The lie could be true, he managed Deoch after all and I collected the tax, the fact it might be close to two in the morning on New Year's Day did not signify much. The other man turned and went out of the room, my shoulders slumped at the rudeness.

Walking towards the drawing room, intending to continue my search, the butler came through another secret door with my frock coat, he held it out and I decided to humour him. As I slipped my arms into its sleeves, he said in a low voice. "Master Logan left the evening's entertainment nae ten minutes past, I believe he meant tae head home fur the evening."

Relief at finding Logan's direction turned to disappointment. I could not follow him home, what excuse did I have for stalking him through the night? "Thank you, I suppose I will also retire, please give my regards to the family."

The butler nodded his reply and opened the door. The evening's chill burned my cheeks. Even though they should have been liberally fortified with Scotch over the past few hours. The large door closed behind me and I stood on the front porch for several minutes. I lost my quarry once again, cursing into the night; I obviously needed some practise navigating ballrooms and parties, yet I felt sure Logan acted as if he followed someone.

Not wanting the butler to open the door and find me still standing on the steps, I descended and walked slowly through the now empty courtyard. The fires in the cauldrons burned lazily, most of them would not reach the morning. Shrugging further into the lined coat for warmth, I walked under the portcullis and looked right and left. No souls remained outdoors, if the butler told the truth of Logan's plans. He might well be home by now, settled in bed for the coming New Year, it might be best if I followed suit.

Striding briskly down the road, I looked out over the fens, remembering the previous evening I dined at the Castle, I had left drunk and in an argument with Phil. This time I might be less intoxicated, yet she and I still fell into an argument. An odd sensation of familiarity came over me as I passed the spot where I previously entered the fens, any trace of the events swallowed by the snow and the changing temperament of the landscape.

Whimsy prompted me to say a prayer under my breath for the McKinneys. I might have shared their grave for eternity without Kieran's bravery. I gave another prayer hoping 1708 would be a year of beginnings rather than endings; I would put the tragedies of 1707 firmly behind me. Turning on my heel, I continued down the road, the first shadowy shapes of Deoch loomed in the distance, the torches lit to guide the revellers now extinguished, only the light of the moon remained.

My thoughts drifted to Phil. She had looked fetching this evening and she might have welcomed a second dance if Beathan had not mentioned the militia. I cheerfully damned him, slipping on a patch of ice invisible in the moonlight. I felt myself falling as a shot rang out above my head, and I hit the solid ground with a heavy thud. The healed gunshot wound in my arm throbbing dully after the impact. Instinctively I rolled to the side of the road as another shot rang out and the lead ball struck the place I fell, heaving myself into the ditch. Luckily it remained frozen in the night air, Freya would never forgive me for another bout of fever so soon after the last one.

Breathing heavily I reached down and unsheathed the dagger at my ankle, I always carried a weapon of some description, never believing I would ever need one at a party, however I thanked Hania for his persistent teachings. Lying in the snow, hiding from an unseen gunman, appeared to be a frequent occurrence for me in Markinch. After a minute, I took stock of my position. Only two shots fired, luckily each of them missed, though the first one only by the luck of providence. If I had not slipped on the unseen ice, my brains would be decorating the road.

I took long steady breaths until I could listen for any noises in the night. Nothing, not even the scratch of small animals; all of them must have been frightened away by the sound of the gunshot. Heaving over onto my stomach, I searched through the hard-crusted snow until I found a clump of heather; I pulled it from the frozen ground with a grunt and slowly lifted it above the lip of the ditch and waited. Nothing happened, the moon only gave enough light to make out shapes in the distance, not enough to lend aid in deciphering the object. After another full minute, I discarded the bush and carefully rose to my haunches.

All remained in silence as I rose to my full height and took in the rest of my surroundings, stepping over to where the lead ball hit the road. I searched through the debris until I found it. Using the knife I dug it from the ground, the force had made it flat on one side, this ball of lead intended to end my life. Once again, I made the choice to take on the fens, would I make it out for a third time? Searching through the side of the road until I found a bridle path. I stepped from the safety of the marked road and into the uncertainty of the Highlands.

A noise from behind forced me into a crouch. Without much brush to shield my presence I remained vulnerable, however, if it were merely a reveller making their way home for the evening, they would miss my presence, if I remained still only a few yards from the road. The light and the way the ground rolled made it difficult to watch for the newcomer. I tried to hide the clouds my breath made, become my surroundings, as I listened to heavy boots rapidly striding down the road.

The newcomer stopped near where I escaped the shooter, it might be a coincidence, yet they stopped for nearly a minute. I watched with shock as the shaded person left the road in precisely the same place I used, presumably following my tracks. Heart beating quicker, I felt my muscles tense, hand-to-hand combat was a specialty of mine. I learned many tricks in the New World, finally a challenge in Markinch I could tackle with experience. I controlled the outcome of this battle, eyes straining, legs ready to lunge, arms and hands ready to grip, the knife held at a deadly angle, mind primed for the challenge, I felt alive again.

The dark shape noticed my presence too late. Without a noise, I pounced, punching the other man in the groin, he immediately fell to protect himself and I kneed him in the face. He howled in pain as I pushed him face first into the icy snow and kicked him in the kidneys. Using my cravat I quickly tied his hands behind his back and used his familiar hair to pull his face from the ground.

Logan coughed and choked. I knew all three blows I gave him would hurt like the devil. I leaned down and said, in a rough voice, ""why are you following me? Did you fire those shots?"

The other man groaned and tried to speak through his newly broken nose. After a couple of failed attempts, he managed. "Heard the shots, came tae investigate, I dinnae fire any weapon, check my hands, nae gunpowder marks."

With my knee pressed painfully in his back, I inspected his bound hands. The lack of light once again made it difficult to see and I leaned down and gave the cuff of his frock coat a sniff, no gunpowder, the smell would linger in garments for days. "So you did not shoot at me, it does not mean you did not have someone do it for you, are you working with the McGreevys? Turner left behind some interesting theories, did you kill the McKinneys? Did you kill Turner?"

Shaking his head vigorously in denial, Logan tried to keep his head from touching the cold ground. "Nae working with the McGreevys, and I dinnae hae anything tae do with the McKinneys' or Turners' deaths. Brought it upon themselves. They operated an illegal still, nobody knew ay it, not even Agnes, I tried tae investigate."

I stared up into the night sky, the stars twinkled back and a shooting star raced across, looking down at Logan's back it all made sense. "You knew the McKinneys received more grain than they could possibly use, you mentioned to Turner something odd might be happening up at the Turret distillery. Unfortunately, Turner was a clerk sent to do a soldier's job and did not have the skills to carry out a proper investigation. He stumbled upon the truth, and confronted the McKinneys, however this does not explain his death."

"Yer half right, I pushed Turner towards the McKinneys. I had nae idea he was nae a foot soldier. Though I should hae known, a scholar by the looks ay the drawing room at the cottage, I was told he could do the job." Logan shook his head. "He never stood a chance, though I dinnae think he killed the McKinneys."

I stood and undid the binds around Logan's hands. "You're Colonel Manners' spy, you are the one who told him of my misadventure and of the McGreevys' possible involvement in operating an illegal still. You are the one responsible for possibly bringing the militia down on us. After all your bluster over how much you hate the English yoke, you are helping us gain a stronger foothold in your own community." I spat on the ground, disgusted by his duplicity.

Hands on his thighs, breathing slowly, Logan spoke to the ground, "It's nae as simple as ye say. I do hate the English, ye took my birthright from me, yet I hate someone more than I hate them. The family who eats, sleeps and breathes in the home I would hae owned if nae fur the English and their damned civil war." Logan stood to his full height. "Colonel Manners promised me I would hae my inheritance back if I provided a service tae him, everyone knows the true King is coming back. Francis Stuart, and he will sweep through the Highlands and trample the English," a feverish light entered Logan's eyes, made all the more disturbing as his nose still bled, "and the Scots will take their rightful place."

"Is Colonel Manners aware of your leanings?" I watched the other man cautiously, uncertain of his motives. "I should not think he would want a spy who hoped for the old pretender to take the English throne."

"Och, well, as ye know, Manners has his spies all over the Highlands, England, the world, for all I understand," Logan rubbed his nose with his sleeve and winced. "He knows I would do anything tae hae Markinch back under its rightful family."

Eyeing the other man warily, "Why did you break into Beathan's office this evening?"

Logan looked unsurprised, "I knew ye followed me, ye certainly hae been awfully interested in my goings ay late. If only Manners told ye I spied for him, ye might hae been able tae catch the real killer."

"And who is the real killer?" If he knew or had a suspicion at least all my week's work would not be in vain.

"I hae a pretty good idea of who it might be, but I cannae make any accusations yet," Logan sighed heavily. "Which is why I came back tae investigate the shots, hoping they might lead somewhere. When I saw the lead mark in the road and evidence someone avoided being shot, well, I followed the path and found ye, lurking in the fens."

Narrowing my eyes, I would not apologise for taking the other man down, I thought he might be the shooter. Instead I said, "I think we better work together. Manners is not one for idle threats, if we do not find the murderer and the McGreevys, he will send the English Militia and I guess you want to avoid this possibility as much as I."

Turning back towards the road, Logan spoke quickly, "I hae a lead, however we must follow it tonight, I think," he looked up at the sky. "There is nae much light, yet we must find the McGreevys with their still. It is the only way tae get the answers we need."

"You know where they might be hiding?" I used long strides to catch up to the other man and we stepped back onto the road again.

Logan turned towards Deoch and walked briskly forward. "I hae a guid idea, there is an auld hermit's cave, a couple of miles through the bush and fens tae the north ay the castle, it is hidden on one side by a waterfall and the other is protected by a steep, narrow road. If we surround it, the villains will not be able to escape. With the two ay us," Logan paused to scrutinise my face, "and yer obvious skill in fighting, we should be able tae take them both easily."

The other man halted in the road between the dark Deoch buildings, forcing me to stop abruptly. He turned to face me. "We are going intae the fens, tae face two ay the most stubborn men in Markinch, they are known cattle thieves and hae committed God knows what other crimes. I suggest ye go back tae the cottage and arm yerself to the teeth. I heard the tomahawks ye carry are mighty ferocious. Perhaps the look of them will hae them surrendering." Logan smiled for the first time in my presence, the same grin as Kieran's when he was up to no good. "Meet me back here in nae less than an hour, we go straightaway, someone wanted ye dead tonight, we cannae risk they will move the still."

Nodding, I felt loath to take orders from a man with dubious loyalties, working as a spy for my own government, under the supervision of Colonel Manners. I did not have many options, Logan presented a straightforward plan and we would follow it through. I started to jog back down the road, I heard doors closing in the distance, I passed a couple of early morning revellers on their way home from the evening's entertainments, oblivious of the danger an unknown marksman might pose.

In my haste, I banged the gate off the fence, the noise following me as I wrenched open the door to the cottage. I picked up the oil lamp I had left burning for my return on the front table and quickly walked into the cottage. I took the first step and halted at a noise from the back of the house. I changed direction and went through the door leading to the dining room and set the lamp on the table, I might need both of my hands if an intruder waited beyond. For the second time, I reached down and pulled the knife from its holder at my ankle, took a breath and lunged through the door into the kitchen.

A quick scan revealed everything remained in order, except the back door lay open, the wind banging it into the frame must have been the noise I heard. I looked out into the darkened garden, the intruder well away, escaping into the night. Turning on my heel, I went straight into the drawing room and lifted the light above my head, papers lay scattered over the floor and chairs, the drawers to the desk lay fallen at awkward angles, someone thoroughly searched all the room's secrets.

A sudden thought made me set the lamp down on the cluttered table between the sofa and my favourite chair, the table where I last set Mr Turner's diary lay empty. In my haste I even looked under the chair.

The diary was missing, I leaned down and picked up the pages of the cipher spread over the floor, whoever took it either already knew how to decode the book or did not care. I raised my eyes unseeing to the knot in the hangman's rope above my head. Only three people I could be sure of knew of the diary's existence: Freya, Phil and now Beathan, yet the possibility any of them would turn the place over to find it, remained slim. All three knew my habits well by now, they would only have to check the places where they often found me at work to find the book. Someone else must have come through, someone who might have heard of the existence of the diary by chance.

For some reason my thoughts went back to Logan. He had been unusually quick to come upon the shooting site tonight, true he could not have fired the weapon, yet this this not mean he could not have an accomplice, or two fugitive accomplices. Feeling duped I turned and ran up the steps two by two. In short order, I raided my trunk and changed my evening clothes for my more suitable tracking gear. Freya still believed the deerskin stank, yet she had cleaned and sewed the bullet hole well enough.

After pulling on my boots, I ran out the front door. Armed with my two tomahawks, the muskets my father gave me and my hunting knife strapped to my leg. I carried a stack of paper cartridges in a leather sack strapped around my back. This time I was prepared. I would be armed and ready to do my duty to the Crown as well as protect Markinch from trouble.

The road remained empty, most revellers having reached their intended destination for the morning of New Year's Day. I reached the buildings of Deoch and found them standing cold, grey and, for once in the early morning frost, eerily silent. Glancing at my pocket watch, Logan still had five minutes to join me. Whether he would or not, remained pure speculation, even though he had revealed his involvement with Colonel Manners and justified his reasons, I still did not trust him, especially with his political leanings.

I walked in a circle, and stamped my feet while I waited to keep warm. Always trying to stay in the shadows, the marksman might be around, hoping for a second chance. Logan could have betrayed my position to the enemy, I was not going to trust him completely. The hour ticked over and I waited another ten minutes, the only sounds remained the settling of the buildings, creaking in the snow and ice. After another five minutes my impatience won out and I stalked back down the road and found the small lane leading to Tavish and Logan's cottages.

An inspection of the imprints in the frost made it easy to spot Tavish's drunken swagger, one leg appeared not capable of keeping up with the other, the old man had shuffled home as best he could. On top of these prints, lay ones at least a couple sizes smaller from worn boots. I would not have to guess and say they belonged to Kieran, which meant it unlikely Logan came this way when he went home.

Anger and frustration propelled me forward, I felt the fool, Logan surely double crossed me, even though at the time I thought his words true, he obviously retained a talent for a lying, a talent I would not be duped by again. I banged on the door for a full three minutes before a bleary-eyed Kieran unlocked the portal and opened it; his eyes still held sleep and he wore a long nightshirt, dirty at the hem.

"Where is your father, boy? Has he come in from the festivities?" I infused my words with authority in the same manner I did when instructing my soldiers in important operations. It affected Kieran in the same manner, and he promptly stood straighter and stepped back to let me into the small cottage.

The room remained dark, and I took a candle from the mantelpiece and used my pocket flint to bright it to life. It sputtered a few times before growing stronger and revealing the remnants of a once great family. Not sure what I expected when I entered Logan's home, I never would have imagined this, all of his family's heirlooms and treasures, jumbled together, one on top of another, stored until one day when they might return to their proper place in the castle. The Markinch coat of arms hung on the wall opposite the fire. I walked over to inspect it further, the design simple, a depiction of the church where Father Tadhg held his services, no arms or plumes distracted from the central image.

Kieran found me frowning over the material. "Faither never returned home this evening, bed's untouched, dinnae know where he might be." The boy's brow furrowed in thought and he took in my costume. "Sometimes he stays late at his office."

I could tell by the growing light in the boy's eye he was gathering up numerous questions to ask over my appearance and I wanted to answer them. Now, however, was not the time. "Where is his office located?"

"In the building with the mash tuns. I can take ye down there if ye wait a minute," Kieran turned to head back into the room he came from.

With a marksman on the loose who nearly took my own life, I would not put the boy in danger too. "Kieran, it is nothing serious, I will find the office myself, go back to bed and I will see you soon." As an afterthought, I added, "Happy New Year, boy."

Logan did not return home to fetch his supplies after we parted, I cursed myself and him for believing his story. I walked back up the darkened road and found the mash tun barn. The main doors remained chained shut and I walked around looking for an entrance, anything, an open window or a loose board. A door near the rear stood open, no need to break into the premises, someone, Logan probably, had gone through earlier in the evening. I was surprised he would not have closed and locked up the barn before leaving. I did not believe any of the villagers might cause trouble, however, the McGreevys still wandered the fens and his obvious lack of worry over their presence only fueled my own speculations over his loyalty.

I looked over the room quickly before stepping through the door, no obvious signs of knaves hiding in the dark. I remained alert, straining for any noise indicating danger; I would be ready this time. Light shone through the row of windows near the top of the wall where it met the ceiling, the moon's light waned as dawn approached. I hardly felt tired even though I had remained awake for an entire day and night. I spied an open door at the far side of the barn, near to where the large doors might be open on workdays, and I cautiously walked over, using the large, silent mash tuns as cover for my progress.

Eyeing the tools on the wall, any one of them could be used as a weapon, and I could not tell if any might be missing, I looked around cautiously before pushing open the door to a small room with my moccasin-clad foot. Darkness greeted me, this room did not have high windows to let in the light, I could not even make out any shapes, turning back towards the mash tuns, I spied an oil lamp on one of the work desks and I quickly went to fetch it. For the second time in the evening, I pulled my flint from an inner pocket and lit the wick, it flashed and created more shadows over the room. I closed my eyes and opened them again to adjust to the new brightness.

No attackers yet and I had given them a large signal of my presence. I still used caution as I went back to the office door. Too many times I had taken my safety for granted or the word of someone up here in the Highlands. I needed to trust in lessons Hania taught me. I thrust the light into the office and found a desk covered in scattered papers, glass lay broken over the floor and a chair fallen over. My eyes could not, did not want to register as I looked up and found Logan hanging by his neck, face horribly purple, eyes protruding.

I turned away from the scene gagging and coughing. As an army man, I had seen worse corpses, yet the sudden impact of Logan's distorted face provoked such a weak response. I could not be getting soft. After collecting my nerve, I forced myself to raise the light again, to inspect the man's corpse, his broken nose bruised in the light, I looked at his hands, scraped and red.

His bloodied hands made me frown. He did not land a single blow on my person. He must have been fighting with someone else. I studied the knot in the rope. I recognised it as the one in my own drawing room. It could not be a coincidence, a man from the south of England with little or no experience in survival, let alone tying ropes, would not have the skill to make the same knot as one born to a workman's life, who probably worked with rope often. The striking similarity between the two gave me enough evidence to shoulder the belief that perhaps one man consigned both these men to death. The possibility Mr Turner's death may not have been a suicide as everyone believed, hung suspended just as Logan's corpse now slowly revolved in the night air, filling the space between hypothesis and reason.

Chapter 15

A guttural cry erupted from behind me and Kieran bowled through the door temporarily knocking me off-balance and upsetting the oil lamp. The boy stared up at his father and screamed again, the shadows moved crazily around the room.

Setting the lamp down on a shelf near the door, I grabbed Kieran's shoulders and forced him to turn and face me. His mouth still open, though no sound emerged, eyes staring he looked as though he could see something I could not. I shook his shoulders, not knowing what to do. "Kieran, boy, look at me."

I dragged him from the room, his feet moving sluggishly and automatically. As a soldier, I had dealt with men who went into shock after their first battle, some even went into a dumb state after years of military action; the mind is a complicated engine. I forcefully shook Kieran's shoulders once again and he blinked. He did not focus on my face, instead he let out a high-pitched keening noise, the unearthly sound tracked its way down my back and I shivered in response. Wrapping my arms around him, I tried to press the shock from his small body, to take it into myself, watching his pain for his father's death, made me relive the terrible morning I found Onatah dead. Our child gone with her, his grief made tears streak down my face.

With a force I did not think he could possess, Kieran pushed away from me and tried to run back into the office. I grabbed the back of his coat with one hand, abruptly halting his progress. "Kieran, do not go back in there, it's not something you should see."

"My faither, we could save him, we only need tae get him down from the rope," Kieran's pleading eyes turned to me. "Ye can help, I saw it once with a coney, I thought it dead with a broken neck in one ay my snares, but when I released the wee thing, it came back tae life fur a moment."

The boy eagerly pulled against my hold and I gripped tighter, "Kieran, it does not work the way you believe. What you saw was some sort of muscle spasm, the rabbit did not come back to life, and neither will your father, I'm sorry, lad."

Kieran began to fight harder and it became tougher to hang onto his wiry body. "Yer lying, a filthy lying Englishman, ye dinnae want tae help him cause he's a Scots, ye hate us, please only get him down."

Logan's body did need to be cut down, however I would have to get help from somewhere and the lad did not need to witness it, I looked up at the windows, weak light indicated dawn fast approached. Unceremoniously picking Kieran up, I walked past the mash tuns and out of the door.

The morning felt different, not only because the rays of the first dawn of the New Year brushed across the barren hills, but also because something fundamental had changed overnight in Markinch. A happening, which would change this boy's life forever, and perhaps the rest of the village. Whether they wanted to acknowledge him or not, the Laird of Markinch was dead. Kieran's fight did not relent as we walked into the main road. I think he screamed, hit, kicked and bit all the harder the further we walked from the office. I needed help fast and Tavish came to mind immediately; he knew the boy and he would know what to do.

"Och, shut yer damned gobs down there! Dinnae ye know its Hogmanay morning, people are dying!" I looked up at a window in the waterwheel building; Angus leaned out of the mantel with a nasty look on his face, shaking both fists.

I needed all the help I could get this morning. "Listen, I need some help with the boy. Are you well enough to come down?"

Kieran quieted for a moment and I heard a loud sniff from above. "It's the first day of the New Year, gauger, surely this means something even tae ye heathens down south? Whatever the boy has done, surely can be mended at the appropriate hour, in fact why not give the boy a clean slate, New Year and all?"

"I am afraid the situation is much more serious than some schoolboy prank." I did not want to upset the boy by shouting his father's fate into the world, instead I tried to impress the importance on Angus. "It involves the future of Deoch, the whole village will be affected."

The mention of Deoch gained the man's undivided attention and he disappeared from the window. Five minutes later, he appeared at the front door wearing his tartan over his nightshirt, the effect much more modest than his usual shirt and skirt.

"Now, what is all this serious talk?" Angus strode over and watched curiously as I kept hold of Kieran, who tried to escape every few seconds. I did not want to speak in front of him, yet I had no choice.

"The boy and I found Logan this morning," I paused and Angus raised his eyebrows for me to continue. "He's dead in his office." Looking down at the squirming boy, "I did not want him to keep looking and I need to alert the proper people."

"Och, I dinnae believe it, man's strong as an ox, drinks like a king, knows how tae handle himself when drunk." Angus rubbed his whiskery chin. "Probably passed out in there, ye probably missed the snoring, I will go in and rouse him, shall I?"

Frustrated with the other man's belief I could not tell if a man were dead, "I think you will have a rather hard time of it, as he went the same way as Mr Turner." I immediately felt like a churl for letting my temper get the better of me, the other man's eyes widening in understanding.

In a halting voice, "If this is the case, I ought tae go up tae the castle and rouse Beathan. He will need tae inspect the body and so forth," the old man stared down at Kieran, pity coloured his gaze. "Poor wee mite, Freya would probably be the best fur him, take him back tae the cottage and I will make sure someone sends fur her from the castle, might as well wake up my brother," the word spat from his mouth.

I watched as the other man hurried up the road, the tail of his night shirt flapping out behind him. I sighed and turned as he disappeared over a rise. Kieran gave up the fight for now, instead he stood motionless, at least the screaming had stopped. We trudged slowly back to the lane and down towards the two cottages, but instead of steering him towards his own place, I directed him with a hand on his shoulder towards Tavish's, I needed someone to help me with him until Freya could be fetched.

The door opened and I stepped through, regretting my choice as I looked around the chaotic room. Tavish did not have time to tidy up after his at home the previous evening. I shouted into the still rooms, "Tavish. you have visitors!"

I sat the boy on a stool by the fire and used a pair of metal tongs to get the blaze going again, I added a couple more squares of peat onto the ashes and watched as they caught fire. A rustling noise from the back indicated Tavish heard my call.

Tavish appeared in the doorway leading to the rest of the cottage, hair tangled and wearing his kilt over his nightshirt, same as his brother. If the situation were not so serious, I might have laughed at the comparison. Hand on hip, he growled. "What in the name of the devil riding on horseback is going on, Captain?" He looked down at Kieran who stared woodenly into the fire, ignoring both of us. "Listen, if he has been up tae nae good, it's only a spot ay Hogmanay fun, I am sure ye can let the lad off with a warning and let the rest ay us suffer our hangovers?"

Glancing down at Kieran, he must get into more trouble than I knew, I looked back at Tavish and indicated he should follow me across the room. The other man sighed wearily, however he humoured me. "Early this morning I found Logan dead in his office." Tavish took a deep breath and before he could say I must be mistaken I interrupted him, "I know a dead man when I see one, gone the same way as Mr Turner. Your brother has already gone up to the castle to inform Beathan."

The other man only nodded his understanding, there might be little love lost between Logan and himself, the younger man took Tavish's position, however, the death of someone so close always left a mark. He turned and watched Kieran for a moment before glancing around the room. He began to clear away the glasses and debris from the previous evening, disappearing into the rear of the cottage. I heard banging and water sloshing.

The boy appeared made of stone and I did not want to intrude in his grief any longer. Turning to the front window, I watched for Angus or a messenger to come and fetch me. In truth I did not know what to do or say, again I would have to tell Beathan I fell victim to a random, failed attack. Would I tell him of my suspicions of Logan, now so utterly wrong, how could my instincts lead me so far from the truth?

Cursing Colonel Manners for his schemes and machinations, I opened the front of my jacket, the cottage warm, and ran a finger down the condensation on the glass. If he had told me of Logan being a spy, I would never have wasted time suspecting him, and I might have the real killer. Or perhaps Manners was suspicious of Logan, even after his confession of being in the employ of my superior, his political leanings made it impossible to rule him out as a suspect entirely, he might still be the man behind the murders. However, I knew there must be more to the story, the way the ropes were tied in both Turner and Logan's deaths, was the clue, I felt positive it could lead me to the rest of the criminals.

I leaned forward and rested my head on the window, tiredness crept into my bones. I needed to explore the hermit's cave just as Logan recommended this morning, today; even if it might have been a ploy to distract me, it remained my only lead. A movement outside the window made me wipe a larger space clear to look through, a maid hurried down the path, a heavy cape over her tartan dress and a large basket in her hand. I went to the door and opened it for her.

"Och, Captain, a sorry business this," the young lady stepped through without any hesitation, she stamped her feet to remove any excess snow and swept into the room. She stared at Kieran, "Poor wee mite," and walked over to squat in front of him.

After whispering a few words of comfort, she turned her head. "Beathan is waiting for ye over at Deoch, in the mash tun building." She quickly checked to see if her words distressed the boy, and called into the kitchen. "Tavish, they want ye down there as well, better get a move on."

Tavish came through dressed in his proper linen shirt and tartan, hat pressed firmly down over his unruly hair. "Thank ye, Maud, take guid care ay the boy," he walked over and opened the door for me.

I hesitated a moment, I knew rationally there was nothing I could do. The boy would be an orphan from now on, no words of comfort could penetrate the fog of sorrow. I took a deep breath and walked out the door. Bringing the person who was responsible for Logan's death to justice would be something at least.

Walking briskly in oppressive silence, neither of us felt the need to make idle conversation; New Year's morning should be a time to take stock, cradle our sore heads and discuss nothing of any concern. By the time we reached the office, Beathan and Angus stood outside the doorway, a couple of men worked quickly and silently to remove Logan's body and cover it with a sheet, at least I did not have to see his face again.

Beathan looked up from his conversation with Angus and nodded to us. I acknowledged his greeting and felt a new wave of frustration mixed with weariness infuse my soul.

"Ye look as if ye could use a week's worth ay sleep, Captain," Beathan studied my face, probably noticing dark smudges under my eyes. "Let us on tae business, and we can try and set the morning tae rights."

The two brothers eyed each other warily for once, rather than with hostility. They both appeared to be hanging on a thread, their mighty hangovers held at bay with sheer willpower. I watched the workmen lift the body and take it outside.

Clearing his throat, "Father Tadgh has been informed," Beathan, announced. "Ye found the poor man, did ye?"

"Yes, as I made my way home from the Castle, someone took a shot at me," the other men watched with keen interest, wearing matching expressions as if they doubted my story. I fished for the lead ball in an inner pocket and showed it to the other men. "It came from the fens and I decided to take matters into my own hands and find the damned fellow." All three men appeared to be taking more interest. "I heard footsteps following behind after only a few yards and I ducked and waited for them to come, thinking it might be the shooter. It was Logan, which is why you may have noticed the broken nose, Logan could not have been the shooter, no powder burns, yet he told me he heard the shots and came to investigate."

"I hae tae say, Captain, ye get yerself intae the most extraordinary adventures," Tavish's bloodshot eyes narrowed. "I cannae think of another man who has suffered as many in such a short space."

Looking over at the other man, I sighed, and turned my attention back to Beathan, "He told me he followed someone, he believed this person could be responsible for the murder of the McKinneys and Mr Turner. However we needed to find the McGreevys to confirm his theory."

Holding up a hand. "Wait, did he tell ye who this mystery person may hae been?" Beathan watched me carefully. "We could end all this now, once and for all, get back tae our normal lives."

I shook my head and grimaced. "He would not say, even when I pressed him, said the truth would only be believable if he had proof," the brothers looked disappointed. "I went home to dress properly and arm myself for a confrontation," I indicated my clothing. "I came back at the allotted time and he did not appear, I waited for a few minutes and came in here and found him. Unfortunately Kieran followed me, damned stupid thing."

The other men nodded, we stood in silence for a few minutes, the others digesting my words. I wondered what they made of my story, as Tavish said, I did seem to fall into more than my share of adventures. I found it embarrassing.

A grim look passed over Beathan's features. "It's obvious Logan perpetrated of all this," he began. I frowned and he held out his hand to continue. "At first we thought he could hae been murdered, the bruises on his face and hands, yet ye admit tae having a scuffle with him." I nodded my head and wanted to tell him he never landed a punch however he cut me off. "There is nae a soul in Markinch who doesnae know ay his hatred fur my family, he would hae done anything tae bring us down. He must a hae some scheme with an illegal still, maybe the McKinneys and Turner knew ay its existence and he did away with them to keep his secret."

"Aye, well, it's certainly possible," Tavish nodded his head. I shook mine, there must be more to the story, why would he go to all this trouble?

Beathan continued, "Perhaps he might have been in league with the McGreevys, they are near impossible tae track down at the best of times. We will probably nae know the full extent ay Logan's plans," he paused and took a deep breath. "I think we better keep Logan's true crimes tae ourselves in the village, accept fur ye ay course, Captain, ye will want tae report the murderer found and deceased."

My brain worked sluggishly, yet the story did not feel right. I watched the brothers take Beathan's turn of events as truth; they would not challenge him and even though I knew something did not feel right concerning his conclusions, I could not think of anything to contradict him.

"Yes of course, Beathan," I said quietly. "I will send word to London on the next packet of our discoveries and our improved circumstances should keep Colonel Manners from taking any further action."

The other men nodded and I followed them from the rear of the building. Once on the main road, we watched the cart make slow progress up to the church and Beathan nodded to each of us. "I will see ye all tomorrow, we must put this tragedy behind us and begin the New Year."

Angus grumbled something and turned towards the water mill, the other Tavish doffed his cap and walked away. I stood alone in the middle of the empty buildings, exhaustion threatened to overcome my weary bones and I turned for home.

The weak sunlight warming my face between the grey clouds scudding past might have cheered me, yet I knew Beathan's conclusions could not be correct. I thought of the same knot in both the hangman's nooses, it was possible Logan tied them both, first to murder Mr Turner and then to end his own life, yet I knew he did not land a single punch on my person last evening; he scuffled with someone else. It sounded stupid when I said it in my head, perhaps Logan punched the ground or scraped his knuckles in another way, I kicked out at a lump of ice in the road to relieve some of my frustration.

I went through the cottage gate and hesitated before opening the door, in my stupor, I forgot to mention the theft of Turner's diary. The fact someone went through the cottage last evening and it could not have been Logan. He would have either been fighting for his life or trying to end it in his office. Passing into the cottage, I stood in the doorway of the drawing room. It looked as if a heavy wind had torn through and I rubbed my eyes, I needed sleep to think.

Trudging up the stairs, I made sure the curtains remained pulled tight, removed my boots, placed my weapons within easy reach and lay down on the covers of the bed fully clothed, too tired to do anything else. I thought of the boy sitting in Tavish's cottage, completely alone before I slept.

A shrill scream made me sit up in bed, eyes full of sleep I jumped up and grabbed the tomahawks laying on the bedside table. Without a logical thought, I half tumbled down the stairs two at a time to face the danger.

I found Freya surveying the damage in the drawing room, she turned to see me in the doorway again and let loose with another scream, eyes rolling up in the back of her head, she fell onto the carpeted floor. Cursing, I hurried to set the weapons aside and went into the drawing room, I crouched down to make sure she had not gained any injuries from her fall. She appeared in one piece and after a minute her eyes fluttered open.

"Captain, what do ye think running around the place like a damned heathen? Especially when the drawing room looks as if it might hae seen a fight." She slowly sat up and gulped in a few breaths of air, "Ye hae taken a few years of my life, ye hae, and on New Year's Day, after such tragic events."

"I'm sorry, Freya" I helped the woman stand and cleared a place for her to sit on the sofa. She fanned herself with a stray piece of paper. "It is all a very long, sordid story, I do not think I could go into it now," I settled into my favourite chair. "You know of Logan?"

She nodded slowly, "I was fetched this morn to collect Kieran from Tavish's cottage, thought it might be best if I watched over the lad, since our boys are couthy, if ye recall," she sighed and looked out the window. "Poor mite, I feel terrible now fur the things I said ay his father last evening," she made the sign of the cross.

My own guilt riding high and my lingering doubts over his guilt in the deaths of Mr Turner and the McKinneys prompted me. "None of us could have known what would happen last night, indeed I have been trying to find clues to connect all these terrible goings on and never thought this might happen."

"Beathan mentioned ye were the body what found him," she grimaced and glanced at me. "A terrible sight, I know," she looked up at the rope and I examined the knot, it looked exactly the same, a twin to the other.

Needing answers, I spoke more sharply than I intended. "Freya, did you tell anyone of the work I did in here, on Mr Turner's diary, trying to decipher the code?"

Freya frowned and looked down into her lap. She played with a stray strand of cotton for a minute before looking up again. "I dinnae think so, Captain, it seemed private, even tae hae ye reading it, well it felt as if it breached Mr Turner's space, yet, I cannae be sure."

"You will let me know if you think of anyone?" I gestured to the upturned drawing room. "It appears someone took great pains in wanting to find the diary, and they did; it is missing."

The housemaid looked around thoughtfully. "In honesty, sir, I believed ye might have fallen intae a fit. Has anything else been taken?" I watched as she checked to make sure all of the valuables remained.

"Everything else is in order," I glanced at the clock on the mantelpiece, the noon hour recently passed and my stomach growled. I had errands I needed to run; I wanted to check Logan's body up at the church and there was another task to complete. "What is the best way to get to the hermit's cottage Freya?"

Her eyes widened, "I cannae think what ye might be about, going up there at this time ay year." She watched my face, my expression did not waver and she continued. "The best way is tae take a path leading from the rear ay the castle through the fens, it will be dangerous this time ay year, if ye go stick tae the path!"

"Thank you, Freya. I will help you set the drawing room to rights when I return." Trying to use my most charming smile. "Do you think I could get a bowl of your porridge before leaving on this mighty trek? I have not eaten a morsel since last evening."

Freya smiled widely and patted my shoulder. Finally, a task she could easily complete, which did not involve dead men or their orphaned children. "Will be ready in a thrice, I will pack some leftover shortbread I brought around, in case ye get hungry."

I set off in the weak New Year sunshine, the birds, unmindful of the tragedy facing Markinch, sang and clambered through the snowy heather. The horizon clear for once, not one cloud appeared to mar its vast beauty. With feet much heavier than the previous evening, I followed the road once again up through Deoch. This time not to meet Logan, yet a strange knot in my gut told me destiny lay beyond, a reckoning at least.

The red buildings were not as silent as the early morning, workers gathered in groups of two, three and five stood and spoke in low tones. I walked through as respectfully as I could, each man wore a piece of black cloth tied to their arm, above the elbow.

One of the workmen shouted, I recognised him as the one who trapped me in a bear hug the previous evening. I wanted to continue, their mourning felt oppressive to me, the men here needed someone to blame for the tragedy, yet when I waved and made to continue, he shouted again.

Not wanting to appear rude, I changed my tack and walked over to the group where he stood, large arms straining under his ill-fitting jacket. I gave them a quick bow. "Gentlemen, a sorry morning to meet upon."

"We're nae gentlemen, Captain, only guid honest folk," the man in the ill-fitting jacket observed wryly. "Ye look tae be on some business. We wanted tae ask ye if there might be truth in the rumour ay a militia coming to Markinch?"

Angry looks appeared on more than one man's face, a few mumbled words I could not catch and one man spat onto the frozen ground. The situation felt more dangerous than I had previously believed and I put both of my gloved hands out in front of me. "I am not sure where you heard this gossip, all I can say is there are no plans for a militia to come here at the moment, none I have been informed of, so if it is true, I am unaware."

A small man from another group came over, his eyes darted from me to the rest of the group, the action reminding me of a ferret. "I think he's lying, Mary Margaret had it from Susan, who said she spoke tae one at the servants up at the big house who works as Mistress Philomena's body servant, and she was told in secret the militia were coming."

My eyes narrowed, I did not have time to put credence into any of this gossip. Never mind it contained a kernel of truth I did not want any of them to know, I felt some of them press forwards threatening me. "Listen to me, the militia will not be coming here if I can help it, and in order to complete my days work, I must be away. I suggest the rest of you get back home and enjoy your last day of freedom before work starts again tomorrow." I lifted my chin, looked several of them in the eye and marched away, hoping I would not get an ice ball to the back of my head.

Upon reaching the church, I found more men gathered in groups, the same as down at Deoch. I nodded to each them as I went through. I felt their hostile eyes burning into the back of my head, however I did not have the time or the resources to try and allay their fears. By the time I opened the door, my mood deteriorated as several of the men I passed called me a gauger arsehole, and I slammed the portal on them. Unfortunately this only announced my entrance to those quietly reflecting inside.

I stomped down the passage I took previously when I came to inspect the McKinneys, I could not see the querulous Father Tadgh in the main room of the church and I hoped he would not be with Logan. Wanting to hide from all the prying eyes staring from pews, I wrenched open the door and stepped inside, this time making an effort to close it quietly. When I turned, I found Father Tadgh and Beathan staring at me from the other side of the slab where Logan's body lay.

Father Tadgh gave me a grimace and he waved his hands in agitation. "There will be nae scientific experiments on this man. He may hae died in sin, going against the laws of man and nature, yet ye will nae use his sin tae benefit, ye evil being!"

Giving the priest the most bored look I could muster. I turned to look at Beathan, who curiously watched Father Tadgh after his outburst; it appeared I was not the only person who thought his accusations absurd.

"Beathan, have you found anything of importance since this morning?" I did not think I missed anything, yet a closer inspection might bring a clue; I remained unconvinced of Logan's guilt and suicide.

The other man shook his big head and let out a long breath before answering. "The only new circumstance is someone spreading a tale the English Militia are coming from the south tae enslave us and we need tae band together with the rest of our Highlands folk tae repel them. I cannae stress how bad this rumour could be fur business."

"I heard on my way here, and all I could do is reiterate what I said the previous evening. With this new development," I paused because I knew the story behind Logan's death could not be true somehow, yet I could not prove it. "Markinch should be safe with the killer dead," I heard the flatness in my tone.

"Right, well, once the men get back tae work tomorrow, all will be well, tae much idle time breeds trouble." Scratching his chin, he went on. "Perhaps we will shorten the break next year," he eyed my clothes. "Are ye off somewhere, Captain?"

"Yes, I am going up to the hermit's cave," Beathan frowned in disapproval, and I continued in order to explain myself. "I have a lead I need to follow, it is important."

"I dinnae know who would send ye on an errand all the way up there at this time of year." I could see Beathan tried to be persuasive. "They are nae friend tae ye, Captain. It is dangerous, I dinnae even know a body from Markinch who might walk all the way up there."

Tired of everyone telling me what I could and could not do in Markinch, using my various near brushes with death as an example I bit out. "Someone tried to kill me last night and a couple of weeks ago. I know it could not have been Logan last night and I will have it from the McGreevys' own lips if they are responsible. Justice will be served." I turned on my heel, walked out of the room and slammed the door, unmindful of any watching eyes.

Chapter 16

Striding through the main doors out of the church, I bullied my way around the men standing in groups. They might have nestled under my skin upon entrance, however my black look sent them scurrying out of the way with quick steps. A couple even doffed their caps at me. I did not think I normally acted the bully, though I will admit to being secretly pleased with the deference. An action I had yet to experience in Markinch, respect for my position and abilities. My crimes may have been great in Boston, yet none doubted my skill at fighting and tracking. Here I remained only another southerner, a Sassenach who could not make it in the wilds of the Highlands.

I walked briskly out of the gate, ignoring Tavish as he came up the road. Turning on my heel, I walked towards the castle, searching for a road or path leading around the stone building, I would not ask for anyone's help. Upon reaching the gates of the castle, I looked around the road on both sides, snow and ice covered most of the ground and in frustration I chose a side and began to walk over the uneven ground. The moccasins might be quiet and warm, yet they did not have the grip of my riding boots and I slipped several times. Cursing under my breath each time, hoping none were watching my haphazard progress.

Reaching the left side of the castle, I turned and followed the wall. The snow remained much more shallow on this side, probably due to the wind commonly blowing from the other direction., This side would be protected most of the time and I made quick progress to the rear of the castle. I spied the midden heap rising from the ground in a large conical shape. The castles refuse pile. I wrinkled my nose and gave it a wide birth while looking for signs of a trail leading north.

I found a door in the wall on the other side of the rubbish and I made an assumption a trail might lead from there. I scanned the ground for any signs of footprints or animal prints leading away from the castle. The place between my shoulder blades itched, and I was conscious of the many windows looking down on the rear of the castle. Anyone could be watching from those castle windows, mocking my efforts, yet I kept going, pride fuelling my feet.

More by chance than skill on my own part, I found a bridle path, wide enough for a person or a horse to walk in single file. I followed it carefully, scuffing snow from it every now and again in order to make sure I did not stray too far. After a mile or so, the terrain became much steeper and I could see the edge of the forest, where the fens ended. I made haste to the cover, as I felt exposed on the fens. With the first of the trees, I stopped and turned to survey the route from the castle, it winded through the marshland, the castle in the distance. I calculated I must have walked for at least an hour and a half, making good progress.

Slipping a waterproof bag from over my shoulder, I scanned the forest ahead. The trees grew fairly densely, yet the trunks were not nearly as thick as those I had encountered in the New World. It would take skill and patience to hide among these skinny obstructions. Under the trees where the snow fell lightest, the trail continued north. I pushed the stopper into the water container, took a deep breath and began to climb through the woods. A feeling of safety and comfort stole over me, the trees comfortable companions, enclosing me within the space of the forest, rather than the harshness of the fens. Which gave a feeling of infinite wasteland, and where every step could be fraught with danger.

I worried I might have taken the wrong path when the sound of water caught my ear. I followed it to the edge of a steep embankment, the edge soft with lose dirt and exposed tree roots. I tried to keep away from the lip, while inspecting the stream. The water around the edges made shelves of ice on either side, yet the stream flowed too quickly for it to become completely frozen. Chasing the water up the canyon, it appeared to follow a path deeply cut into the earth, the banks remained high on either side with no footpath.

Cursing under my breath, I rejoined the footpath, I hoped to use the stream as we did in the New World. As a path leading us around the known trails, hiding our passage. I did not want to take the only route up to the hermit's cave, if the McGreevys happened to be waiting for me, a flintlock in hand.

The way became even steeper until the trail turned into a switchback and my breath became more laboured under the stress of effort. Aware I needed to try and conceal my presence for as long as possible, when the path narrowed between large boulders, I crouched as I turned blind corners, hoping to catch anyone waiting off-guard.

The incline began to even out and I stopped, my back resting on one of the large boulders, taking out a couple of paper cartridges. I primed both of the flintlocks. Whatever met me at the hermit's cave, I would be ready. I might go down, yet I hoped I would not be alone. I took the first corner and jumped around, legs braced and pistols primed and found another corner. With a sigh of disappointment, I walked to the end of the visible path and waited. Heart thumping with excitement, I felt the familiar rise of nervous anticipation infuse my body; it made a lump in my throat. I once again launched myself around the wall of rock, to find success, the entrance of a cave.

None stood in the mouth of the cave, yet I would not take any chances. In one move, I crouched and turned so my back pressed against the wall on the right side of the cave, clearing my throat. "Come on out, boys, there is only one other way out of this cave and it involves a drop and a bath."

Nothing, not a single noise to indicate another person's presence. I waited a minute more and peered inside the gloom of the cave. I could make out stationary shapes, however the only way to prove my lack of company meant exploring further. I remained in my crouched position, better to make a smaller target. I replaced one of the flintlocks with a tomahawk; it had much more use in close quarters hand-to-hand fighting, as well as being a weapon neither of the boys would have come across.

The cave smelled dank, as did most others I had explored in my time, yet another smell pervaded the clammy air. Something I knew every well, after walking through the four yards of the cave, to the end, where water fell in great icy sheets. I realised I remained alone, for the moment. Weak light filtered through the water and I stuffed the flintlock into the front of my belt and used the tomahawk to pry open the lid on one of the wooden crates. The cave was too dark to read the writing printed in black paint along the side.

Letting out a low breath, I searched through the faintly damp hay inside the box until my fingers found what my mind did not want to believe. I pulled a flintlock musket from the box and, from a quick inspection, I could see it was new. I smelled the flintlock ignition, never been fired. I set it back into the box, fixing the lid back into place, each casket might carry a dozen or so weapons. I looked around the cave and counted at least thirty boxes of guns, enough to arm a highly trained force who could carry out highly effective raids.

A sick feeling filled the pit of my stomach, much more than an illegal still operated in Markinch. I may have uncovered a true conspiracy to aid Francis Stuart to the throne, and someone in Markinch with money and resources lay behind this scheme. I stumbled to the entrance of the cave, my head felt light and I needed some air. On the way, I passed several stacks of smaller boxes, from the smell I knew they carried the new paper cartridges, enough gunpowder and ball to arm a secret militia.

At the cave's entrance, I took several deep breaths, hoping to dispel the feeling of stupidity now closing in on my consciousness. This scheme appeared to have been in operation for months, and I never realised. The conspirators would have been operating under my nose: how many were involved? Could I trust anyone in the village?

The sound of a lock clicking into place made me freeze for a moment. With as much speed as possible, I brought my own flintlock up to face the new arrival. A second of relief passed when I realised Beathan stood in the narrow entrance to the lane. He did not lower his weapon, and military instinct drove me to keep my own held aloft until the danger passed, whether it came from friend or foe.

"Ye shouldnae come up here, Captain," Beathan's voice grinded out. He looked hard, none of the previous friendliness I had come to expect from him lit his features. "Now we hae a problem."

Cold realization gripped my heart. It felt as if I could not breathe for a moment; betrayal from strangers I knew well, however, the same from someone I considered a friend, inconceivable. "Beathan," I gave a short bark of nervous laughter. "I think we must have stumbled into a situation requiring explanation, surely not everything is as it appears?"

"Ye know fur an army captain, a highly decorated one, I made inquiries ye might be interested in knowing." Beathan half-smiled without warmth, remaining cold, calculating. "Ye are a naïve fool when it comes tae folk, ye really hae nae clue."

Concentrating on Beathan's stance, the way he held his weapon, I knew I needed to keep him talking. "Tell me you know nothing of the weapons in this cave, you mean to destroy them, for all your talk of Logan being a fool for supporting the Stuarts, I cannot believe it of you."

"I suppose ye cannae believe it, someone born tae privilege, yer own uncle, though ye dinnae say a word, is a very wealthy and powerful peer, did ye believe ye could ever escape it?" Beathan frowned at me. "The belief in yer superior breeding infuses everything ye do and why ye do it, just as it did the lads when I attended college."

"Come now, Beathan, we are friends. I make no secret of my past." The lie did not fall easily from my lips and Beathan sneered. "I have never played Lord of the Manor with you. I am here as the tax collector, a lowlier position in any village could not be held, or more hated."

"A runaway lordling, disgraced soldier come gauger, I suppose we hae more in common than I previously thought." Beathan leveled his weapon at my head, and I did likewise, at his heart. "I hae powerful friends, Captain, men counting on me tae support Francis Stuart when he makes his triumphant return tae Scotland and conquers England, there is nae going back fur me."

"Everyone has a choice," I said slowly, the fanatic look in Beathan's eye struck me as the same I saw in Logan's eye the night he died. What was this strange loyalty the old pretender conjured? "We could destroy the weapons and inform Colonel Manners of the conspirators, you might be dealt with leniently."

"It is far tae late fur comprises and promises, Captain." Beathan's grip on the flintlock remained steady, though his voice shook. "I hae committed terrible deeds fur these weapons, fur my loyalty tae Scotland, who do ye believe killed the McKinneys and Turner? Logan Markinch? The man full ay bravado and words, yet I am a man ay action, someone who has done something fur the cause."

Intent on saving my own skin, any shock over his admission was lost. A part of me acknowledged it as a mundane reality. "Why did you kill the McKinneys?"

"Daft buggers wanted out," Beathan sighed for the first time and regret passed through his eyes for a moment. "I knew the Turret struggled tae meet its debts, they made guid Scotch however, they never sold all ay their product. I came in and offered them a deal. I would pay fur their grain, in return they would operate a portable still and nae ask any questions," he sighed. "They soon realised I traded the Scotch fur weapons and they felt the noose around their necks. I took them out tae the fens and killed them both."

I listened to the hardening of Beathan's voice, he may not have come to his decision to be a murderer easily, yet he became accustomed to it over time. "Why Turner? Surely a clerk turned tax man could not endanger you, he spent most of his time puzzling over maths equations."

"Someone put a bug in his ear over the McKinneys' new grain suppliers," Beathan shook his head. "He asked tae many questions and came tae close tae the truth. In the end he gave me nae choice, damned fool, as ye give me nae choice now, Captain, ye know tae much."

I blinked several times. "It was you out on the fens when I went to investigate the explosion. You followed and shot me, you bastard, and I would guess it was also you last night. If not for slipping on the ice you would have killed me, as you did Logan," the hand holding the flintlock never wavered.

The grim smile Beathan wore turned into a grimace. "Yer a damned lucky man, Captain, I only wanted tae scare ye, give ye a warning, yet for all the trouble ye kept up yer pursuit. Last evening after returning from yer cottage with Turner's diary, I knew I had the perfect opportunity taw rid myself ay yer damned nosy presence. Foiled again, how many lives could one man hae? I guess we shall find out now."

Thinking frantically, I spoke, "The death of the second tax man in as many months will bring the English down on your head, Beathan. Do you think you can escape their wrath?" Calculating a moment, I used the one piece of information I knew of which he must not be aware. "You killed their spy and they will come looking for answers."

Beathan searched my face, confused. "Spy fur the English in Markinch? I do nae believe it, everyone has lived here fur more years than I can count. We hardly hae any newcomers, ye are only trying to spin this confrontation out longer. I cannae blame ye in wanting live fur a few more short moments."

"I am not lying, someone has been feeding Manners information from the happenings of Markinch. Someone who I now realise knew what you might be up to and reported it to him." With no idea if it might be true or not, I spun the lie, Logan might have shared his suspicions with Manners.

"Logan," Beathan spat the other man's name out. "Should hae guessed he would be a traitor, his whole family were traitors, trying tae profit from the English. It is nae matter," he straightened. "We are at a stalemate, we shall each fire; perhaps we will both be killed."

Lifting my chin, I forced a smile. "Death for me would be as comforting as falling into my mother's arms," I trained the flintlock on his chest, my hand never wavering.

I watched the other man hesitate. I could take him now my rational mind thought, there remained a small chance of escaping a life threatening injury, yet after all Beathan revealed, I needed to give him another chance. I opened my mouth to speak and he cut me off abruptly.

"I am nae a coward, Captain, I am a business man. Perhaps there is something or someone I might offer ye in return fur yer loyalty?" Beathan's insinuation brought a sickening feeling to my stomach. "Ye hae nae love ay the English Militia, yer practically a traitor already after attacking them. Join us, we will need experienced military men tae fight, and perhaps my sister could be persuaded intae yer arms."

"You would sell Phil to me for my loyalty?" I spat the words out, my honour affronted, Phil's respectability laid bare between us. Here Beathan proved he could never be the man I thought he was. I sniffed. "You are a great actor, sir, however I am not, I may not have much respect for the English and their methods, yet I would never betray them. As for Phil, I would never do her the dishonour of forcing her to be my bride out of some traitorous deal with her murdering brother. You are not the man I thought you." I took a deep breath. "Prepare to test your mettle," I clicked the lock back, ready to strike the flint.

Phil came barrelling around the corner in the next instant, another second and I would have pulled the trigger and Beathan his, our stalemate over. However, Phil looked around Beathan's shoulder with wide eyes fixed on the flintlock. "What the devil! Put down yer weapons!"

The demand went unanswered, I could tell by her rosy cheeks and heavy breath she must have made the journey as quickly as possible. I could not fathom any reason bringing her up here. Now I only wanted her gone, my stomach tightened at the thought of standing over her lifeless body, the image almost brought me to my knees.

"Get the hell out of here, Phil." I shouted the words, infused them with as much authority as I could. "This is none of your affair, leave this place and do not look back, you understand me?"

Unfortunately her years of bucking all authority made her oblivious to my demands and she tried to step around Beathan. Who saw his opportunity, reached behind him with his free hand and grabbed the front of her tartan, pulled her in front of him.

"Are ye going tae let another woman die under yer watch, Captain?" Beathan smiled grimly and pointed his flintlock at Phil's temple, for a moment she remained shocked into stillness.

"Beathan, unhand me at once. I know the game ye are playing, why ye stole the diary, perhaps the captain can help ye." Phil tried to squirm from her brother's grasp. He only pressed the muzzle of his weapon harder into her skull, the sight made my mouth dry.

"Let us be reasonable here," I tried to keep my own flintlock pointed at Beathan's head rather than his body, such a shot was not without its risks. "You are not going to shoot your only sibling, she is your family after all."

His barked laughter echoed through the cave and around the stone walls. "A sister who never does what she is told, who refused to marry into the wealthy and well-connected family ay my friend. Who spends her days reading and largely making a nuisance of herself, she is nae family tae me, she cannae even be used as a pawn."

Phil struggled all the harder to free herself from Beathan's grip, the hurt caught in her voice broke my heart. "Ye are my brither, ye are supposed tae protect me. Stop this foolishness now, let me go, we will never speak ay it again, I promise," she turned tear-filled eyes to meet mine.

"As I said tae the captain, it is tae late tae turn back fur me, the only way is forward. I must see my tasks through, whatever the consequences," Beathan looked at me and I knew he asked me to make a choice.

My life for another's, I wish I had been given the same choice in Boston. I would have traded my existence for the life of Onatah and the child. I would have made it in a heartbeat, my life for hers. Now looking into the frightened and confused face of Phil, I could detect no subterfuge, she remained truly innocent. I took a few steps back into the cave and pointed my weapon to the ground, watching as Phil shook her head at me. She pulled away from Beathan as far as her tartan would allow, the material tearing.

"Dinnae back away, Captain, he doesnae know what he does, he will kill ye," Phil sobbed on the last words. Her body racked with tears and she started flailing her tiny fists at Beathan with all her might. "Stop this at once, stop it!"

Done with his sister's hysterics, he cuffed her on the side of the face and she fell into the rock wall. I made a couple more steps back into the cave, my eye catching the boxes of paper cartridges.

"You and I are going tae hae a long discussion over loyalty when we return tae Markinch and ye are going tae agree tae marry the man I chose fur ye." Beathan aimed his flintlock at my head. "Do ye hae any last words?"

I tried to catch Phil's eye, she stared at me, terrified over what the next seconds would bring. I slowly brought both my arms out to my sides, looking into Phil's eyes all the time, hoping she would catch onto my plan, my weapon faced the boxes on my right. She looked away for a second and her breath caught.

It felt as if I watched the next minute take place from a great distance, through a glass bent to make all the objects appear much smaller. Phil turned abruptly and pulled away from Beathan, ripping her tartan from her shoulder. The yellow dress stretching behind her as she ran to safety in the narrow lane of tall boulders.

Beathan only had time to look at her in puzzlement before turning back. I ran several steps back and fired my weapon into the boxes of premade ammunition. For the next ten seconds nothing happened, Beathan laughed at my efforts. As the first round went off, followed by an ear-shattering explosion I dove through the opening under the waterfall, unmindful of the cold or where I might land.

Water from the falls blurred my vision and I closed my eyes tightly. Praying Phil made it past at least the first turn in the rocky lane. It would offer protection from the debris flying through the air, though the flames would make breathing hard. With my arms crossed in front of my face, I hit the water in an ungraceful flop; shards of ice cut my exposed skin. Even my clothes held no protection from the sharpness of some of the projectiles.

The impact of the half-frozen pond knocked the wind from my lungs, and my first instinct in the water was to take a deep breath. I fought it as I sank lower into the cold pool. I thought once my feet reached the bottom I could push back up to the surface My clothes felt ten times heavier with the water soaking in and I knew I could not stay above water for long. I opened my eyes, the clear cold water burned them, my ears rang from cold and I felt water seep under the layer of fur. Trickling at first, before filling with more urgency into the space between my skin and clothing; this would only make it more cumbersome to swim.

Still my feet did not reach the bottom, I tried to peer below me, all remained in darkness. Above, a faint orange glow illuminated the surface of the water. I realised the whole cave must have caught alight, from below the water, it looked beautiful, without the noise of the cartridges exploding, nearly peaceful. I thought back to what I had said to Beathan, dying would be as easy as falling asleep in my mother's arms, peaceful from down here, waiting to be lifted above, perhaps I might be religious man after all.

The stillness broke sharply, my body needed air, I had been under water for at least a minute. I convulsed violently and commenced shaking in great racking fits with cold, my body fought for life, death might not be as easy as I thought and with a thrust of my legs I tried to reach the surface, my clothes weighing me into the water, acting as a talisman for death. I felt my energy wane; in the same way as in the bog, yet there would be no child to save me this time.

Lungs burning from the effort of not breathing, nose pinched, I gave two, three good pushes with my legs and tried to work my encumbered arms. I looked up and I could see the surface, one more and I could at least breathe. I broke the surface as a fish might spluttering, coughing and moaning as my body tried to fill itself with air, every muscle screaming out for oxygen. I felt my deerskin clothing and moccasins dragging me back under the water. Impossible to tread above the surface with this weight and I prepared to take a deep breath before going under again. I tried to push towards the side of the pool, the thin ice close to the middle broke easily and several shards cut my hands.

The surface of the water reached my eyes, yet I refused to close them. If I could still see, I thought irrationally, I might have a chance to survive. As I tried to push my numb, tired limbs into action I heard a shout, my given name from the lips of a woman, something I had not heard in a long time.

"Esmond, Esmond, hold on, I hae a branch." Searching around frantically, I could hear Phil sobbing. I turned back to face the cave, and watched as Phil wrestled a branch haphazardly from the bank and trudged down to the river.

Her face smudged with dirt and soot, the dress looked burned, yet her features remained set in determined lines. Her forehead wrinkled in concentration, a look I knew well, and in a voice hoarse from holding my breath and effort from staying afloat, I cried. "Don't get too close to the edge, the ice will not hold you!"

Phil studied me with narrowed eyes, "I think I know how unstable ice can be." Adopting the tone of an old lecturer, she continued, "I once did a study as a child using several buckets ay frozen water and weighted instruments tae guage whether the pond down in Markinch were safe tae sledge upon." She pushed the branch out over the water as my head slipped below the surface.

I could hear her yelling at me dully through the filter of the water. I wondered if she expected to fill the rest of my life with such lectures. Followed by a severe reprimanding as she gave now. Using my numb hands, I grasped the wood and held tight, hoping for salvation.

Phil might be small, yet she was tenacious, a slow inch at a time, I felt the branch move, until I could crane my neck and breath carefully above the water. If I did not feel so cold and numb, I might laugh at her efforts. After what felt like an eternity, the ice at the edge of the pond bumped into my face, with one hand still holding tight to the wooden lifeline. I swung my numb arm around and hoped it would land on the stable ledge in front of me.

"Good, Esmond," Phil did not quit her litany of praise, and I felt her small gloved hands grasp my own numb hand. She pulled hard, trying to wrestle me from the water, after a few minutes she cried out in frustration and I lifted my head to see tears streaming down her face.

"Ye must try," she begged. "Ye must at least get yer torso out ay the water. I cannot lift ye further and help will still be ages away. Hopefully someone saw the explosion from Markinch, they will come. Ye must nae give up," she shouted the last bit.

"I am tired, Phil, I can't feel my legs, my arms, I can barely feel the warmth of your hands." I let out a shuddering breath, I saw she shook from cold, her clothing wet from helping me. She would not last long out here without shelter or warm clothing. I made my decision. "Phil, look at me, I am too heavy for you to pull out, you have to let go now. Make your way back to Markinch as fast as you can. The cold will take you soon, without your cape and tartan you are a martyr to the elements." To show I my resolve, I let go of the wood and released my grip on her hand.

"Nae, I will nae let go," she sobbed, tears running furiously down her cheeks, pooling at her chin and dripping onto our clasped hands. "Dinnae ye see, ye great fool, I came fur ye, Beathan showed me the diary, told me I must translate it fur him. It was then I knew he was behind it all, I saw him come up here, I came fur ye, I made my choice."

Trying to smile through frozen lips, I hoped the effect did not appear as grotesque as it felt. "And here I believed all along I must save the damsel in distress. You have to let go now, be strong, get down to the village and protect the people of Markinch. The fact a small cell supporting the Stuart cause flourished here will not go unnoticed to the English."

Phil grimaced and gripped my hand in her small ones all the tighter. "That's why we need ye, I need ye, give one more great push, I know ye can, ye made it out of the bog, ye can make it out of this."

I fixed my eyes on hers and I tried with the last of my strength to throw my arm out of the water, it dragged heavily beside my body, as I tried to pull from Phil's grasp, a large hand and arm appeared between us and I heard Phil give a shriek of surprise before the collar of my deerskin coat grew tight and I felt myself being slowly lifted from the water.

Chapter 17

A man as large as Beathan set me on the side of the bank, he studied me curiously, head cocked to one side, wide strangely innocent blue eyes searching for something in my face. He was startled for a moment by the barked order of another man I could not see.

"Levy, get the man out ay his clothes, and right quick with it now." The other voice sounded sharp, as if he might be accustomed to giving the large man direction. Levy did not waste time in questioning his instructions, he bent over and began divesting me of my wet, heavy clothing. I tried to make a feeble protest with unresponsive limbs. A heavy blanket flew at the man's head, and he caught it before it fell onto the snow-covered ground. He handed it to me and I tried to cover my shivering body while he helped me to my feet.

Grateful I could not feel the sharp pebbles and ice underfoot, I watched another man light a fire and Phil throw fuel onto the flames in order to make it larger. She appeared to know these men and a thought struck me. Between chattering teeth and racking shivers, I managed. "You are the McGreevy brothers," a statement more than a question.

The other man looked up from the fire and smiled grimly. "At yer service, Sassenach. Levy help him over tae the fire, there's a guid lad," he added as the larger man took my elbow and roughly steered me towards the flames. "Name's Roth, this here is my younger brother, Levy."

Levy pushed me down onto a rock near the fire and smiled a toothless grin when I looked up at him. I tried to give him a nod in return, however I did not seem to have much control over the spasms in my body. "Thank you, Levy, you saved my life."

"Listen to this, Levy, a Sassenach gauger thanking ye," the big man looked at his brother curiously. "Ye should remember this day, as I dinnae think ye will ever be in such guid graces again," Roth began to laugh at his own joke.

Phil looked uncomfortable wrapped in a second blanket. She studied each of the McGreevys' faces and tried to avoid my eye. I thought she might be embarrassed over my nudity. Clearing my throat, I asked. "How did you manage to get here so quickly? Markinch is a way off."

Roth watched me intently as I tried to wiggle my toes, stamp my feet and rub my hands together all at the same time. He appeared to make a decision, "I guess it'll be best if we make a clean slate ay it." He looked up at Levy and continued. "We were working with Beathan, after the McKinneys." Phil looked at him sharply and I studied his face. I wondered how much he would admit, and to how much of the conspiracy he might be privy.

He held up his hands. "I want tae say neither Levy or I had anything tae dae with the McKinneys' or Turner's death, we may be thieves, but we are nae murderers, especially ay our neighbours. Beathan came tae us after the McKinneys disappeared," Roth said the last word with some doubt. "Said he'd teach us tae make Scotch and we could get out ay the cattle business."

Beathan chose his marks well I thought with self-pity. First he came to the aid of the McKinneys making them a simple offer, work a second still and have a major cost of Scotch production deferred. He used the same approach with these boys, learn a new skill, perhaps have a chance at a better life, I had been the easiest target of all, befriend the outsider excise man.

Roth interrupted my thoughts as he continued the story, "Levy and I know cattle, we're nae Scotch men and we found the intricacies difficult." He shrugged his shoulders as he looked at me. "Ye may recall the still explosion, the night ye found the McKinneys. We knew what all in the village didnae, Beathan must hae been behind their deaths. We decided it would be better fur our health if we ended our arrangement with Beathan, but he said he wouldnae let us go."

My eyes flicked to Phil's expression; she watched Roth tell his story with a mixture of sadness and disbelief. I could not be sure how she would take all the revelations, the shock at finding him standing at the entrance of the cave, flintlock pointed to my head burned into her memory.

"What happened after? Surely, he could not force you to continue working for him? You obviously did not have the skill to help with the Scotch and as you probably already know from the contents of the cave, he needed it to trade for weapons from the French."

Phil took a sharp intake of breath and buried her face in her hands. I wanted to get up and comfort her, however my jellied legs wobbled at the thought of standing again. I could feel the pins and needles burn in my toes and fingers and underneath this blanket I remained naked, hardly proper conduct for a gentleman.

"We found the weapons in the cave and tried to use it as leverage," Roth shook his head. "Clever man, Beathan, told us our lives wouldnae be worth spit if we ratted on him, he's got powerful friends in Auld Reekie who would protect him and we are known criminals. The best I could do was hide out with my brother and hope everything might come tae a head without us. And it did, we're safe enough, I think. We watched him the day ye came up tae the fens and poked around our auld still site, we couldnae help ye without exposing ourselves. Ye made it out all right in the end."

I narrowed my eyes; "I knew someone watched from the woods, if I had not been so intent on exposing you, I would have realised Beathan stalked me from the rear." I continued angrily. "After the story you have told me of your goings-on, you should be lucky I do not seek warrants for both your arrests for public mischief at the least." With the word arrests, Levy stirred beside me and I looked up into his frowning face.

Looking at his brother steadily and until Levy made eye contact, Roth continued shaking his head lightly. "We tend nae tae use the word arrest, it makes my brother uncomfortable. We hae a couple ay run ins with the law down south," he sighed and tried to smile encouragingly at his bigger brother. "Some men want tae try their luck with a man as large as Levy, but he can hold his own."

I studied both of the boys, I knew they were guilty of cattle rustling, it remained an ill-kept secret amongst the villagers of Markinch. Yet they had failed in their attempt to be Scotch runners and did not have to be linked to Beathan's crimes, which would end with their heads on spikes if the English had any say in the matter.

The burning in my feet and hands felt so intense I nearly shouted in pain, instead I tried to regulate my breath. After a minute I had it somewhat under control, looking up I met Roth's eye. "I will make you a deal, I do not want to see more bloodshed, I have seen enough to last me many lifetimes over." Cautious interest passed over Roth's features as I continued. "As of now, there is no evidence linking you to Beathan's crimes, there has only been a rumour you might be trying to operate a portable still in the fens in order to avoid the duty. I will leave your names out of the official report, however you must do something for me."

Roth's eyes narrowed in suspicion, used to dealing with men who tried to cheat him and his brother. "You and your brother need to take up some form of gainful employment and I know Agnes McKinney could use a man's help over at the Turret, if you are keen to help your neighbours."

Scratching the whiskers on his chin, Roth peered into the fire for a couple of minutes. The only sound in the small valley the waterfall, the crash of liquid on ice and the crackling of burning twigs and peat, he eventually looked back up and stared me in the eye.

"Ye hae a deal sir," he grimaced as he watched me tremble. "I would shake yer hand, but I think ye need it tae stay warm," he laughed. "Ma will be happy for us to spend more time around the farm in any case, she is getting tae auld tae be on her own. Eh, Levy, time tae go and see Ma, get yer things ready." He told his brother, and the large man stood up and went over to where two rucksacks sat side by side and heaved one onto his back.

"I warn you now," I used my military captain's voice, "if you or your brother start up any trouble with the villagers, I will be forced to take action."

The other man laughed as he set his own bag on his back, turning to me with a cheeky smile. "Sassenach, you'll hae tae find us first, mind I've given ye my word as a true Highlander." He bobbed his head and began to walk down the stream, his brother following behind.

"Bloody Scots, will be the death of me." I shivered out as I watched the two brothers disappear around a bend. I looked back at the fire and pulled the blanket tighter around my large frame, help could not come fast enough.

Out of the corner of my eye, I watched Phil step closer to the fire. She appeared to be puzzling over some question and she finally spoke as she stepped close enough to unwrap the blanket she had over her shoulders and put it over my own. "I hope we're all nae in yer curse, Captain."

Gathering the remnants of my dignity to my person, I lifted my chin. "You saved my life, not only today, in other ways too." Never being a man who expressed emotion, a lump in my throat prevented me from going on further. Phil understood and she shuffled over and sat on the rest of the log in front of the fire.

Phil rubbed a hand across her forehead, squeezed her eyes shut. "I think I am so superior with all ay my books and machines," she took a hitched breath. "I never suspected Beathan ay all this, tae me he was just a boy, the one who lost the mother he worshipped. I never gave him the sympathy he needed, I only mocked him fur loving such a hurtful woman."

I valiantly tried to put my unease over my nakedness aside, adjusted the blankets over my person again, and with one fluid motion I scooped Phil closer to my side, my naked arm anchoring her there, the heat from her body adding to my comfort, the acrid smell of gunpowder in her hair making my nose twitch.

"How could you know of any of your brother's plans?" I squeezed her closer for a minute. "I, a trained soldier sent to ferret out such plots, had no inkling until the end. Now it makes perfect sense, we will have to work together to protect the town, the English will never believe the plot is finished."

Phil rested her head on my shoulder, the action so trusting I felt a fierce protection rise up in my stomach. "I know ye will dae yer best tae protect us, it is in yer nature. Captain, fur all yer worldly faults, we will protect Markinch together." She looked up at the smoke coming from the cave, staining the sky overhead. "We will have tae explain somehow, make people understand."

"We will try and stay as close to the truth as possible." I told her, my mind going over various possible explanations, "in order to satisfy my superiors and the villagers, yet we will keep the McGreevys' name separate from this. We do not need any more bloodshed. Hopefully when word reaches Edinburgh of Beathan's death. The cell will be paralysed for a few months before it can operate again, unfortunately I do not believe any of the ring leaders will be caught."

"A search through his office may reveal something," Phil mused. "Somehow I cannae believe he is dead, and a traitor. He placed us all in danger." Her voice broke and the tears she had fought against since the explosion erupted. I held her as she cried and shuddered her pain into the already damp woolen blankets. "He broke the promise our faither made tae the English never tae take up arms against them, or conspire, how could he risk Faither's word?"

This is how the Tavish brothers and the rest of the village folk found us, huddled around the fire on a small ledge of the riverbank, Phil in my arms crying and I trying valiantly trying to cover my modesty.

"Thank the good Lord above sitting in his golden chair," Tavish burst out when he saw us. I immediately pulled away from Phil and she jumped from her seat, a red stain appearing on both her cheeks. "And what has happened here?"

I remained speechless for a minute, what *had* happened here, I asked myself. I watched as Angus and three men wearing black armbands looked between Phil and the cave billowing smoke and I sighed. It was going to be a long day and I could feel the familiar heat of a fever coming on.

"An accident, Tavish, a terrible accident, do you have any extra blankets or clothes I might use? I am afraid mine are a bit wet," he only continued to stare at me.

"How ye ever survived fighting in the New World, I'll never know, Captain," Angus came forward and immediately began to tug on the blankets. I fought him weakly, my strength had not returned. "Here, give me one ay the blankets and we can fashion a kilt fur ye, put the other around yer shoulders."

In the midst of all the men, Phil straightened and looked them in the eye, without a quaver in her voice, "Beathan is dead." The other men studied her with incredulous looks on their faces. "I know it will be hard tae believe, he was a traitor, against the English and against us, he would hae placed us between two formidable enemies, neither ay which cared fur the folk of Markinch."

I watched Phil as she made her statement, she made her choice, as she had when she rushed to rescue me from Beathan. She chose her people, not the promise of social or monetary rewards from dubious men in Edinburgh. I never respected a woman as much as I respected her in this moment. I wanted to take her up and kiss her. Though such an action would probably end in both of us in a heap on the stony ground, my strength low. I needed to get back to the village, my warm bed and sleep for a long time.

It was not to be however, it took Phil and me at least another half-hour to explain how all the events of the past year, culminating in my appearance in Markinch, had led to the explosion in the hermit's cave and the death of the prodigal son. After which two of the men and Angus agreed to stay with the cave until the fire burnt out, in order to recover Beathan's body. Phil helped me put my damp moccasins on before we walked back to Markinch. An arm over her shoulder, as she explained the workings of a mantelpiece clock her father recently purchased, her worry and nerves soothed with explanations of science.

Phil walked me to the door of the cottage, past all of the curious stares and calls from the villagers. Into the hands of Freya, who caused an even greater fuss over my appearance than she had with the state of the drawing room earlier, and bullied me up the stairs and into bed immediately. I argued the whole way, knowing a fever would soon set in and I would be incapable of writing the urgent letter I needed to send to Colonel Manners. It would be the only way to save the town from a militia, I needed to tell him of all the recent events.

After arguing for at least an hour, Freya threw up her hands and relented, bringing up my writing case and setting it on the bed, with a dire warning over my further health if I tried to get out of bed. She stomped down the stairs to make her feelings known. Now I sat staring at a sheet headed with the date and the direction of Manners written over the top, several different openings rolling through my brain. Through my increasingly painful headache, I wrote out the events as I saw them, giving as much detail as I could, leaving out the McGreevys. I reassured him all would be well from now on, although I knew he would be disappointed at not knowing the names of the conspirators in Edinburgh.

I promised him I would search through Beathan's papers, yet I knew he would not be clumsy enough to leave evidence behind. His Scotch arms scheme worked for a year and it might have continued if not for Logan's suspicions. Informing Manners of Logan's death, I infused my words with as much annoyance as possible without stating how disappointed I felt in his lack of trust. If only I knew he had acted as a double agent, perhaps Beathan might have been caught earlier and Kieran would not be an orphan now.

With my last burden finished, I sealed the envelope with wax and set it next to the bed. Freya would know to send it off immediately and I fell to sleep, my body burning from fever. I watched as different nightmares passed through my brain, confused images of Phil's body lying dead as Onatah's, of Beathan's burnt body as my own, until peaceful rest kept my mind calm.

Sleeping through the night and into the next day, I woke with a sneeze and fell back into the soft pillows. I cracked one sore eyelid open and looked around the darkened room and waited until the pounding in my head lessened before sitting up. My muscles felt sluggish and by the soreness in my throat. I knew the grip of fever possessed me, probably from all the time spent out of doors yesterday and being wet for most of it. I shivered lightly, remembering how cold I had been. I weakly checked under the blankets and realised Freya, probably with the help of the barber. Must have dressed me for bed, by the subtle noises downstairs I realised she must be around.

I tried to pour myself a glass of water from a carafe on the table next to the bed, and only succeeded in knocking the whole pitcher over. For a second I thought perhaps my clumsiness might have gone unnoticed, yet it was not to be. I heard Freya's familiar heavy steps on the stairs and braced for her arrival.

With a motherly frown placed firmly on her face, she looked at me differently. I wondered if her look had anything to do with Beathan's death.

She bustled over to the side of the bed and hardly gave the carafe a glance, instead she put a hand to my forehead. "Och, Captain, yer still burning with a fever," she smiled and patted my shoulder. "Though the barber disnae believe ye are in any serious trouble this time, only cold and tired, need tae get yer rest."

My voice cracked and sounded rough as my throat felt raw from sickness. "Tell me, Freya, did you post the missive I left on the table to London? And what has happened since yesterday?" I made to sit up straighter. "I need to speak with Phil."

"Ye created such a fuss over the letter, I posted it this morning on the packet to London." Freya smiled reassuringly, "and as fur the rest, the tale of Beathan's doings has been making the rounds, and his part in the McKinneys, Logan and Turner's deaths."

I sat and watched Freya think for a minute, a myriad of different emotions passed over her features and curiosity made me ask. "There seems to be more to the story than what you are telling me. Why don't you say, since I will be up from this bed soon enough?"

"Nae without having a long rest, Captain," Freya assumed her best motherly tone. "The barber left strict instructions fur ye tae take yer time in recuperating. Ye had tae many near-death experiences, yer system is in shock, fever, gunshots, drowning, fever!"

I lay back on the pillows in an action of appeasement. "As you can see, I am resting now, so what is it you're not telling me?" I grew worried, I could usually ferret anything out of the woman.

"It's only the whole village is in a state over Beathan and his schemes, Logan's death, people are divided, some say he is a martyr." I looked at Freya hard and she continued quickly. "Nae everyone, mind, nae me, I liked Mr Turner though he was a Sassenach, some say he shouldnae be buried on sacred ground."

Frowning, I said, "Beathan's burial is a matter for the church, Father Tadgh should have everything in order." I thought of the fanatical priest. "He seems to know his business."

"He does, though he is saying Beathan's actions are not treason, they are the work of the Lord on earth to aid Francis Stuart to the throne of Scotland and England, and drive out the heretics." Freya remained quiet for a minute. "Logan's funeral is this evening, I am sure he will use it to gain supporters."

Using both hands I rubbed my forehead, pressing my fingers into my eyes. Everyone has an agenda, whether I am in the New World, in ballrooms in London or in a small village in the middle of the Highlands.

My second thought made me lift the covers on my bed and slowly shift my legs to the side. I could not let Phil face all of this alone, I needed to be with her. I had promised her yesterday, we would face the future together. I gave Freya a stern look. "I know I need rest, however some things are too important."

After a moment's hesitation, she turned and walked out the door, throwing over her shoulder. "I will wait fur ye downstairs, Captain, we can walk up together." It was her way of showing allegiance.

It took twice as long to dress in my formal red dress uniform as normal. My fingers clumsy from sickness and the cuts and bruises from where I fell through the ice. For the most part, they looked as if they would only leave minor scars. I shaved with care in the mirror once again avoiding the cuts left healing on my cheeks and forehead. I looked much more battered than I had previously thought.

Buttoning up my red frock coat, I wore it to make a statement. A continuation of the decision I came to when faced with Beathan's choice: I would no longer run from who I am or what I represent. Even though they took someone I loved, here I had an opportunity to be the man I always wanted to be.

Freya and I walked slowly up the muddy road, the weather grown milder in the last day or so. Melting the snow and frost making some places in the track impossible to navigate, we used the verge on the sides to pass. Deoch stood quiet, the workers beginning to walk to the church after the day's work. The buildings looked forlorn to me, not the usual bastion of solidity I had come to know, only shells.

A crowd gathered in the churchyard, workers and their families dressed in their Sunday best stood in groups. The men, with black cloth still tied to their arms, spoke in low voices as children played and were scolded by their elders.

I waited at the gate, Freya went through, and looked back at me before continuing to meet a group of women chatting and minding children. I waited and watched until Phil finally looked up and saw me standing at the gate. She smiled and relief made my eyes water; I had worried our promises might have only been part of the fever. I might have read her feelings incorrectly or she changed her mind after the shock of her brother's death.

Excusing herself from the group of men, she walked through the people. Some watched curiously, others ignored her completely until she came and stood at the gate. She smiled again and held out her hands, "Esmond, please join me."

I assured myself the explosion left no lasting damage to Phil's face; a few scrapes marred her otherwise perfect complexion. I took a deep breath, and hauled her into my arms, burying my face in her shoulder; the embrace lasted only a few seconds, my strength sapped.

"You are safe and whole." I cradled her face in my hands and watched as tears formed in the corners of her eyes. "I could hardly think of anything other than you from the moment I woke."

Phil smiled, and stepped away brushing efficiently at the tears on her cheeks. "I am as well as can be expected, my brother is dead, the foreman of Deoch is dead, my father is tae ill tae rise from his bed." She looked at me, "I worried fur his health when I broke the news."

The bell in the church tower began to toll and mourners broke away from their groups and entered the church. I looked up at the dusky sky and frowned at the dark, bruised, clouds. "A storm is coming, we should get inside before the first drops fall."

In response Phil tucked her arm under mine and led me through the small graveyard and into the church, her warm body next to mine reminding me I was not alone.

Author's Note

This is a work of fiction, in saying this I have tried to stay true to the atmosphere of the time. The early 1700's were an incredibly important period, not just for England and Scotland but also for the world over. The excitement over scientific discoveries made by pioneering scientists would have lasting effects on society and where man saw himself positioned in a world that appeared to be getting smaller. The characters and Markinch itself are products of my imagination set in the historical context of the story's time.

PRETENDER AT THE GATE

COMING IN
NOVEMBER 2014

Esmond's fight to save Markinch and the women he loves takes him from the small highland village he has come to call home to the dangerous streets of Edinburgh in the Spring of 1708. Commanded to bring the rest of the Scotch smuggling ring to justice, Esmond searches through the dangerous back alleys and the glamorous drawing rooms of Edinburgh's capital.

His loyalty to the English crown in question, Esmond desperately enlists the aid of a pair of old foes from Markinch. Along with a man whose own loyalties appear obscured, Esmond fights to find the truth under the ever-present threat of invasion from France.

Esmond's growing fears and paranoia over whether one of his closest confidences has been betrayed is fuelled by the news Francis Stuart has left the French coast. The old Pretender has enough French mercenaries and Scottish allies to take Edinburgh and most of the highlands. Esmond will face the ultimate choice, save the woman he loves and the town that saved his life, or stay in Edinburgh and fight alongside his English brethren.

The sequel to Scotch Rising, Pretender at the Gate will be available to purchase on Amazon. Check back soon for more details!

Please come visit me at http://sjgarland.wix.com/s-garland

Title:	Scotch Rising
Author:	S. J. Garland
Publisher:	Maple Kakapo
Address:	2069 Pakowhai Road, Napier, New Zealand 4183
Format:	Softcover
Publication Date:	5/2014
ISBN:	ISBN 978-0-473-28490-9

Made in the USA
San Bernardino, CA
29 April 2014